Praise for Ann of Sunflower Lane

Julie Sellers' *Ann of Sunflower Lane* is a love-letter to books and reading, and especially to the power of *Anne of Green Gables* to reflect and to shape life. When abused fifteen-year-old Ann Alwyn is forced to live on a Kansas farm with grandparents she has never met, who could have imagined that her mother's copy of *Anne of Green Gables* would offer her a way to live her life differently? Sellers' Ann "without-an-e" has an eye for beauty and justice; the novel features some gorgeous landscape descriptions as well as wisdom: "'Never, never give anyone the benefit of the doubt if they hurt you.'" Julie Sellers' characters are believable, even lovable, and her literary allusions (quite apart from those to *Anne*) are welcome invitations to explore new worlds through reading and writing.

> —Elizabeth Rollins Epperly, Professor Emerita and founder of the L.M. Montgomery Institute at the University of Prince Edward Island

Ann Alwyn is a true kindred spirit to *Anne of Green Gables*! I love how vividly this book conjures up contemporary rural life in a small town, chronicling how the transplanted Ann comes to terms with her troubled family history by putting down new roots and reinvigorating old ones. Full of humor and heart, this engaging story will appeal not only to those who are already familiar with classic girls' books by Louisa May Alcott and L. M. Montgomery, but also to less experienced readers for whom this lively tale could serve as a wonderfully inviting entrée into that world of older and often less accessible literary riches. A treat for all ages!

> —Dr. Marah Gubar, author of *Artful Dodgers: Reconceiving the Golden Age of Children's Literature* (2009), Associate Professor of Literature at MIT

"I have been exiled to a veritable wasteland," 15-year-old Ann Alwyn of Denver sighs as she finds herself whisked away to live with her newly-found maternal grandparents on their Kansas farm. Now, Ann must walk a narrow path set by her strict grandmother if she wants to stay out of foster care. I loved this character, this book. Readers of all ages will fall in love with *Ann of Sunflower Lane*.

 —Cheryl Unruh, author of *Gravedigger's Daughter: Vignettes from a Small Kansas Town*

Ann of Sunflower Lane

Julie A. Sellers

Meadowlark PRESS
Emporia, Kansas, USA

Meadowlark Press, LLC
meadowlarkbookstore.com
PO Box 333, Emporia, KS 66801

Cover image by Onalee Nicklin
facebook.com/StoryBookExpressions
instagram.com/onaleenicklin

Ordering Information: Special discounts are available on quantity purchases by corporations, associations, and others. For details, contact the publisher at info@meadowlark-books.com.

YOUNG ADULT FICTION / Girls & Women
YOUNG ADULT FICTION / Family / Multigenerational
FICTION / Coming of Age

ISBN: 978-1-956578-23-2 (hard cover)
ISBN: 978-1-956578-22-5 (paperback)
ISBN: 978-1-956578-24-9 (ebook)

Library of Congress Control Number: 2022942983

For Lesley Sieger-Walls

"Wherever you are,

there is another door"

—William Stafford

Table of Contents

1

Only for the Summer

"It's only for the summer," Ann Alwyn assured herself. "I won't have to spend the rest of my life here in the middle-of-nowhere Kansas. In a couple of months, Dad will get a real job and this whole neglect thing will be cleared up so I can go back to Denver. I'm positive of it."

It was May, 1989, and the days of summer stretched before fifteen-year-old Ann like the wide-open Flint Hills surrounding her as she sat stewing on the swing in the oak tree at Sunflower Lane Farm. The sweet scent of nearby irises and peonies floated on the warm afternoon wind blowing across all that emptiness. There was plenty of space to contemplate the injustice of having her life upended and being abandoned with the grandparents she didn't know. If she'd just kept her mouth shut, no one would've bothered her. But she'd let a comment slip to their nosey neighbor, and now, here she was.

"Who's ever even heard of Storey, Kansas?" Ann said with a sigh. "I have been exiled to a veritable wasteland."

She relished the dramatic tang of the words, and she let her imagination fly. She envisioned a scene where her repentant father begged forgiveness for his distance all these years and for disrupting her world now. He'd really change this time, and she'd forgive him. It would be a happy ending, just like in a novel.

Ann heard the back screen door creak open and close. She looked across the yard to see her grandfather, Bernard Holmberg, stoop to pet the farm dog, Sam. She studied him from a distance, still unable to believe this man she'd never known was any relation to her. He was dressed in faded overalls and a plaid button-up shirt, something Ann thought only people on television wore. His face was wrinkled but tanned under his thick shock of gray hair, and his blue-gray eyes sparkled from behind his glasses when he smiled, which was often.

Ann wound the rope above her as she remembered the conversation that she'd overheard her grandparents having on the drive to Kansas yesterday. They'd thought she was asleep, but she'd caught every word: how she was "the carbon copy" of Amelia—Ann's mother and their youngest daughter—with her long, wavy, strawberry blond hair and clear, blue eyes. How they still missed their daughter, dead all these years. Grandma had cried, but she'd tried to hide it.

"If they cared so much, how come they never even tried to contact me before?" Ann grumbled aloud as she let the swing unwind, the world a blur around her. She heard the crunch of Grandpa's boots on the path and glanced at him.

"That old swing still works, I guess," Grandpa called as he approached. He swept off his cap to wipe his brow in the heat.

"Yeah." Ann dragged her feet in the dirt to slow herself to a stop. He seemed nice enough, but then again so had their neighbor, Mrs. Dansbury, and look where that had gotten her. It didn't pay to be too trusting, Dad always said. But Ann found people so interesting; she always wondered what each person's story was, and if she didn't find out, she just imagined a fitting one for them.

"Found something for you, since you said you like to read." Grandpa held out an old book to show her.

She'd meant to keep tight-lipped, like Dad warned her. But once Grandpa got her talking about her love of reading on the drive back from Denver, she unwittingly thawed. She was so used to being alone and talking to herself about whatever popped into her mind that she wasn't very good at being quiet.

"*Anne of Green Gables*," Ann read the title aloud. She ran her fingers across the pale green cover and traced the silhouette of the young woman's face framed on it. She did love a good book, and something about that title called to her. Wouldn't it be thrilling to belong to somewhere, anywhere, to such a degree that you could call yourself "of" it?

"It was my mother's, and she gave it to your mother when she was a girl. It was tucked away in a trunk in the garret, just waiting for you," said Grandpa.

Ann peered up at her grandfather, squinting one eye against the sun. She'd never met her grandparents before the hearing. As soon as Mrs. Dansbury got child services in the middle of things, Grandma and Grandpa showed up in Denver, prepared to take her in and save her from the Colorado foster system. They'd never cared before, so she wasn't sure why they got involved now. But Dad said it would only be for the summer. He'd get a job to prove he wasn't neglecting her by traveling with the band and that they had a stable home life. His in-laws never thought he was good enough for their daughter, so he'd show them.

Just a couple of months, and I can go back, Ann reminded herself. Then, things would go back to normal—at least, as normal as things ever were for them. Life in Denver might not be perfect, but it was at least familiar, and Dad could be very charming when he wanted to be.

"Thanks. I do love to read," Ann said, flipping through the yellowed pages. Grandpa seemed nice enough, and maybe once he got to know her, he wouldn't mind having her around. Grandma, on the other hand, might be another story.

"You're welcome," he said. He turned to gaze thoughtfully off across the fields that had been in the Holmberg family for three generations.

Ann followed his gaze over the greens and browns of earth and fields to the gray ribbon of the highway, trying to see what he was looking for. Clumps of trees hinted at other farms, and above, a clear sky stretched out to the intangible threshold between it and the earth. There was just so much space. It was all so different from Denver and the other cities where they'd lived chasing her father's dream of being a musician. It was kind of unnerving, after spending her life inside the walls of a school or an apartment. Still, it reminded her of what her English teacher, Ms. Miller, told her when she'd gone to clean out her locker before they left.

"Consider it a new adventure, Ann, a chance to broaden your horizons and see what you can discover to write about there," Ms. Miller said. "William Stafford was born in Kansas. Remember the poem of his you liked so well? It said, 'Wherever you are, there is another door.'"

Ann still felt the same tingling exhilaration at the perfection of that line of poetry. She looked far out across the great expanse of uninterrupted landscape before her, wondering exactly where that optimistic door might be. All she saw was miles and miles of farmland and sky. She felt very small.

"Suppose it must be pretty hard to have to come somewhere so different and not know anyone," Grandpa said, breaking the silence as he turned his eyes from the land.

Ann shrugged.

"You know you can write or call your friends in Denver if you want."

"I don't really have any close friends in Denver."

"Well, wherever they are."

"We've moved around so much I gave up on the whole best friend thing."

"Well, maybe your half-sister then."

"Sabrina and I aren't really close. It's fine—I'm used to being by myself. Besides, Dad will have everything straightened out by the end of the summer, so it's not like the few people I know in Denver will forget me."

Grandpa didn't contradict her rosy outlook. "I know you like to read. What other hobbies do you have?"

"I like to write. Other than that, I mainly just do homework. Ms. Miller gave me extra reading and writing assignments since she knows I love English. I like school, so I don't mind studying. Besides, I'm not allowed to go out much anyway, in case someone realizes . . . " She stopped short.

Grandpa seemed not to notice. "Don't worry, there'll be plenty to do here to keep you busy. We always have chores on the farm."

"You mean, like milk a cow or chop wood or drive a tractor or something? That would be so *Little House on the Prairie*—well, other than the tractor."

Grandpa stifled a smile. "Not exactly. Although we do have a woodburning stove we use in the winter. This old house doesn't have central heat or air."

"You don't say," Ann said drily, thinking back to the suffocating wall of humidity that had awaited them inside the ancient white farmhouse when they arrived and opened the door. That was what had driven her out to the garden in the first place—that, and the uncomfortable feeling of finding her own face staring back at her off the wall of pictures above the piano.

Ann had never seen her mother's photograph before that day. Her half-sister, Sabrina, who was five years older and remembered everything, told her Dad had destroyed all of her mother's pictures after her death. Ann never knew her mother, but she'd imagined what she must have looked and been like more times and ways than she could remember. In Ann's mind, she was just like Marmee from *Little Women*: sweet and kind and such a lovely person that her father was devastated by her death; that was why he had trouble expressing how much he loved her, his own daughter. Sometimes the mother of Ann's imagination had long hair, others short; sometimes she was a brunette, others, she had black hair or blonde or red. But despite all the different forms Ann's imaginings had taken, she had never dreamed she resembled her mother so much, even though she looked very little like her father and nothing like Sabrina. Maybe the reason Dad never talked about her mother was because Ann did look so much like her. That had to be it.

"Ann?" Grandpa was asking.

"Huh? Sorry. I let my mind wander."

"I was just saying we don't have any cows to milk, and I'll take care of the wood. I'm mostly retired and rent out my land now, so you don't need to worry about driving tractors either."

"That's good because I'm only fifteen and can't even drive a car. Dad's always really busy, and he's never had the chance to teach me to drive."

"Fifteen? I thought you were going to be a junior this year."

"I don't turn sixteen till August."

"Guess I just lost track of time. But anyway, it's not a problem. I'm sure Grandma will have some chores in the house that don't require driving."

Ann said nothing. Her first impression of her grandmother was that she was quaintly old-fashioned and proper, with her prim print dresses, short gray hair, and a large handbag with her initials stitched on the flap. Now that she'd had more time to study Grandma, Ann decided she was also very reserved—nothing like she'd have imagined for the mother of the perfect mother she'd dreamed of all these years. She remembered the enthusiastic hug Grandpa gave her when the order came down, while Grandma merely patted her hand.

"Do you like to cook?" Grandpa asked, drawing Ann back to their conversation.

"I really don't know how. I pretty much survive on mac and cheese and soup from a can. Oh—and I can make tacos when I have the ingredients."

"Hmm . . . Well, Grandma is a good cook, and she can teach you."

Ann had the distinct impression that Thelma Holmberg would not be an easy person to please, especially in all questions of housekeeping. She seemed inflexible about the way things were done. This was going to be like *Rebecca of Sunnybrook Farm* or *Up a Road Slowly*, Ann decided, with a strict relative taking in the heroine. Thank goodness Grandpa seemed less demanding.

"I'll try my best," Ann said.

"That's all you ever can do."

Ann wasn't convinced her grandmother would agree.

"You needn't worry. We'll take good care of you," Grandma had told Ann that afternoon when they arrived at Sunflower Lane. They had just showed her what would be her room on the second floor of the broiling house.

Ann cringed at feeling someone was merely doing their duty by her, just like when Sabrina reminded her that she'd had to babysit her all those years while Dad was away and before she got her own apartment. But it's not like Ann had much of a choice. It was Sunflower Lane or a foster home. Even with the lack of modern conveniences and Grandma's critical eye, her grandparents' 1880s farmhouse in the middle of nowhere had to be better than a foster home, Ann decided. She'd have to make the best of it.

"Welcome to Kansas," Grandpa said, his eyes trained back on the shimmery horizon.

Ann stood and followed his gaze, looking out across the green fields. The freshness of spring wafted on the breeze around them, and yellow and black butterflies flitted among the flowers. The quiet was punctuated only by a tangle of birdsong, the hum of tires on the nearby highway, and the lonely wail of a distant train. Maybe she would discover something elusively beautiful about all that space once she got used to it. It was like stepping into a landscape portrait or a page from a novel set in a long-ago time and place. Oh, she wouldn't want to live here forever, of course, but she wouldn't have to. She was only here for the summer.

2

The Rules

The morning breeze danced through the south window in Ann's room. It rustled the pink and white checkered curtains before slipping over the bed where she still lay reading and out the north window to the fields beyond. Sunlight glanced off the windows, reflecting Ann's current mood, for she was in considerably better spirits than the previous afternoon by pure and simple dint of a good book.

"Ann!"

Ann sucked in her breath and stared at the yellowed pages of *Anne of Green Gables*. Marilla Cuthbert was so aggravated at Anne Shirley's outburst at Mrs. Lynde for criticizing her red hair that she, Ann Alwyn, could almost hear Marilla's voice leap off the page all the way from Green Gables. Now that was some talented writing.

"Ann Alwyn!"

Ann's head snapped up. She glanced at the clock. It was seven-thirty. Grandma had told her they lived by the philosophy of "early to bed, early to rise," but surely seven-thirty wasn't late. Ann left her book on the nightstand beside the white, Jenny Lind bed and dashed from her room to the top of the stairs. She peered over the banister at her grandmother below. Thelma Holmberg stood, hands on her hips, an embroidered apron covering her cotton dress.

"Good morning," Ann said, hoping she wasn't in trouble already.

"You can't lay abed all day on a farm. Breakfast is ready and we're waiting on you."

Ann caught her breath. Hadn't Marilla just said something like that in the novel? Who said fiction was stranger than truth?

"I wasn't asleep. I just got caught up in the book Grandpa gave me and lost track of time." *Just like Anne Shirley,* she added to herself.

Ann had a habit of growing attached to her favorite literary characters, and she was already smitten with the heroine of her novel. Anne Shirley seemed so real to Ann Alwyn, given more similarities than merely the fact they'd both gone to live with elderly people on a farm, that the latter was sure the former must exist somewhere.

"Well, enough of your reading for now. Put on some clothes and come down," said Grandma.

"I'll be right there."

Ann hurried back into her room and opened the stiff closet door. Everything in the 1880s farmhouse seemed out of square and off-kilter.

"You are a curmudgeon," Ann told the house. "My door doesn't really shut, it sticks. These old wooden windows fight me when I try to open them, and this closet door drags. Grandpa said he put the closets in himself, and they used to have wardrobes in here. It's rather a shame, because a wardrobe would be more literary, like something out of *Jane Eyre* or C.S. Lewis. But on to the real question: what on earth does one wear on a farm?" She surveyed her few clothes.

Five minutes later, Ann descended the steep staircase in faded jeans and a blue T-shirt. She slipped into her chair on the side of the kitchen table, Grandma and Grandpa on the ends. They each reached for her hands, bowed their heads, and Grandpa said grace.

Ann cringed at the memory of her first meal with them, when she had picked up her fork from habit, oblivious to her grandparents' unshakeable rule of praying before every meal.

"Did you sleep well in your new room?" Grandpa asked.

Ann nodded, watching as Grandma served scrambled eggs, ham, and thick, toasted slices of homemade oatmeal bread with butter and wild plum jelly. Ann was used to pouring herself a bowl of cold cereal with milk, if they had any, or eating a toaster pastry for breakfast. Her mouth watered at the scent of home-cooked food swirling in the low-ceilinged, homey kitchen.

"That was your mother's room," Grandma said.

"Was it?" There had been nothing in the room to associate it with her mother. In fact, the only thing hanging on the wall was a cross-stitched sampler. Her mother must have taken everything with her when she married and left Sunflower Lane.

"Yes, it was, and the one across the hall was your Aunt Janis's room," said Grandpa.

"It's a nice room. It's much larger than my room in Denver, and I like the two big windows that reach almost all the way up the wall. In Denver, I didn't have any windows in my room, so it was always dark. I'm glad there's a nightstand and lamp beside my bed for reading. And that reminds me: I love the book you found for me, Grandpa."

"Never mind about your books right now. I like to read as much as the next person, but I think you might have stayed up too late reading," said Grandma.

"I swear I didn't. I went to bed at ten when you and Grandpa did. But the sun woke me up, so I thought there wouldn't be any harm in reading only a few more pages."

Grandpa chuckled. "I'm glad you like it. It was always one of your mother's favorites, and my mother's, too."

"I can see why. Have you ever read it?"

"No, can't say as I have. What's it about?" asked Grandpa.

"It's about an orphan named Anne, with an 'e', who goes to live on Prince Edward Island with a brother and sister named Matthew and Marilla Cuthbert. Only, they hadn't wanted to adopt a girl, they'd wanted a boy to help on their farm—it's called Green Gables. And Anne has a vivid imagination and loves to read."

"Sounds like someone else I know." Grandpa grinned.

"Maybe. Only I was named after Nana Alwyn, so my name isn't spelled with an 'e' like the girl in the book."

"Ann was your mother's middle name, too," Grandma said.

"It was?"

Grandma pursed her lips. "Yes. And remember: Pretty is as pretty does, so I don't suppose it matters much how you spell your name."

Ann was learning that Thelma Holmberg was every bit as fond of maxims as Marilla Cuthbert and the Duchess of Wonderland had been of morals. Still, she was trying to stay on Grandma's good side, so she didn't argue.

"Now, you two quit chattering about books and finish your breakfast before it gets cold," Grandma said with a frown.

Dutifully, Ann returned to her plate. She was already full but didn't want to run the risk of offending Grandma by wasting food. She studied the kitchen as she ate the last bites of her meal. The pale-yellow walls reflected the morning sunshine. Simple print curtains with sunflowers hung at the two windows, one above the sink and the other looking out onto the laneway. The oak table was polished and still shone, despite its years of use and a few scratches along the way. A yellow clock, shaped like a skillet, ticked loudly above the stove.

"Would you like me to clear the table?" Ann asked when she had finished. She could at least do that right.

"That'd be real helpful, but first, we need to talk about our expectations here," said Grandma.

Ann swallowed. "Sure."

"First and foremost, no boys."

"What?"

"There's a time and a place for everything, and you'll have plenty of time for boys later," Grandma said crisply.

"Where would I even meet a boy?" she said.

"We do have boys here in the country, and they do attend school," Grandma said. It was the first time Ann had detected so much as a spark of humor in her grandmother.

"But I won't be here when school starts. Dad promised to have this resolved by then."

Grandma shook her head. "Now, you know that's not likely."

"But . . ."

"No buts. It doesn't matter how long you're here, I don't want you having a boyfriend."

Ann's temper flashed. "Oh, don't worry. I never had one before, so I can't imagine I'd have one here. Boys don't tend to like bookworms."

"It's for your own good," Grandma said.

"Fine. It's not like it will be a hard rule to keep," Ann said.

"Next, no wandering off or going anywhere without permission."

"Well, that ought to be easy. I've been going nowhere but from home to school and back my entire life, so I shouldn't think it would be difficult to stay locked in this house either."

"You won't be locked in anywhere. We just want to know where you are," said Grandma.

"Don't worry. I can't even drive, so you're safe." Ann's cheeks were flushed.

"We also don't condone drinking. Or drugs."

"Never have done either; wouldn't start now," Ann said shortly. She crossed her arms and glared. Did they think she'd snuck out and chased boys all over the country and been a complete party animal? Little did they know what her life had been like. Straight to school, straight home, with Sabrina watching her every move, always waiting for a chance to pounce and get her in trouble with Dad, even after she'd moved out last year. The whipping Dad gave her the one time she dared to go to a friend's house after school had been enough to convince her not to try that again. And she'd seen enough of the effects of alcohol on him and his bandmates to ever consider following in his footsteps.

"You'll have a few chores around the house. Many hands make light work, you know. Grandpa says you'd like some cooking lessons . . ."

Ann raised her eyebrows at Grandpa. He shrugged.

" . . . and you can help me clean. You can also work with me in the garden."

"I don't know anything about gardens, but I'm not lazy. I'll try my best at all of my chores."

"I'm sure you'll learn real fast." Grandpa gave an encouraging nod.

"You'll go to church with us on Sundays . . ." said Grandma.

"I don't usually go to church."

"You will now. And when school starts, we'll expect you to study hard and make good grades."

"But I won't be here when school starts." Ann said, face flushed.

Grandma sighed. "That is not what the judge said."

"He said Dad had to get a stable job, and Dad said he'd fix this by the end of summer." Ann's voice rose.

"Let's not argue about it," said Grandpa.

"We're not arguing," Grandma and Ann said in unison.

The statement hung in the air for a moment. Ann looked back and forth between her grandparents, awaiting a harsh dressing down. Would she have to pay for her outburst for days, like she did when Sabrina's passive aggressive barbs made her explode? She swallowed and offered Grandma a weak smile.

"I'm not a bad kid, Grandma. I promise," Ann said.

Grandma studied the frank eyes, the tilt to Ann's chin. "I know it must be real hard to have your life disrupted, but this is for the best. And so are the rules. I just want to keep you safe," Grandma said.

"Safe from what? We're in the middle of nowhere."

Grandma ignored her. "Let's do these dishes."

They washed the dishes by hand—there was no dishwasher in the old farmhouse—while Ann dried them, and Grandpa put them away. Ann's frustrations cooled as she worked. She would just have to prove to Grandma she was no juvenile delinquent. Her gaze wandered out the open window as her grandparents chatted and she mechanically dried plates, glasses, and silverware. Outside, a pink flowering crabapple tree swayed in the morning breeze.

It's just like the cherry tree outside Anne Shirley's room at Green Gables. She called it the Snow Queen because it was white, so I guess this one is more of a Rose Queen, she said to herself.

How like Green Gables this place seemed. Ann had spotted a small orchard off the garden, and Grandpa said there was a creek that ran through the farm. She could imagine it was a brook, and not a "crick," as she'd heard her grandparents call it. Grandpa was a lot like the kind Matthew Cuthbert, and Grandma certainly had all the strictness and practicalities of Marilla. It was almost enough to make you believe fiction was true.

Come to think of it, Ann imagined the house must be similar to Green Gables, too, although there wasn't a parlor. The front door opened into what her grandparents called the dining room, but now, it held only a piano, Grandpa's desk, and a hutch filled with dishes. The living room was to the right of the front door and just past the door leading to the stairs. The shadiness of its dark paneling was mitigated by the large picture window facing the front yard and laneway. In it was a small television, Grandpa's recliner, Grandma's rocking chair, and a well-used couch. The bathroom, the one and only in the entire house, had been shoehorned into a hall between the dining room and her grandparents' bedroom, but of course, bathrooms were not mentioned in *Green Gables.* Upstairs, there was the room where Ann had slept, Aunt Janis's old room, and the "cold room" used as storage, so called because its location on the northwest corner of the house made it susceptible to the chill from winter winds. And somewhere up above, there was the garret where Grandpa had gone to find her book. Still, this was a rambling farmhouse, even if there wasn't a single green gable to be found on it. There had to be plenty of scope for the imagination out here on the prairie in all this space.

"Ann," Grandpa said, but got no response. "What is it the kids say these days? Earth to Ann."

Ann snapped to attention. "Yes? Was I talking to myself?"

"No, but you've been drying that same plate for about two minutes straight, staring off into space," said Grandma.

"Sorry. I was just admiring that tree."

"The flowering crabapple? Yes, it's pretty this time of the year," said Grandma.

"If Anne Shirley were here, she'd tell you that 'pretty' doesn't 'go far enough.' But I agree, it is lovely."

Ann did not fail to intercept Grandma's quizzical look around her to Grandpa who was smiling and whistling a cheery tune as he put away the last of the dishes. Grandpa seemed to be a kindred spirit; of Grandma, Ann was not entirely certain.

"Wipe the table, please, and then you can go with Grandpa. He wants to show you around the farm," Grandma said when they'd finished the dishes.

The sound of car doors closing out front filtered in through the open window. Grandpa looked out.

"Oh, no. It's the Page sisters," he said.

"Of course it is. No one else would come calling at this hour, and they're dying to see Ann. Please behave," Grandma cautioned.

"Grandma, I'm almost sixteen. I think I can behave," Ann said, bristling. "And who are the Page sisters?"

Grandpa said, "The two nosiest gossips in the county. And be forewarned: they're here to grill you."

3

The Misses Page Come Calling

"**G**rill me?" Ann asked, but her grandparents were already at the front door. A novice at living in a small, rural community, Ann had no earthly idea what interest the Page sisters, whoever they were, could possibly have in her. She peeked out the window to see a shining white Cadillac parked in the drive. She wondered if she could have found even so much as a speck of dust on its gleaming exterior.

"Why, Miss Genevieve and Miss Winifred. What a lovely surprise," Grandma greeted the two visitors.

"Good morning. We brought some chocolate chip cookies for your granddaughter," said Miss Genevieve.

"Thank you," Grandma said, the picture of the gracious hostess. "Please come in. Ann, these are some of our neighbors, Miss Genevieve and Miss Winifred Page."

"How do you do?" Ann asked politely, as she knew any heroine worth her salt would say. She shook the hands of the two diminutive women standing before her clothed in their Sunday best dresses with white sandal pumps. They each wore a hat that had been stylish decades before—Miss Genevieve in a green pillbox that made her eyes seem that much more piercing, and Miss Winifred in a pink cloche with a bunch of mauve flowers on the band that bobbed each time she nodded her agreement with her older sister. As a rule, Ann, like most teenagers, was not inclined to be "grilled," but surely two elfin ladies in their eighties couldn't wreak much havoc with a simple visit. It looked as if a gentle puff of breeze could blow over both of them with little effort.

Grandma ushered everyone into the living room, and the two sisters sat, one on each end of the couch, looking expectantly at Ann.

"Come sit with us, dear," said Miss Winifred, patting the space between her and her sister.

Accordingly, Ann sat, and Miss Genevieve and Miss Winifred openly studied her face.

"I still can't believe they got a granddaughter. At their age!" said Miss Winifred. She glanced around Ann to her sister and gave a prim shake of her head.

"Oh, they've always had the granddaughter. She just wasn't here," Miss Genevieve said. She peered around Ann from the opposite end of the couch. "Please forgive my younger sister, Ann. Sometimes she has a terrible habit of missing the obvious."

"Of course, you're quite right, Genevieve," Miss Winifred conceded. She leaned over and whispered loudly in Ann's ear, "It's just easier to agree with my older sister."

Miss Genevieve ignored the comment. "She's the spitting image of Amelia when she was that age. Wouldn't you say, Winifred?"

"The very likeness. And Amelia always had Bernard's smile, so the mouth is definitely his."

"Let us hope she isn't as mischievous as Bernard was," Miss Genevieve said with the air of one who expects her hopes to be dashed.

"Miss Genevieve and Miss Winifred were my teachers in grade school," Grandpa explained.

"Really?" asked Ann.

"Oh, yes, dear, and your grandfather could be a very ornery little boy. I had to pull his ear many a time when he was my pupil," Miss Genevieve said.

Ann saw Grandpa touch his ear as if he could feel those bony fingers itching to pull it from across the room and the decades.

"One day, he left a frog in my desk drawer," said Miss Winifred.

"Grandpa!"

"What? I was young once," Grandpa said.

"But he was a bright little boy, wasn't he, Genevieve?" Miss Winifred continued.

"Indeed, he was. Are you a good scholar?" Miss Genevieve turned a piercing gaze at Ann over her wire-rimmed glasses.

"Uh, yes, ma'am," Ann faltered, caught off guard. The honorific rose naturally to her lips although she had never ma'amed anyone before in her life. She sat frozen in Miss Genevieve's hypnotic gaze.

"Ann's quite a bookworm," said Grandpa.

"As was her mother," Miss Winifred said.

"A point in her favor. Do you use profanity?" Miss Genevieve asked.

Ann started at the sudden change in the conversation. "No."

"Never?" she said, clearly unconvinced.

"Not at all. I strive to speak like the great heroines of literature. They do not swear, and therefore, neither do I," Ann said in a tone utterly befitting one of those heroines.

"You're not into punk rock, are you?" Miss Winifred continued the third-degree.

"No, of course not," Ann said, her irritation rising. Who did these two think they were, showing up to pry into her personal life?

"Are you in a gang?" Miss Genevieve asked.

"No." Ann's answers were getting crisper. It was clear she was indeed being interrogated by two seasoned sleuths. A background check seemed imminent.

"No drugs? Alcohol? Cigarettes?" Miss Genevieve pressed.

"No." *When had the room gotten so hot?* Ann wondered. The sweat pooled in the small of her back.

"Good," Miss Genevieve said. She leaned back and placed her hands in her lap.

Ann let out the breath she hadn't realized she was holding. Was the interrogation by the Storey Inquisition finally over?

"You know, I think Ann might be around the same age as John Alexander's stepdaughter," said Miss Winifred.

"Who's John Alexander?" asked Ann.

"John lives on the farm just north of here," Grandpa explained.

"He was a confirmed bachelor all his life, but then he surprised us all and got married last year," Miss Genevieve said. She sounded as if she were offended that John Alexander hadn't asked her permission to make such a life-altering change.

"Ellen Alexander is a veterinarian medications representative. She was a Tucker, and her family was originally from this area. She was back here for her job, and she decided to explore her family history. She had a flat tire out near the old Tucker farm—John Alexander owns that land now, you know—and he came to her rescue. Isn't that lovely?" said Miss Winifred.

"There's hardly anything lovely about a flat tire on a country road," Miss Genevieve said. "Please keep your feet firmly planted on solid ground, Winifred."

Miss Winifred ignored her. "This is Ellen's second marriage, so John got a ready-made family. I'm sure you'll get along well with them, and won't it be nice to have some friends before school starts?"

"But I won't be here . . ."

"We'll make sure Ann meets all the neighbors," Grandma said. She shot Ann a look.

Fine, thought Ann. *But Dad will get everything straightened out by the end of summer. Won't he?*

Miss Genevieve glanced at her watch. "My goodness, would you look at the time? We'd better be on our way. We have other places to be this morning.

"It's been lovely catching up with you," Miss Winifred said.

"A granddaughter at your age. Well, I guess all you can do now is hope for the best, Thelma," Miss Genevieve said. Her tone indicated she still harbored some serious doubts.

"I think it's real nice Ann has come to stay with you," said the more optimistic Miss Winifred.

"It's not like she had a choice from what I hear. She's just lucky she has grandparents who know how to do their duty, even though they didn't know where she was all those years before," Miss Genevieve said.

"What?" Ann was taken by surprise. That wasn't right. Their detective skills must not be as good as she'd thought. "But . . ."

"It's a miracle it all worked out," Miss Winifred said, the flowers on her hat bouncing as she nodded.

"Yes, it is. Well, we need to be off, but we really do need to do this more often. We just don't neighbor around like we used to. Come, Winifred."

Ann rolled her eyes. No doubt their guests had a full morning of poking about the countryside planned. They seemed to know everything about everyone for miles around. But what had they meant about her grandparents not knowing where she was? Maybe she'd ask Grandpa; she was more likely to get an answer out of him.

"Well, that's out of the way, and it's a relief," Grandma said after the sisters left.

"Now, Thelma, you knew they wouldn't stay away for long," said Grandpa. "They can't help themselves."

"No, but they're best taken in small doses."

"Are those two always like that?" Ann said.

"Always. Except when they're worse." Grandpa rubbed his ear gingerly. "Come on—let's go look around the farm like we planned," Grandpa said.

Ann collected her shoes from the mat by the back door and sat on the bench to put them on. The Page sisters' visit was so like what she'd read in her novel. At least she'd held her temper, which had been no small feat. The scene she'd just endured carried her mind back to the thorny question of how Anne Shirley would be punished for her outburst to Mrs. Lynde. They must not send her back to the orphanage, or the title of the book would be different. What if . . .

"Ann?" Grandma said, shattering Ann's reverie.

"Hmm? Oh, sorry. I was thinking about Anne Shirley in my book again."

"You'd be better off to worry about Ann Alwyn," Grandma said. "She seems to need all your attention."

4

Horizons

Ann followed Grandpa down the back steps and around the house to the laneway, giving the dog, Sam, a pat on the head as she passed him. He was an Australian shepherd mix with grayish fur and haphazard spots, and his clear eyes and bobbed tail made Ann smile. She'd never had a pet before, but she could get used to the happily wagging tail each time Sam saw her.

"We'll take Bessie," Grandpa said.

"Bessie?"

Grandpa stopped and gestured to the weathered green pick-up parked beside the gray Buick they'd driven to bring Ann back from Colorado.

"Why do you call it Bessie?" asked Ann.

"Just look at her. Could she have any other name?"

"I'm not really an expert at naming vehicles, but sure. Bessie fits."

Grandpa chuckled as they opened the creaking doors and climbed into the truck. He backed out and maneuvered Bessie down the long, rutted laneway to the county road. The pickup had known better days, Ann decided, with its rust and dents and muffler-less roar.

"Sorry there's no A/C. It hasn't worked for years," Grandpa said as they bounced along with the windows down.

"The springs in the seat seem to be fine," Ann said.

Grandpa laughed. "That they are."

"So where are we going?"

"I figured we'd go up to the pasture and count the cattle."

Ann stared blankly. "Why? I'm sorry if that's a dumb question, but I don't know anything about cattle. Or farms in general, for that matter."

"You can't know things if you don't ask."

"That seems to be the philosophy of the day. Anne Shirley said that, too."

"Who?"

"The character in the book you loaned me."

"Of course. Well, you have to check on your cattle to make sure you're not missing any, so I help out our renter, Arthur, by counting his cattle. Besides, it gives me something to do. I don't like being retired." Grandpa raised his voice as they rumbled across the bridge over the creek and up the hill to the pasture.

Ann peered at the barbed wire fence bordering the swaths of land as they rode by. Three strands of the prickly wire stretched menacingly between each fence post.

"How could they ever get out of that?" she asked.

"You'd be surprised. There are miles of this fence to keep up, and sometimes a section comes down. Or, now and then, someone forgets to shut the gate."

"Mental note: Always shut the gate."

"Always." Grandpa pulled off the road and into the pasture entrance. "Hop out with me, and you can walk the gate out of the way after I open it."

Ann did as she was told, and she began to feel more confident in her ability to fit into life on the farm. Why, it would be a breeze! Ann thought, allowing herself the luxury of thinking in exclamation points, just like Mrs. Lynde did in the scene she'd read that morning, and Anne Shirley, for that matter. So what, if Ann's English teacher told her she used too many exclamation points in her writing? Ms. Miller was miles away in a different state. If exclamation points more perfectly expressed her thoughts at Sunflower Lane, Ann decided, she would use them with abandon, along with italics. She ran through the prairie grass to the waiting truck.

"Now that we're off the road, I thought maybe I'd give you a driving lesson," said Grandpa.

"What?"

"I taught both our girls to drive up here in this pasture. There's nowhere safer."

"Are you sure you want to risk it? Sabrina always told me I was a danger on a bicycle and would be in a car. Dad let me drive just a little the one time when we went up into the mountains, but he got frustrated with me pretty quickly. I'm not very good at anything hands-on."

"Let's give it a try," Grandpa said.

They changed seats, and Ann held the steering wheel in a death grip. "What do I do first?"

"Looks like you'll need to scoot the seat forward. Now, put your foot on the brake and pull the gearshift down into drive. No, your right foot."

"Sorry. Are you sure you want to try this?" Ann asked, some of her apprehension returning. But Grandpa seemed more patient than her father; he surely wouldn't yell and criticize or hit her if she made a mistake.

"We all have to learn sometime."

Ann put the truck in drive and awaited further instructions.

"Press the accelerator and follow these ruts through the pasture."

The faithful old vehicle lurched forward with a groan as Ann let her foot off the brake and stomped on the gas.

"Not so hard," said Grandpa, reaching up to steady himself against the frame, but Ann had already let off the gas and slammed her foot back down on the brake.

Ann reached out a tentative foot and pressed the accelerator. The truck moved, turtle-like, down the rutted path worn across the prairie by countless years of similar trips.

"How do I know where I'm going?" Ann asked.

"Just follow the ruts to that windmill. The cattle will be around there."

"Do we just drive up and count them?"

"Yes, moving slowly. We don't want to spook them."

They drove in silence as Ann fixed her gaze straight ahead in concentration. Suddenly, a flutter of wings crossed in front of them, and Ann followed its flight with her eyes and hand.

"Look at that bird," she said, pointing.

"Eyes on the road and both hands on the wheel."

Ann's head snapped forward, and she gripped the wheel with both hands.

"What kind of bird was that? It was beautiful."

"A meadowlark. That's the Kansas state bird. Watch it here, there's a bit of . . . "

Ann felt her stomach drop as the truck pitched downward and a pair of pliers Grandpa kept on the dash sailed through the air and landed with a thud on the floorboard.

" . . . a dip," finished Grandpa, retrieving his pliers.

"I didn't see it," Ann said, cringing in anticipation of a rebuke.

"No, you can't see it," Grandpa said without a trace of frustration. "You'll just have to learn where it is and avoid it next time. Let's go."

"Is that a pond?"

"Yes, but the water's not reliable, so that's why we have the windmill and tank."

"It makes me think of the Lake of Shining Waters in my book."

Grandpa looked doubtful. "It's just a pond but call it the Lake of Diamond Waters if you want."

"Why not?" Ann said, smiling at Grandpa's adaptation. This naming places was creative and kind of fun. She could see why Anne Shirley enjoyed it. She'd never lived anywhere that had places worth naming before. "I love all these flowers," she said, her eyes darting to the splashes of color nestled among the waving blades of grass.

"There's a lot of wildflowers in these pastures."

"Why do you call the farm Sunflower Lane? I haven't seen a single sunflower."

"Let up a little," Grandpa said at Ann's increased speed. "It's too early for sunflowers, but you'll see them all along the roads later in the summer. My grandfather picked the farm's name because he thought it was a hopeful symbol for his future. He'd saved up his money to buy this place. He didn't come from a family of farmers, but that was his dream."

"That's a fantastic story," Ann said, thrilling at the daring image of an ancestor who had been master of his fate and captain of his soul.

"It's your family history. These are your roots," Grandpa said.

Ann considered his words. "I never thought of it that way. I've always felt pretty much rootless my entire life."

The truck wound up a slight rise to the windmill and water tank, and there were the cattle, great red animals with placid white faces.

"Stop here and put it in park so we can count," said Grandpa.

Ann complied and began to count to herself. The job was harder than it had sounded. Just when she had a tally, one of the animals moved and she confused it with another. She was also finding it difficult to keep her attention off the wide-open vista all around her. The grass in its shifting tints stretched as far as the eye could see, broken only by daubs of wildflowers and the mirage of a horizon somewhere beyond. It still made her feel a little unmoored, but there was definitely what Anne Shirley called "scope for the imagination" in all that space.

"Looks like everyone's here who needs to be," Grandpa said, bringing Ann back from her musings.

"It's really peaceful up here. I feel like I could see to the very ends of the earth."

"If you can appreciate a view like that, you're a Kansan at heart, Ann," Grandpa said.

"I doubt it, if I'm only here for the summer. But I do love nature. I always enjoyed the few times we went out of the cities where we lived, and especially our school field trips. Of course, you don't get many of those in high school. But Nana had a nice flower garden, and I tried to take care of it after she died, and we moved back to Denver to live in her house."

"Didn't you have any activities at school?"

"Not really. Dad didn't want me to 'run around' after school."

"I see."

They sat in silence, looking out across the pasture, each with their own thoughts.

"Grandpa, can I ask you a question?"

"Sure. What is it?"

"What did the Page sisters mean when they said you didn't know where I was?"

Grandpa gazed back toward the horizon as if looking for the answer written somewhere upon it.

"Just that: we didn't know where you were. Your father left Kansas City right after you were born."

"After Mom died?"

"Yes. We tried to find him, but we couldn't. We contacted your Nana Alwyn, but she wouldn't tell us where you were either."

"But Dad said you didn't approve of him. That's why you didn't want anything to do with us."

Grandpa sighed. "It's no secret we didn't think Jake was the best match for our daughter. But we always wanted to be a part of your life. He didn't let us know where you were."

Ann sat digesting the information. None of it was what she'd heard from Dad and Sabrina, and some things still didn't make sense to her.

"Then how did child services find you?" she asked.

"It was thanks to your neighbor. Your Nana finally responded to one of our letters several years ago. She wouldn't go against your father's wishes and tell us where you lived, but she did let us know you were OK. We'd written several times after that without a response, but we didn't give up. We didn't know she'd passed away or that you'd moved back to live in her house. When we wrote this last time, the letter was misdelivered to your neighbor."

"Mrs. Dansbury."

"Yes."

"Did she open the letter or what?"

"No. She remembered our name from the return address, and she said she couldn't forget the town because Storey sounded so 'quaint.'"

"But how did she know who you were?"

"She gave the letter to Sabrina. Seems your half-sister had some colorful things to say about us. She let it slip that we're your grandparents."

"Yeah, Sabrina has a temper."

"Sounds like it."

Ann sat quietly digesting the information. Could it be true? Had these grandparents she'd never known been looking for her all her life? If so, Dad and Sabrina had both hidden the truth from her. Sure, Dad had lied about some things in his time, and Sabrina was a habitual liar. But surely her own father wouldn't lie to her about something so important as this. Would he? And why?

Grandpa reached over and placed a weathered hand on her shoulder. "It's a lot to get your head around."

Ann shrugged. "I'm fine. Should we head back? I think I'm getting the hang of this driving thing."

"You sure are. Just circle around the tank and follow the ruts to the gate."

"We're off," Ann said, putting the truck in gear.

"Just watch out for the . . . "

Ann saw the group of limestone rocks and slammed on the brakes. Once again, she and Grandpa lurched forward on the old bench seat.

" . . . rocks," Grandpa finished, fishing his handkerchief out of his overalls pocket and wiping it across his forehead.

"Are you absolutely positive you want to teach me to drive?" she asked.

"Not a doubt in my mind."

Ann took a deep breath and coaxed the truck into gear.

"Ready?" she asked.

The intrepid Grandpa never hesitated for an instant before he answered. "Ready."

5

A New Departure in Biscuits

"'**P**oetry is the achievement of the synthesis of hyacinths and biscuits,'" Ann quoted Sandburg as she moved the rolling pin back and forth with enthusiasm over the snowy mound of dough. It was a muggy, rainy afternoon, and Ann was having her first baking lesson from Grandma in the low-ceilinged kitchen at Sunflower Lane. Perspiration beaded her forehead, partly from the heat but mostly from concentration. She wanted her first attempt at baking to go well.

"Gently," Grandma said, ignoring Ann's cryptic reference to flowers. "And only roll the dough to a half-inch thickness. That will make your biscuits light and fluffy and not tough as shoe leather."

"I've never made biscuits from scratch before. And I should probably tell you I messed up the ones out of a can once."

"If you pay attention and do as you're told, you'll learn."

"I hope you're right," Ann said.

"You'll have to. We aren't in the habit of making biscuits out of cans in this house," Grandma said as she demonstrated how to cut the biscuits. "Practice makes perfect, and you'll have plenty of practice here."

Ann nodded dutifully. No matter how accurate Grandma's proverbs and morals might be, they still chafed because they were usually directed at her correction.

"Now, we'll pop these in the oven for ten minutes, and we'll set the timer so we don't forget them," said Grandma.

"That's how I messed up the canned ones," Ann said.

"Burned them?"

"To a crisp."

"Always set a timer, especially in your case. You do seem to be easily distracted. Let's set the table for supper while they bake."

"I know how to do that at least. Miss Simmons taught me how to do a full formal place setting in junior high home ec, but we moved before I got to any of the cooking lessons. But I usually only set out what I need since I eat alone so often."

Grandma sniffed. "You won't find many meals around here where you don't need all the silverware."

Ann nodded and undertook the task of setting out plates, napkins, glasses, and all the silverware.

"I've been meaning to ask you, is there anything you need? Any clothes? Or something for your room?"

"There's no need to go to any trouble since I'm only here for the summer," Ann said.

"We've talked about this: it will probably be longer than just this summer."

Ann continued to set the table in silence.

"We have other furniture around if there's anything you could use. Maybe a desk? You said you like to write."

"I've never had a desk," Ann said.

"No desk? Where did you do your homework?"

"At the kitchen table. Unless the apartment or house we were renting had a decent window. Then, I'd sit there. Nana's house in Denver has a tiny window seat. That was my favorite place after we moved there when Dad inherited the house."

"Sitting at a window doesn't sound real comfortable."

"Sometimes it wasn't, but I liked the light and looking out and watching the world go by, even if I wasn't out in it. It was like I had my own personal painting, and it was constantly changing. At Nana's, I could open the window and let the perfume of her flowers float in on the breeze. It was heavenly, especially when the lilacs were in bloom. Anne Shirley—that's the girl in my book— would say that there's 'scope for the imagination' in a window. Sitting at one always gives me ideas for my own writing. At Nana's, I'd go sit in the window seat and write furiously whenever 'genius took to burning.'"

"Your mother's desk is still around. You could have it."

"Really? I've never had anything that was hers."

"She liked school real well. She saved up her money and bought a little desk at an auction when she was about your age. She was real proud of it. It's up in the garret now, so we'd need to get it down and clean it."

"Awesome." Ann sniffed the air. "The biscuits already smell delicious."

"Baking isn't hard. You just have to stay focused."

"I guess. Is there anything else I should do?" asked Ann.

"We need more jelly. Run down to the cave and fetch another jar, and I'll call Grandpa in for supper. He's out there puttering around in the shop again."

"The cave? There's a cave here?"

"The limestone storm shelter. You know, the door on the west end of the living room? It leads to the stairs."

Ann swallowed. "Is it dark down there?"

"Not if you turn on the light. The switch is at the top."

Ann went as one resigned to her duty from the kitchen, through the dining room, and to the back wall of the living room. She gingerly opened the door to the cave. The gray light of the rainy afternoon filtered in the western window at the end of the wooden structure over the steep limestone steps. A cobweb stretched across the black hole yawning before Ann's feet. She turned on the single bare bulb, toed the spiderweb out of the way, and began her descent to the cave, one hand steadying herself on the roughhewn stones of the wall.

At the bottom, Ann pushed open a sagging wooden door whose creaking hinges made the hair on the nape of her neck stand at attention. Another unshaded lightbulb glared from the domed limestone ceiling, casting weird shadows off the narrow stone walls and floor. She shivered in the eerie coolness belowground. Ann made her way to the center of the room and stopped, listening to the utter silence that surrounded her.

"It's like a dungeon down here," Ann said aloud. Her voice echoed off the stone walls. "I could totally see this as the setting for a gothic novel. I absolutely will not think about that time Sabrina locked me in the basement at Nana's when I was little. It was just like *Jane Eyre*."

"Ann!"

Ann jumped, startled by Grandma's rebuke from the top of the stairs.

"Coming," she called.

Ann dashed the last few steps to the wooden shelves at the back of the cave and reached for a jar of Grandma's homemade jelly. She hurried to the stairs, only to find her grandmother standing resolutely at the top of them, arms crossed. Ann pulled the bottom door closed and hurried up.

"What on earth took you so long?" Grandma asked. She stepped out of the way as Ann exited and handed her the jelly.

"I was just thinking."

"Quit your woolgathering and go wash your hands. Supper's on the table. We don't want it getting cold because of your lollygagging."

Grandma returned to the kitchen where Grandpa was waiting at the table. Her voice carried into the bathroom where Ann scrubbed her hands.

"I found her. She was 'thinking' down in the cave," said Grandma as she pulled the biscuits from the oven.

Ann rolled her eyes.

"Thinking? About what?" asked Grandpa.

"You'll have to ask her," Grandma said.

Ann sighed and dried her hands. There would be no pleasing Grandma, she thought as she returned to the kitchen.

"Ann, set the basket of biscuits on the table, and put the rest back on the stove to stay warm," Grandma said.

Grandpa asked the blessing on the food, and they began to pass the bowls and plates back and forth.

"I hear you made your first trip down to the cave," said Grandpa.

"Yes, and it's kind of creepy. Why do you have a cave here anyway?"

"That's what we call that kind of storm shelter in the Flint Hills. My grandfather and his neighbors cut the rock out of the pastures and built it when they built the house."

"Have you ever had to use it?" asked Ann.

"Of course," Grandma said.

"Have you ever seen a tornado?" asked Ann.

"Sure have," said Grandpa.

Ann shuddered. "That's terrifying."

"Tornadoes are nothing to take lightly," Grandma said. "If you should ever be here alone and a bad storm comes up, you go straight to the cave lickety-split, you hear?"

"Don't worry, Grandma. I have no desire whatsoever to be swept away like Dorothy in *The Wizard of Oz*."

Grandma and Grandpa chatted about the local happenings and the weather which, as Ann was learning, was a common topic among the farmers in the rural community. It always seemed there was either too much or not enough rain.

After some time, Grandpa sniffed the air and wrinkled his brow. "Thelma, is there something still in the oven?" he asked from his chair nearest that appliance.

"No, there shouldn't be," Grandma said. She sniffed the air. "But I do smell something."

She opened the oven to reveal the blackened remains of the last biscuits sitting like so many lumps of coal.

"Goodness sakes, Ann. Why did you put them back in the oven?" Grandma asked.

"You said to put them in the stove to keep them warm," Ann said.

"I said to put them on the stove, not in it." Grandma sighed. Her eyes flicked momentarily to the copy of the Serenity Prayer she kept on the refrigerator. "Why on earth would you think it was a good idea to leave the oven on and put food back in it?"

Ann crossed her arms, tilted her chin down, and looked steadily at Grandma with both eyebrows raised.

"I am doing the best I can, but I've never baked, and I can't read minds," she said.

Grandma blanched and her mouth dropped.

"We know that," Grandpa said quickly.

"I assure you I'll learn as quickly as I can," Ann said.

Grandma swallowed before speaking. "Yes, of course you will."

"Now, should I clear the table? I can do that tolerably well."

Grandma nodded, and Ann stacked the plates carefully beside the sink while Grandpa scraped the scraps into a small bucket.

"Run this out and feed Sam," he said. "And be sure to give him some attention while you're at it."

Ann carried the scraps out the back door and across the patio to Sam's dish. She emptied the bucket and scratched Sam behind the ears while he ate. Her grandparents' voices carried out the open kitchen window, but she pretended not to hear.

"Did you see that look?" Grandma said.

"I did."

"Just like Amelia." Grandma's voice caught.

"The spittin' image."

Ann didn't want to hear any more, so she gave Sam one last pat and stomped up the steps so they'd know she was coming.

"I've been thinking," she said, hoping to make peace and stay out of trouble. "I do know how to make one thing: tacos. I could make those one night if you'd like."

"I don't think we've ever had tacos." Grandma sounded unconvinced.

"But they say variety is the spice of life," Grandpa said.

"I don't think we'll be hurting for much of that." Grandma glanced again at the Serenity Prayer. "Not with Ann around at any rate."

6

Great-Uncle Pete is Surprised

“What did you think of our little country church, Ann?” asked Grandpa.

They had just finished a traditional Sunday dinner at Sunflower Lane, complete with pot roast, potatoes and carrots, homemade crescent rolls, and Grandma’s cherry pie for dessert.

“I’ve never really been to church before, so I don’t have much to compare it to. But it was fine. I really like Pastor Walsh’s wife, Mabel. She seems like a kindred spirit. She said she teaches the teen Sunday School class, but I was the only one there this week.”

“I thought Ellen Alexander’s children would be there, but she said they were visiting their father in Kansas City,” said Grandma.

“Who?”

“Our neighbors—the ones the Page sisters mentioned,” said Grandpa.

“Oh, yeah. I remember.”

The phone rang, prompting a sniff from Grandma. “Who could that be during the dinner hour?” Grandma asked as she made her way in no apparent hurry to the phone in the next room.

She answered the black rotary phone that looked to Ann as if it belonged in a museum.

“Hello?”

Anyone who has ever lived in an old farmhouse with one telephone in its very heart knows the entertainment value of any call. Grandpa and Ann listened to Grandma's half of the conversation, not because they were nosey, but because it was impossible not to hear.

"Why, hello, Janis . . . Yes, we just finished . . . That'd be real nice . . . Yes, we can come. What can I bring? . . . Now, I know I don't have to, but you know I can't just show up empty-handed … Of course, I have an extra loaf of bread made. I'll bring that. Thanks again, honey."

Grandma returned to the kitchen. "Janis invited us over for supper tonight. She wanted to do something to welcome Ann."

"We can combine it with a Sunday drive," said Grandpa.

"What's a Sunday drive?" asked Ann, unfamiliar with that pillar of entertainment in rural Kansas.

"You drive around and look at the crops, maybe visit someone," Grandpa explained.

"She's invited Pete, too. We haven't seen him in ages," said Grandma.

Ann didn't know who Pete was, but she suspected he must be another relative she had yet to meet.

"Who's Pete?" she asked.

"My older brother," Grandma said.

"He likes to tease, so take everything he says with a grain of salt," said Grandpa.

"Great," Ann said. "Because I love to be teased."

As Ann discovered later that afternoon, Sunday drives in Storey were never the shortest distance between two points. Grandpa drove a winding path along back roads to make the drive last longer, for Ann's grandparents adhered to the proverb that "a Sunday well spent brings a week of content." They believed Sunday work should be kept to a minimum, and to avoid any temptation, they could make even a short drive last almost infinitely.

Ann rode drowsily in the back seat, only half listening to her grandparents speak the names of people and crops she did not know, catching snatches of their conversation. She was trying to remember Kansas authors and heroines, other than Dorothy. Laura Ingalls Wilder lived somewhere in Kansas for a time, she recalled, and Ms. Miller told her William Stafford was from Kansas. That was probably why he knew so much about new moves and other doors, Ann decided. She snuggled her head against the window, sleepy eyes watching the line of haybales alongside the passing field melt into a single umber blur.

"Wake up, Sleepyhead. We're almost there," Grandpa said.

Ann yawned and stretched, peeling her eyes open against the afternoon sun. She looked out as they rolled down Storey's bricked Main Street. She had been into the grocery store once with Grandma and thought she'd stepped back in time. She'd never been in a store that had an honest-to-goodness butcher and baggers who would carry your groceries to the car for you.

"There's a lot of history on this street," Grandpa said. He slowed and began to point out buildings. "That's the old Opera House—where the bakery is now. My mom remembered when it drew the most fashionable shows to town. We did our class play there when we were juniors, but it was so cold no one could get their cars started, and we lost money. We were flat broke when we started our senior year. There's always been a bank in that building, and that's the hardware store. That's the dime store—it was a general store when I first started delivering milk to town."

"You delivered milk?" said Ann.

"Sure did. We had dairy cattle up until a few years before I retired completely. I met a lot of interesting folks that way. I could tell you all kinds of stories."

"I want to hear them," Ann said. Grandpa was a natural-born storyteller, and his remembrances opened her imagination to other times and worlds.

"That's the library, the greenhouse, and there's the post office. The Dairy Crème is there, across from the park, and the café is right beside it. And that's all there is to downtown Storey."

"The café is Grandpa's unofficial office," Grandma said with a hint of humor.

"In my defense, that's where all the farmers go to get the news. I have to stay up-to-date."

Ann grinned. "Thanks for the narrated tour."

They turned off Main and followed a shady street into a residential neighborhood.

"We're here," Grandma said after a couple of blocks.

"Here" was Aunt Janis and Uncle Edward's trim, white, ranch-style house. A sea of colorful yard ornaments and whirligigs blanketed the front lawn. A slightly short, slightly round woman with permed brown hair streaked with gray waved from the porch.

"Hello! Welcome! And you must be Ann. I'm your Aunt Janis," she said. She wrapped Ann in a tight embrace.

"Hello," Ann managed to say.

"Oh, let me look at you. Edward, doesn't she look just like Amelia?" Aunt Janis ran a gentle hand down Ann's face.

"She sure does. Nice to meet you," Uncle Edward said. He was tall and had a wide, friendly smile. His salt-and-pepper hair was cut short, and he had deep laugh lines around his brown eyes.

"It's too hot to stand out here. Let's go inside where it's cool." Aunt Janis opened the door and shooed them inside.

Ann looked curiously around the living room. It was decorated with a profusion of overstuffed throw pillows in bright hues, and crocheted doilies and antimacassars anywhere one could imagine— and a few places Ann never would have imagined, which, given her proclivities along those lines, was a feat not to be taken lightly. Ann perched in the middle of the couch between Grandma and Grandpa, a hard pillow wedged behind her.

"Uncle Pete isn't here yet so we'll just take this chance to get to know you. We'll tell you all about ourselves first so you don't feel like you're getting the third degree," Aunt Janis said.

"Thanks," Ann said.

"I'm the head cook for the school district, and your Uncle Edward owns the farm implement dealership and parts store here in Storey. Our twins—your cousins, Mary Beth and Junior—are both in college up at Kansas State. Can you believe this will be their last year, Mom?"

"Doesn't seem possible," said Grandma.

There was a loud knock at the door, and Uncle Edward went to answer it.

"That'll be Uncle Pete. He's a little deaf, so you'll have to speak up," said Aunt Janis.

Ann's great-uncle Pete, who had farmed until his sons took over the land, now lived in a house on a quiet street in Storey.

"Come in, Uncle Pete," Uncle Edward shouted. "Everyone's in the living room."

Great-Uncle Pete hobbled in supported by a knobby, well-used walking stick. He wore overalls and a faded plaid shirt. His face was worn and grizzled, and his white hair stuck out from under his fraying seed cap.

"Pete, this is Ann," Grandma said to her older brother.

"Eh?"

"This is Ann," she repeated, louder.

"How do you do?" Ann asked politely.

Uncle Pete adjusted his glasses and openly stared.

"Well, I can't believe it. She looks exactly like Amelia did," he said. "Here—let me shake your hand."

Ann dutifully offered him her hand and felt him slip something into it. When she looked, she found a butterscotch candy.

"Thank you," she said, but Great-Uncle Pete was already making his way to the recliner.

"The candy is his standard trick," Grandpa explained.

Ann helped Aunt Janis and Grandma set the picnic table, amazed at the variety of food. There was grilled chicken, browned baby potatoes, fruit salad, Grandma's oatmeal bread, green beans, and a steaming dish that Aunt Janis described as Aunt Hazel's cheesy grits.

"The grits were your great-uncle Pete's wife's signature dish. I think everyone in the family has one," Aunt Janis explained.

"I suppose mine would be burned biscuits," Ann mumbled to herself as the others filed out to the deck and took their places.

Grandpa asked the blessing, and the meal and conversation continued. Aunt Janis made an effort to include Ann by asking her about her grade in school and hobbies. From there, the conversation followed the usual lines in rural Kansas: crops, weather, livestock, the markets. Ann's mind began to wander.

"Got any boyfriends, Ann?" Great-Uncle Pete asked.

But Ann's mind was elsewhere. She had rationed her reading time since coming to Sunflower Lane, partly out of necessity and partly because Grandma had kept her busy. Each evening, she read a little before bed, and she spent the following day wondering what would happen next in the world of Green Gables. Her thoughts were far away in Avonlea when Great-Uncle Pete began his interrogation.

"Must be thinking about him right now. See them starry eyes? So who's the lucky fella?" said Great-Uncle Pete.

Ann glanced up. Was he talking to her? "Huh?"

"What's your boyfriend's name?" Great-Uncle Pete shouted.

"I don't have a boyfriend," she said.

"What? Ain't got a boyfriend? Why, you're gonna be an old maid."

Ann's cheeks turned pink, and she leveled him with the same look she'd given Grandma after the biscuit incident.

"Great-Uncle Pete, Grandma has made it very clear I am not allowed to have a boyfriend. And as far as being an old maid goes, I can assure you I would much rather be a spinster than ever be married to a crotchety old grouch such as yourself," she said.

Great-Uncle Pete's mouth hung open. "I guess they teach different manners in the big cities these days."

"If we're speaking of manners, let's revisit the topic of meanness," Ann said, her temper still aflame. "Because let me assure you, Great-Uncle Pete, that teasing a newcomer is the height of insensitivity."

"Well, I never," said Great-Uncle Pete.

"Well, you have now," Ann replied.

An uncomfortable silence filled the air.

"Pete, boyfriends are no laughing matter. Ann is not allowed to have one, and that's that," Grandma said shortly.

"Well, I guess I can see why, after what happened with Amelia. But she don't need to be so touchy about it," said Great-Uncle Pete.

Ann furrowed her brow. "What do you mean 'what happened with Amelia?' Just because my father isn't perfect doesn't mean you have any right to insult him."

"Hmph." Great-Uncle Pete grunted and shook his head.

"Let's not let talk about boyfriends ruin our evening. It's time for dessert, and I made homemade ice cream and my prize-winning chocolate cake with chocolate cream cheese frosting," Aunt Janis said. She stood and began clearing the table along with Grandma, chattering about a new recipe she'd found for banana bread.

"Ann, please take these plates in," Grandma said.

Ann stacked the last of the dishes and carried them to the kitchen. Aunt Janis was still talking, now about her garden, as she and Grandma sliced the cake and dished ice cream.

"You're going to love this strawberry ice cream," Aunt Janis said. She wrapped her arm around Ann and held her close. "I froze strawberries from my garden last year, and I'm just so excited to get to share them with my niece. I sometimes wondered if I'd ever see this day."

"Thanks," Ann said.

"Ann, you'll need to apologize to your great-uncle," Grandma said.

Ann sighed. "I know. But he had no right to tease. Besides, you should be happy with me. I told him I'm not allowed to have a boyfriend. Isn't that what you want?"

"Yes, but you need to hold your temper. I understand Pete's teasing can be trying, but he's lonely. Your Great-Aunt Hazel passed on to a better life last year, you know," Grandma said.

"Probably any life would be better than one married to him," Ann mumbled.

"What?"

"I just said he's grouchy and his comments were out of line—especially the way he attacked Dad. I know he isn't perfect, but he's not even here to defend himself."

Grandma turned away and said nothing.

"Ann, honey, sometimes we have to make allowances for elderly people," Aunt Janis said.

"I know. 'Angry people are not always wise.' I've certainly seen the repercussions of losing my temper with my father and Sabrina, so you'd think I'd learn. Besides, I suppose I should be glad Great-Uncle Pete didn't insult my hair."

"What?" asked Grandma.

"Nothing. It's from my book."

"Never mind your book. Fill the pitcher and you can go apologize before we have dessert."

Ann retrieved the pitcher and filled it from the sink. She watched out the window as Grandma and Aunt Janis passed out plates loaded with dessert. When she stepped to the screen door, Great-Uncle Pete was still going on about the no boyfriend rule. Her hand was on the latch when his words filtered to her ears. She stopped abruptly at them.

"That rule is a good thing, Thelma. 'Specially considering the way Amelia just up and took off."

Aunt Janis glanced up and saw Ann at the patio door. "Oh, dear, your hands are full. Let me open that for you," she said.

There was a beat of uncomfortable silence before the conversation turned back to the weather. But Ann knew what she had heard. Leave it to Great-Uncle Pete to decide that leaving Storey to get married was a cardinal sin. As if this were the only place on the face of the planet that mattered! But why was everyone so uncomfortable anytime the topic of her mother came up? Why didn't anyone ever talk much about Mom? There was just so much Ann still didn't know or understand. But if they were going to criticize her mom, maybe it was better that way.

7

The Enchanted Forest

“Don’t stay up too late reading,” Grandma said as Ann bid them goodnight.

“I won’t. I’m just going to read a few minutes like I do every night, and then I’ll go to bed,” Ann said.

She changed into her pajamas and crawled into bed, the lamplight falling on *Anne of Green Gables* on her nightstand. She had tried to pace herself to make the novel last longer, but now, only a few chapters remained.

“I’ll read one chapter,” Ann said. But as the story unfolded, she became so engrossed that she kept turning the pages. Suddenly, she stopped short.

“No! Not, Matthew! How can they possible kill off Matthew? I refuse to read another page.” Ann resolutely placed the book on her nightstand and shut off the lamp. But the moonlight filtering in through the window illuminated the room around her, and Ann could see the novel beckoning.

“Oh, all right,” Ann said at last. “I don’t suppose it could get any worse than Matthew dying.”

She switched the bedside lamp back on and resumed her reading. A few pages later, Ann sat bolt upright in bed.

“Sell Green Gables? If they sell Green Gables, I’m not reading another word.”

But she continued to turn the pages.

"Not go to college?" Ann shrieked. She quickly snapped her lips together, listening for a reproach from Grandma to be called up the stairs. The only sound was the night breeze blowing the curtains at the window and the distant croaking of frogs along the creek. Ann returned to the last scenes of her book.

"So she forgave Gilbert Blythe. Well, he seems to have learned to be less of a jerk. At least there's some consolation. But I won't put too much hope in any budding romance, for fear of running the same bitter disappointment I suffered when Jo March turned down Laurie in *Little Women*. I still cannot fathom what she was thinking."

Ann turned off the lamp again, but sleep eluded her.

"This is ridiculous," she said as she stared at the ceiling in the moonlight. "I feel half lonely now that I've finished *Anne*. But it's just a book—even if Anne Shirley and Green Gables do seem so real."

When her alarm sounded the next morning, Ann swatted it into silence, pulling the covers over her head.

"I should move. I know I should move. But I'm so tired. Why did I put myself through that last night?" she said.

She rolled to the edge of her bed and dangled her feet, her head still on the pillow. She scooted her feet around, feeling for her flip flops, slipped them on, and finally sat up in bed. A glance in the mirror showed that her hair had tangled into a knot with all her tossing and turning.

"Well, I certainly look like anything but a literary heroine this morning," Ann said. She pulled a brush through her hair and braided it, then slipped on some cutoffs and a T-shirt.

When Ann scuffled into the kitchen, Grandma was pulling a pan of blueberry muffins from the oven and Grandpa was listening to the markets on his 1960s vintage radio.

"Morning," she said, dropping into her chair at the table.

"Ann, are you ill?" Grandma asked, having come around the table to get a good look at Ann's dejected face and tired eyes. She reached a hand to Ann's forehead.

"I'm not sick. I'm sad because Matthew died." Ann sighed.

"Who's Matthew?" asked Grandpa.

"And how did you find out he died?" said Grandma. "I didn't hear the phone in the night. Bernard, did you hear the phone?"

"I never heard a thing," Grandpa said.

"No, Matthew Cuthbert," Ann said. Her grandparents stared blankly at her. "In my novel. He died, and Anne Shirley isn't going to college. The only bright spot is that she and Gilbert made up."

"Well, at least there's some good news to be had," Grandpa said with smiling eyes.

"Ann Alwyn, you seem to half believe what you read. You had me worried with your dying Matthews." Grandma sat down and reached for Ann's hand for grace.

"I thought you liked that book," Grandpa said after the blessing.

"Oh, I do. I've never identified so strongly with a book before. But now it's over, and I feel like I lost my best friend. Even if I reread it, it will never be the same. I'll get swept up in the plot all over again, but I'll always know what's coming. I'll secretly hope it might end differently, and Matthew won't die, but it won't, and he will, and then I'll be sad all over again. Do you know what I mean?"

Grandpa nodded. "I do. That's the sign of a truly good book. But experience has shown me I find something new every time I reread a book that means a lot to me."

"I suppose you're right," Ann said.

"We need to leave for Grandpa's dentist appointment, so I'll leave you the dishes. And for goodness' sake, go take a walk. You look pale as a ghost," said Grandma, interrupting the literary conversation.

"A walk? Are you sure? What if I get lost? I never took a walk alone before."

"You'll be fine. Take Sam with you, and he'll show you the way back," Grandpa said.

"Where should I go?"

"Out the lane and down the road. Use that imagination you're always talking about," Grandma said.

Ann watched her grandparents pull out of the laneway and turned to the dishes. As she washed, dried, and put them away, her mind wandered back across the pages of *Anne.* It really was a satisfying book. If she'd known a girl like Anne Shirley somewhere in all her moving about, they'd have been bosom friends.

"She sets the bar kind of high for best friends," Ann said aloud as she put away the last dish.

Ann looked at the clock. It was early; maybe she'd be able to catch Dad at home. She'd tried to call several times since coming to Sunflower Lane, but all she ever got was the answering machine. Ann dialed, but the result was the same.

"I hope that means he has a job and is busy working. Well, I guess I might as well take that walk, since I don't have anything more to read."

Ann slipped on her tennis shoes and set out down the dusty gravel laneway. Sam trotted along beside her, wagging his short stub of a tail contentedly.

"It's a beautiful morning," Ann said to Sam, raising her face to the sun as she walked. She stopped at the end of lane and looked both ways. "Which way from here?" she asked. Sam turned left and continued down the county road, so Ann followed. They crossed the bridge to a field entrance at the foot of the hill where Sam turned in.

"This is Grandpa's land, but I haven't come here before. Let's explore, Sam."

They followed the tire tracks running along the field. The dog led the way for a few feet before turning and crawling under the prickly strands of a barbed wire fence. He stopped and looked back at Ann with a bark. She could see a narrow path winding into the woods beyond.

"Are you sure?"

Sam answered by crashing through the undergrowth and starting up the hill.

"Why not? Exploring the woods would totally be something Anne Shirley would do," Ann said.

She climbed carefully between the wires of the fence as she had seen Grandpa do and paused in the dance of shade and light cast by the canopy above.

"It feels like I've stepped into some enchanted forest. In fact, that's exactly what Anne Shirley would name this place: the Enchanted Forest. What do you think, Sam?"

He barked his agreement.

Ann followed Sam along the rocky path, worn into the hillside by generations of deer. They meandered along, stepping through the tangle of vines and shrubs. A kaleidoscope of sun and shadow, birdsong and breeze played around them. After several moments, Ann found herself at a point where the path split, one trail leading up the hill to the open pasture beyond, and another winding down in the direction of the creek.

"'Two roads diverged in a wood.' Which one should we follow?" said Ann.

Sam answered by taking the downhill path. It snaked through more undergrowth, back through the fence, and into a clearing at the end of the field. There, a tall, gnarled lilac bush awash in fragrant blooms swayed gently in the warm morning breeze. Its perfume floated across the clearing, and Ann breathed deeply of her favorite scent. She watched a Monarch butterfly flitting gracefully from bloom to bloom as she crossed to the bush and rested her hand on a rough limb.

"How did you get back here?" she asked the bush. "There has to be a story here. I might have spent my life in cities, but even I know lilacs don't just grow in forests. Or maybe they only grow in enchanted forests. What's this?"

Ann took a step toward a round depression in the ground. She was studying the shape and imagining it as the foundation of a former turret when a bumblebee buzzed by her head. She screamed—and not in affectation of a literary heroine, for Ann was terrified of anything with a stinger. She took to her heels and careened down the path toward the creek, Sam barking along beside her. She never paused nor glanced over her shoulder before plunging across the shallow waters of the creek, tumbling into them right at the mid-point of her hasty retreat. While Sam frolicked in the cool water, Ann righted herself, stumbled the rest of the way, and scrambled up the steep, muddy bank on the other side, grasping handfuls of undergrowth and low-hanging branches. At last, she found herself, hot, shaky, and dirty, on the opposite bank, heart still pounding.

"I don't see how you can be so calm," she said to Sam as her canine companion came crashing up the bank through the weeds to stand at her side.

He answered with a healthy shake to clear his drenched fur, covering Ann.

"I'd be very grumpy with you if I weren't already soaking wet."

Sam nosed Ann's knee where she discovered a gash from her fall on the rocky creek bed.

"Wonderful. This is not going to help me convince Grandma I'm not a disaster at pretty much everything. But in my defense, I had no idea there were killer bumblebees around here. And this really hurts."

Ann picked her way slowly along the field. She had reached the county road when she heard the approaching crunch of gravel. She ducked behind a tree at the edge of the field and peeked out to discover a sparkling white Cadillac inching toward her: the Page sisters.

"Oh, what did I do to deserve this?" wailed Ann. "Those two gossips will be all too happy to tell everyone in town, the county, and the entire state of Kansas what happened to me. And worse yet, they'll tell Grandma."

Ann dropped to the ground, burrowing behind the prickly bushes she later learned were wild roses. She grasped Sam by the collar and stared into his eyes.

"Please do not bark," she begged as she listened to the car approach and creep by at a snail's pace.

When all was silent, Ann peeked out between the thorny branches to see the Cadillac turn slowly onto the highway. She let out a breath of relief.

"Let's go before someone else comes along."

Ann slipped from behind the bushes and trudged along the lefthand side of the road. She was between the bridge and the entrance to Sunflower Lane when she heard another vehicle approaching down the hill. This time, there was nowhere to hide, so she kept walking, trying to be as dignified as possible when soaked, covered with mud, and with a cut on her knee. The vehicle slowed as it drew alongside her.

"Need a lift?" said a voice.

Ann turned to see a boy about her own age leaning out of the window of a well-used red Chevy pick-up. His wavy, brown hair was windswept, and his hazel eyes seemed to laugh at her predicament. Just her luck, he would be cute—the perfect dashing hero for any novel. And here she was soaked, muddy, scratched, and bleeding.

"No, thank you," she said and kept walking.

"You look like you fell in the creek or something."

Ann's nose tilted upward. Good-looking or not, he was being a royal pain.

"Not the talkative type, are you?"

"Haven't you ever heard you shouldn't talk to strangers?" she said coolly.

"You must be the Holmbergs' granddaughter. I heard you came to live with them."

Silence.

"Ann, right?"

Ann had reached the entrance to the laneway. She stopped, and the pickup stopped.

"Sure you don't want a lift in?"

"Have you never heard not to get into a vehicle with strangers?" Ann asked.

He grinned. "You don't give up, do you? All right then. I'll be seeing you." He waved and spun out, throwing gravel as he raced down the road.

"I certainly hope not!" Ann yelled after him. She turned to Sam and shook her head. "What a jerk! And can you imagine what would have happened if the Page sisters had seen me talking to him? They'd tell Grandma, and I'd be grounded for life. It's hard enough for me to stay on her good side as it is. I sincerely hope I never see that annoying boy again in my life."

8

The Phone Call

"This is miserable," Ann said from where she lay listlessly on the couch reading, a fan blowing over her legs.

"Agreed." Grandpa sat in the nearby recliner with a second fan trained on his swollen face.

Several days had passed since Ann's stumbling romp through the creek, and in that time, she had developed what Grandma declared a record-setting case of poison ivy. The itchy rash covered broad swaths of Ann's legs and arms, made worse by the scratches from the unforgiving thorns of her wild rose bush camouflage. It even had the audacity to make a mild appearance on her face.

"How was I to know there was poison ivy?" Ann had asked when Grandma identified her ailment.

"Leaves of three, let it be," said Grandma as she handed her a bottle of calamine lotion.

Ann dearly wished her grandmother's proverbs wouldn't always be directed at her. Of course, there was no one else around to get into the kind of scrapes Ann seemed to constantly find herself in, so wishing for someone else to be lectured was a lost cause.

"No offense, Grandma, but I was being chased by a killer bumblebee. I didn't stop to count the leaves on every plant around. I'd think you could have a little sympathy for me. I've never been taught what poison ivy looks like. And this stuff really itches."

Each morning the poison ivy had brought what seemed a new degree of discomfort. This was the first day Ann felt that the pestilence, as she called it, had not surfaced in any new locations. Temperatures in southcentral Kansas had shot into the 90s, and life with a case of poison ivy in the unairconditioned farmhouse gave a new meaning to uncomfortable. Ann's only consolation was that she was not alone in her convalescence that evening. Grandpa was recuperating from a root canal, and they commiserated together while Grandma was at a church meeting.

"How's your mouth feel?" Ann asked.

"I've felt worse," was Grandpa's stoic reply.

Ann and Grandpa smiled in the companionable relationship that was developing between them. Ann staunchly refused to compare Grandpa to Matthew Cuthbert, given the latter's untimely demise, but she felt wholeheartedly that her grandfather was a kindred spirit and sympathetic listener. Besides, Grandpa was anything but shy, like Matthew was.

"I'm probably lucky I don't have poison ivy any worse than I do. Grandma says the Enchanted Forest is full of the stuff."

"Enchanted Forest?"

"Yes, where I walked the other day."

"Oh, along the timber," Grandpa said.

"It was so peaceful! But I won't be able to explore there as I'd like. Grandma says it is full of poison ivy in the summer, and I'll be back in Denver before it freezes."

"You could walk along the field on our side of the lane—down Lover's Lane. There's no poison ivy there."

Ann sat up. "There's a Lover's Lane here?"

"That's what my mother called the path along our field. She and my father would walk there when they were courting, and my brother, Clarence, used to walk down it to court Lily Bellerose. They'd sit in the clearing along the creek and talk. The Belleroses' house was across the road."

"Did Clarence and Lily marry?" Ann asked, caught up in the story.

"No, she died of influenza, and he died the next year in a farming accident. My mom was so upset she stopped the mantel clock at the time he died, and it's never been wound since. But, if you look at one of the trees down there, you can see Clarence's and Lily's initials carved on the trunk."

"It's so romantic—just like a novel. But what happened to the Bellerose house?"

"It burned down decades ago. It sat back in a clearing at the foot of your Enchanted Forest. We own that land now."

"Where the lilac bush is?"

"That's it. You probably saw the spot where the old well was filled in."

"The circle on the ground?"

"That's right."

"How did the fire start?"

"I think it was a chimney fire," Grandpa said.

"That all sounds tragic," Ann said.

She hadn't written much since the neglect mess had brought her to Sunflower Lane, but now that she had her very own desk, maybe she could write about one of Grandpa's stories. A young love thwarted by death and the decades-old lilac bush hidden away back off the road where a house had burned did offer plenty of scope for the imagination. And to think, there was a Lover's Lane right here, just like in Avonlea. It seemed she was constantly learning something new about her family and Sunflower Lane.

"Grandpa, can I ask you something?"

"Of course. What is it?"

"Why does no one want to talk about Mom? I mean, other than telling me I look just like her."

"And you probably already knew that."

"No, actually I didn't. I'd never seen a picture of her before. Sabrina said Dad was so heartbroken after she died that he didn't keep any of them."

"That doesn't sound . . ." Grandpa stopped short. Only the sound of the fans broke the silence. "Well, that's too bad."

"Is there some reason no one says anything? I mean, do you blame me since she died when I was born?" Ann said.

Grandpa sighed. "No, of course not. No one blames you. It's just that it's still hard for us to talk about your mom, even after all these years. Especially for Grandma."

"I noticed."

"I think we're all just trying to sort things out. She's been gone for fifteen years, and we've never had the chance to get to know you before now. Give us time."

Ann wanted to ask him about what she'd overheard Great-Uncle Pete say, but she couldn't bring herself to do it. What if the truth was worse than the fiction that she'd woven in her mind about her mother all these years? Maybe it was better not to know.

"You know, your mom loved to read—that's why she became an English teacher. There's some more of her books up in a trunk in the garret. Once we both feel better, we'll go look for them. I know she'd want you to have them," said Grandpa.

Ann smiled. "Thanks. I'd like that."

A plaintive mewing came from the open front door. Ann went to investigate.

"It's poor Tiger. He climbed up and is hanging off the screen on the storm door."

"Poor Tiger" was a half-grown kitten Ann and Grandpa discovered hidden in the same wild rose bushes where Ann took refuge from the Page sisters' prying eyes. His piteous cries pierced the air, and only after much calling and pleading from Ann had he ventured out on trembling legs. Ann's heart went out to the frightened creature in that instant, and it melted even more when

Grandpa explained that someone likely had dumped him there to be rid of him. Ann empathized with the unwanted animal and adopted him for Sunflower Lane on the spot.

"I wish Grandma would let me bring him in the house," Ann said. She stepped out and peeled Tiger from the screen in a purring bundle of silky fur and claws. She had already suggested this more hospitable welcome for the kitten to Grandma, only to be firmly informed that animals on a farm remained in the great out-of-doors. She felt comforted that Tiger and Sam had become fast friends and enjoyed the comforts of a shared blanket out in Grandpa's shop at night.

"That battle's lost," Grandpa said.

"I think he's hungry. Can I give him a saucer of milk on the porch?"

Ann had read about kittens drinking saucers of milk many a time and thought it only fitting.

"You can give him some milk, but you'd better not use one of Grandma's saucers," Grandpa said.

"Well, all right, but it won't be authentic," Ann said. She deposited Tiger on the porch to go in search of one of the plastic butter containers Grandma kept for food storage in her economizing efforts of waste not, want not.

"There you go," Ann said. She patted the little head as Tiger lapped up the milk. "I'll stay with you for a while so you don't feel so lonely."

She sat in a lawn chair with Tiger walking circles on her lap, butting his head against her hand as her mind wound back to everything Grandpa had told her. Ann hadn't lived in Storey long, but it didn't take keen powers of observation to know that anyone who did anything slightly differently than the status quo ran the very real risk of social censure. No one had probably even liked Dad or his dreams of being a famous singer, although he could be very charming when he wanted to be.

The phone rang on the other side of the open window where Ann and Tiger sat. She heard Grandpa's step on the creaking floor as he rose to answer.

"Hello . . . Oh, Jake . . . "

Ann sat up expectantly. It was the first time Dad had called since she'd come to Sunflower Lane. Maybe he'd already gotten a job and things were going to be resolved sooner than later. Maybe he did care enough to change after all. Soon, she'd be back in Denver, albeit in a confined existence of home to school and back. She felt a strange mixture of hope and regret.

"Yes, she's here. Hold on."

Ann heard Grandpa step to the screen door and open it on creaking hinges. "Ann, your father is on the phone."

Ann detected a sharp undercurrent she had never experienced in Grandpa's usually cheerful voice. But she didn't care; Dad was surely calling to tell her he'd finally kept a promise to her and that she'd soon be back in Denver. She ran inside and answered.

"Hi, Dad!"

"Hey there, kiddo. I'm calling because I have some good news." He slurred his words.

Ann cringed. He'd called her "kiddo," and he only did that when he was drunk.

"Did you get a job?" she asked.

"Well, it's more complicated than that."

Ann felt a knot take root in her stomach. "What do you mean?"

"I've had an offer from this really great band. They're going places, even cut an album that got some airplay."

"That doesn't sound like a steady job to me."

"Well, no, not exactly. But you wouldn't want your dad to miss the chance of a lifetime, would you, kiddo?"

"What exactly are you saying?"

"I'm saying that I have to follow my dreams, you know? This is the one. I can feel it. Besides, your grandparents made such a big deal about not having been part of your life they ought to be happy to have you there."

"But you said it was only going to be for the summer."

"Technically, that's not what the judge said."

"No, it's what *you* said."

"I'm not going to give up this chance because of you." His voice was suddenly hard.

"Of course not. We couldn't expect that." Ann tasted the bitterness of the words on her tongue. Thank goodness he couldn't reach through the phone and smack her.

"Watch your tone with me, young lady."

"So how much longer will it be?"

"As long as it takes. But you should plan on at least the school year there. Maybe longer."

Ann bit her lip but couldn't stop it from trembling.

"Well, I've got to get to practice. I'll call when I can, but you know how it is on the road. Not much time. See ya' later, alligator."

Ann heard the click before she could think of anything to say. Slowly, she placed the receiver in the cradle as tears streaked her face. All the stories she'd imagined about her father and told herself were nothing but a fiction. He wasn't distant from a broken heart; he was distant because he only cared about himself. She felt Grandpa's work-worn hand on her shoulder and heard Tiger's orphaned cries at the door as the full weight of realization sank in: Dad cared so little for her that he hadn't even tried to do anything to get her back. He had abandoned her in Kansas, and it wasn't only for the summer.

9

A Kindred Spirit

"I am genuinely in the depths of despair," Ann said to her reflection in the tarnished mirror above her dresser as she brushed her hair one morning not long after her father's phone call. "I suppose it's only fitting I feel like Anne Shirley, considering I basically *am* an orphan."

Ann leaned her elbows on her dresser and rested her chin on her folded hands, studying her reflection.

"Oh, I know it's not like life with Dad was great, but there's nothing like hearing that your father's dream of being a famous singer is more important to him than you are. So whether I like it or not, I guess this is home now."

Ann glanced around her room in the early morning light. Already it displayed evidence of the truth of her statement. She ran her finger over the two doilies the Misses Page had brought her on their second visit. Ann smiled as she held the small enamel box that had belonged to Great-Uncle Pete's wife. Even he'd softened when he heard the news, and he gave it to her with a rusty hug. Aunt Janis was busily sewing white, ruffled eyelet curtains for her room, and Grandma had offered to help her repaint it from the too-girly pink to Ann's favorite pale lilac.

Ann turned and knelt at her north window, looking out across the yard and fields and railroad tracks and highway to the horizon—clear to infinity, it seemed.

"So much space," she said. "Sometimes I feel like it's the other door Ms. Miller told me about. And sometimes, I feel so small. But I guess I'd better get used to it. For better or worse, I'm staying. Even I have to admit it's better to be Ann of Sunflower Lane than Ann of a Foster Home."

"Ann?" Grandpa called up the stairs.

"Yes?" Ann hurried to open her door and peered over the banister.

"I'm heading up to the pasture to check the windmill. Why don't you come along, and we'll have another driving lesson?"

"If you want to."

"Course I do. You know what they say: Don't put off till tomorrow what you can do today."

"Et tu, Grandpa?" said Ann, wondering how anyone in Storey could ever communicate without their warehouse of sayings.

"Is that a 'yes'?"

"Yes, it is."

"Then come on! Day's a wastin'."

Ann and Grandpa had spent the better part of an hour on her driving lesson in the pasture. They went back and forth, her ability and confidence growing with each trip down the rutted path across the prairie. By the time they drove back through the gate, Ann knew the location of every dip, rock, and potential pitfall that awaited her between the entrance and the windmill and tank. Now, Ann put the truck in park and stepped out so Grandpa could take the wheel for the drive home. She leaned against the bed and looked back across the pasture while Grandpa closed the gate.

A dilapidated pick-up pulled up in a cloud of dust and stopped. It looked vaguely familiar to Ann, but she couldn't place it. She'd probably seen it on Main Street of Storey on their Sunday drive. A tall man wearing jeans, a blue Western shirt, and a cowboy hat and boots climbed out and ambled over to where they waited.

"Mornin'. Saw your truck and thought I'd stop," he said. He started as he looked at Ann.

"Mornin', John." Grandpa shook the other man's hand. "Ann, this is our neighbor, John Alexander. This is my granddaughter, Ann Alwyn. She's come to live with us, and we couldn't be happier."

"Nice to meet you," said Ann.

"Nice to meet you, too. What grade are you?" John said.

"I'll be a junior."

"You're right in between my stepkids. Corrie'll be a sophomore, and Cameron's a senior. You should come over and meet them. They've only lived here a year, and they still feel new to these parts, too. Bernard, you and Thelma bring Ann on over this evening after supper."

"We'll do that," Grandpa said.

"See you then." John touched the brim of his cowboy hat.

"Sounds like you might have some new friends before school starts," said Grandpa.

"Well, maybe one. Grandma probably doesn't even want me to have boys as friends."

"She might tolerate Cameron. He's done a little work for our renter, Arthur, so she knows him."

"I don't think I'll risk it. And who knows? I might not even have anything in common with his sister."

"You never can tell until you meet her. You might find she's— what is it you said your book called it?"

"A kindred spirit."

"That's it."

"I guess we'll see," Ann said, trying to sound nonchalant. In truth, the prospect of meeting someone else her own age in Storey made her feel a tiny spark of hope for the first time since her father's phone call. If she was going to stay at Sunflower Lane, she might as well try and make some friends. Being the new girl was never easy, and Anne Shirley and her bosom friend, Diana Barry, had rekindled her dream of having a best friend.

And so, after supper that evening, Ann found herself standing with her grandparents on the Alexanders' doorstep in nervous anticipation. Ellen Alexander answered the door. She had a bright smile and a prominent dimple that put Ann instantly at ease. She invited them into the living room where John was reading a farm paper. A teenage boy in a T-shirt and jeans with brown, wavy hair and hazel eyes was stretched out on the couch with a magazine. He clambered to his feet as they entered.

"This is my son, Cameron Addair," Ellen said.

And that was when Ann remembered where she'd seen John's truck before: that insufferable boy who'd mocked her after her accident in the creek had been driving it, and that boy was Cameron Addair.

"You!" Ann said darkly.

"So it *was* you," Cameron said.

"You've met?" said John.

"Not officially. I offered her a ride the other day on the road, but she turned me down."

"It was the day I fell on my walk. He saw me on the road, but I told him I was just fine," Ann said in a rush. She didn't want Grandma thinking she'd done anything wrong.

"Nice to meet you officially," he said with a crooked grin as he shook Ann's hand. He was much taller than she.

"Likewise," she said. She finally managed to slip her fingers away from his grasp and quickly stuffed her hands in her pockets.

"Cam, go get your sister. I'm sure she'd like to meet Ann," Ellen said.

With a grin Ann-ward, Cameron walked to the stairs and yelled, "Hey, Corrie. Get down here."

But no Corrie appeared.

After a few Corrie-less moments, Ellen excused herself and walked to the stairs. "Corrie," she called.

"I'm reading," was the grouchy reply from somewhere above.

"Cordelia Addair, come down here. We have company."

"Cordelia?" Ann said. That had to be a good sign. Anne Shirley had asked to be called Cordelia when she first came to Green Gables.

"Coming," said an exasperated voice.

Ann's ears registered each cranky footstep descending those stairs, her eyes first discovering the bare feet, then the long legs, cut-offs, arms crossed over a plain T-shirt, and finally the face, framed by long, wavy, black hair.

"Ann, this is my daughter Corrie. This is the Holmbergs' granddaughter, Ann," said Ellen.

"Nice to meet you," said Ann.

"Same," said Corrie.

"Why don't you kids pour some lemonade and go out on the back deck so you can talk? It's a nice evening," said Ellen.

"C'mon," Corrie said with a smile, her bad mood gone.

Ann followed her to the kitchen, aware of Cameron's presence behind her.

"So," said Corrie as she set out glasses. "I have to ask: is it with or without an 'e'?"

"Without."

"Well, that will be a 'lifelong sorrow' for you."

Ann's ears perked up. "I take it you've read *Anne of Green Gables*?"

"Like, a thousand times. My dad—my real dad—gave me the book. He's an English professor, and he picked my name from the book. But no one calls me Cordelia unless I'm in trouble."

"I'd never read it until I came here this summer. Grandpa gave it to me," said Ann.

"I have the rest of the books in the series if you want to borrow them."

"Really?"

"Sure. It's the least I can do for a real-live Ann."

"Cordelia, could you stop talking long enough to pour the lemonade?" asked Cameron.

"Are your hands broken? Pour it yourself," Corrie said.

Cameron poured a tall glass of lemonade for himself and sauntered out to the deck.

Corrie rolled her eyes. "Brothers. Do you have any siblings?"

"Just a half-sister. She's five years older than I am, and not really very nice. We're not close."

"How old are you? I'm fifteen—I'll be a sophomore."

"I'll turn sixteen in August, so I'm a junior."

"Wow—I'm sure you'll be the youngest in your class. It's almost like you're a year ahead in school. Too bad we won't be in the same grade, but it's OK. We can still do stuff together. Let's go outside. Sorry we have to put up with Cam."

Corrie slipped on her flip-flops, and Ann took her glass and followed her out of the sliding patio doors to the deck. Cameron was reclined in a lawn chair with his eyes closed.

"Just ignore him," Corrie said.

"Yeah, sure, just ignore me while Corrie tells you all about how boring Storey is and how she wishes she could move back to Kansas City."

"Is it even possible for you not to talk?" Corrie said.

"It's possible, but not likely. Besides, your life would be oh, so boring if I didn't talk."

"Is it really that bad here?" asked Ann. "I mean, I haven't gone anywhere other than the grocery store, the library, church, and my aunt's house."

"It's OK, I guess. I mean, I've made some friends here. It's just a whole lot smaller than Kansas City. And John can be such a grouch sometimes. But my stupid brother thinks country life is great because he wants to be a vet. Where are you being exiled here from?"

"We moved around a lot. But I lived in Denver for the past year."

"Denver's cool."

"It's OK. So you'll show me all the ins and outs of life at Storey High?" Ann asked, steering the conversation away from any questions about why she'd ended up at Sunflower Lane. They probably already knew—Cameron had known some about her that day on the road—but she didn't know them well enough to want to talk about that kind of information yet.

"Better let me do that. She goes back to Kansas City as often as she can," said Cameron.

"Shut up, doofus," Corrie said, tossing a flip-flop at her brother. "Ann, please ignore my brother. He specializes in being a pain and in teasing. He can be such a Gilbert," said Corrie.

Cameron opened his eyes and sat up. "I thought Gilbert was the hero of your stupid story. You did force me to watch that dumb movie when we were stuck inside during the blizzard, you know."

Corrie ignored him. "Come on. Let's go to my room where we can talk in peace. And don't come bothering my friend and me, or she might just break a slate over your head like Anne Shirley did to Gilbert Blythe."

Cameron stood. "I'd like to see her reach my head."

Ann followed Corrie past Cameron's mocking eyes. His laughter mingled with the night sounds of crickets and frogs and breezes, following them all the way into the house.

10

Of Caterpillars and Butterflies

"Corrie invited me over tomorrow evening. She's having some of the other girls from school come for a barbecue and wants me to meet them. Is that OK?" Ann asked one morning at breakfast.

"As long as you finish your chores," said Grandma.

"Sounds like you and Corrie have hit it off," Grandpa said.

"Yeah, we have a lot in common. We both write, and we love to read. We have our own little book club of two going. Right now, we're talking about *Pride and Prejudice*. Have you ever read it?"

"I think so, many years ago," Grandpa said.

"I really can't stand Mrs. Bennett. She's a disagreeable creature."

"Must be the name. The Bennetts up the road always were disagreeable creatures. Caroline Bennett sold me a goldfish that died within the hour when I was seven. She cheated me out of a whole nickel for it, too. Can't say as I've ever really forgiven her for it," said Grandpa.

"Bernard," Grandma said, warning in the tone of her voice. Grandma staunchly believed "we shouldn't hate anybody," and she felt obligated to remind everyone of that gem of wisdom, herself included, with a frequency Ann found both astounding and frustrating.

"Not those Bennetts, the ones in the novel. It's a wonderful book. Corrie and I had a debate about Mr. Darcy versus Gilbert

Blythe as the perfect literary hero. We both agreed on Gilbert. He sets the standard pretty high for heroes, both literary and flesh-and-blood ones."

"There'll be time enough for boys. 'A place for everything, and everything in its place,' and that includes young men," Grandma said.

Ann refrained from sighing. "Yes, Grandma. I know the rules. Besides, I'm positive I couldn't find a Gilbert Blythe or anyone even close to a literary hero in Storey. No need to worry."

"I'm glad you and Corrie are friends. I don't know her as well as her brother, but she seems real nice. Cameron's helped Arthur some, and he's a hard worker," said Grandpa.

"He drives me crazy. He's refined the ability to be annoying. But I'll just have to endure the presence of that caterpillar as I become better acquainted with the butterfly of his sister."

"He's a good kid," Grandpa said.

"He seems like a nice boy, and I don't mind if he's around when you're with Corrie—as long as he knows you're not allowed to date."

"Trust me Grandma, I have no interest in Cameron Addair. His one goal in life seems to be to annoy his sister, and now by extension, me. He teases us and makes fun of our literary interests, and I loathe being teased. But Corrie and I do not dignify his utter lack of aesthetics with a response."

"I've always found that's the best option when faced with an utter lack of aesthetics," said Grandpa with a grin.

"I think it's nice you're going to get to know some other girls before school starts," Grandma said.

"Me, too. I'm excited about meeting them. I usually didn't let myself get attached to anyone because we moved so often. But Corrie says to stop being so negative and think *carpe diem*."

"*Carpe* what?" said Grandma.

"It's Latin for 'seize the day.' Or in this case, tomorrow evening. Isn't that a great philosophy?"

"Why don't you work on seizing the rest of your breakfast? 'Sufficient unto the day is the evil thereof,' and you can worry about your get-together tomorrow. Just be sure to behave yourself," said Grandma.

Ann sighed. "Yes, Grandma. And don't worry: As long as no one pulls my hair or calls me 'Carrots,' I can probably hold my temper."

The next evening, Grandpa dropped Ann off at the Alexander farm to help Corrie set up for her barbecue. The two girls chatted as they worked with Ellen to prepare hamburgers, potato salad, coleslaw, and baked beans. Ann was arranging chocolate chip cookies on a tray when Cameron sauntered through the kitchen to help himself to a handful.

"Your brother," Ann said with a shake of her head and in a tone that she'd inherited from her grandmother.

"Yeah, he's perfected being a pain. He's best buddies with John now. All he ever wants to do is hang around this lame farm with him. But he always liked going to my uncle's farm up near Atchison, so I guess I can't expect anything better from him now," Corrie said.

"Tell me about the other girls you've invited," Ann said.

"Well, there's Laura Robbins. She's my age and lives on a farm on the other side of Storey. She's one of the most practical people I've ever met in my life. Very little imagination, but nice. Ginny Lewis is also my age, and she's really pretty. She's the boy-crazy one of the bunch. She constantly talks about boys, but to be fair, she's had quite a few admirers, despite the fact she's always on the honor roll."

"Kind of like Ruby Gillis in *Anne*?"

"Exactly like Ruby Gillis. But she's nice, and really smart, and I like her. Molly Milner is your age. She's quiet, but sweet. I think you'll definitely find she's a kindred spirit. And then, there's Acacia Thorne." Corrie rolled her eyes.

"Who's that?"

"One of the popular girls. She's your age, and no one really likes her. Her mom was a Storey, and her family's just as rich as her ancestors were when they named the town after them. She's stuck-up and nasty."

"Why'd you invite her if you don't like her?"

"I didn't. She invited herself when she overheard me talking to Molly in the grocery store last week. She broke up with her boyfriend, and now she tries to flirt with Cam all the time. I think that's the only reason she wants to come hang out with the bookworm crowd."

"Great."

The doorbell rang, and Corrie ran to greet her guests. Ann peeked out the window to see a used car and directly behind it, a shining red sports car.

"Any bets as to who owns the red one?" Ann said to herself.

Corrie and her friends returned to the kitchen in a chattering group. A green-eyed girl with long, black, spiral-permed hair and designer clothes followed them, glancing around as if looking for something.

Or someone, thought Ann.

"Ann, this is Laura and Ginny and Molly. And this is Acacia," Corrie said.

"Hi," said Ann, suddenly feeling shy. Corrie had told her all about the others, but what had they heard about her?

"Hi," said Laura. She had a frank smile and a sweetheart face framed in long, brown hair.

The practical one, Ann reminded herself of Corrie's description.

"Nice to meet you," Ginny said with a grin. She was petite, with chestnut-colored, curly hair reaching to her waist. Her dark blue eyes crinkled when she smiled.

The Ruby Gillis one.

"Welcome," Molly said simply but with a warm smile. She was about Ann's height with light blond hair and dark brown eyes.

The sweet one.

"Yo," said Acacia.

The nasty one.

"OK, everything's ready out on the deck, so let's eat," Corrie said.

The girls chatted as they served themselves and found their places on chairs and benches. Much to Ann's dismay, Acacia sat down beside her with a flounce.

"So you're the long-lost granddaughter," Acacia said with a sneer.

The deck grew suddenly quiet.

"Acacia, I really don't think we need to talk about that," Molly said.

But Acacia continued. "What? It's not like the whole town hasn't heard."

"You're out of line," said Laura.

"Yeah. Zip it," Corrie said.

Acacia flashed a venomous smile. "What? It's not my fault I heard how her good-for-nothing father neglected her. Left her home alone for weeks on end. No food, no money. The neighbor had to bring medicine to her when she got a cold. Seriously, who thinks they can make it as a musician these days? And it's, like, so totally embarrassing that you ended up in court. Does that make you a juvenile delinquent?"

"Enough," Ginny said.

"Oh, but that's just the tip of the iceberg. You ought to hear what they said about her mother. Why, hello, Cam." Acacia switched tones as Corrie's brother walked out on the deck.

"Hi everyone. Hope you don't mind if I grab a plate," Cameron said, surveying the food.

"Are you joining us this evening?" asked Acacia.

"Well, maybe," he said.

"No, you're not," said Corrie.

"Oh, come on. Just sit down for a little bit. Pretty please?" Acacia said. She pouted and fluttered her heavily mascaraed eyelashes.

"Sure," Cameron said. He dropped into the narrow space between Acacia and Ann on the bench.

Ann turned her back to him and continued her interrupted conversation with Molly. As the evening wore on, she avoided Acacia. It wasn't hard, considering she spent the rest of the time talking with Cameron.

"Those two deserve each other," Ann said to Corrie after the others had left and they were cleaning up the deck.

"Yeah, I don't know what's up. He usually can't stand her," Corrie said.

"How did she know all about me? Have you heard anything else about my mom?" Ann asked. She stared off into the darkness of the yard where the first sparks of dancing fireflies showed.

"This is a small town, and Acacia loves to gossip. What she doesn't hear, she makes up. I wish I could say she 'hadn't a spark of imagination,' but she does. She just doesn't put it to a positive use. So don't worry about it. I told you she's nasty, and she was probably just trying to upset you to see what you'd say."

But Ann worried anyway, even after Grandpa had picked her up.

"How'd it go? Did you make some new friends?" he asked.

Ann looked out the window as they drove, watching the stars blink out as in Longfellow's Acadie, "one by one in the infinite meadows of heaven."

"Yes, I really liked them. Well, all but Acacia Thorne. She is one of the most hateful people I've ever met, and that includes my sister, so that's saying something. I definitely don't like her. That girl is going to be a thorn in my side—no pun intended."

"She can't help it. She's Frank Storey's granddaughter, and that man is a snake. But don't tell your grandmother I said that. You know what she always says."

"Yes: 'we shouldn't hate anybody.' Well, I suppose there must be a Josie Pye in everyone's life. She's the mean girl in *Anne of Green Gables*, and I have a sneaking suspicion Acacia is going to be mine. Great."

She looked at Grandpa, wondering if she should ask what Acacia had meant with her comment about Mom. There was just so much that was never said about her mother.

"Grandpa?"

"Yes?"

Ann paused. What if Acacia knew something she didn't want to know? Besides, Corrie said she just made stuff up. It had to be that. Didn't it?

"Nothing."

11

A Lily Maid on Storey Creek

"This is totally like the Lily Maid scene in *Anne*," Corrie said.

Ann opened one eye from the large tractor tire innertube where she lay lazily floating in the shallow waters of Storey Creek near Corrie's home. Her friend was draped across another innertube nearby. In the face of a string of hot summer days, they had improvised at the lack of a swimming pool by spending the afternoon in the creek, but they'd sworn never to let Acacia Thorne find out. She of the in-ground swimming pool would never let them live it down if she knew.

"How do you figure? I'm wearing cut-offs, an old T-shirt, and canvas tennis shoes to keep from cutting my feet on the very unromantic rocks in this creek. And in case you hadn't noticed, this isn't a boat," said Ann. She thumped the innertube.

"Ann Alwyn, I thought your imagination was better than that."

"Besides, I doubt there are any Gilbert's poking around," Ann said.

"You'd better hope there's one if that innertube sinks."

"The water is only four feet deep here, and it gets even shallower before it goes over the riffle. Besides, I can swim. My father threw me into a swimming pool when I was four, and I learned fast. So I think I'm safe."

"But you have to admit it would be romantic."

"I suppose. Although a 'crick' isn't as romantic as a Lake of Shining Waters."

"That is very true," said Corrie. "But then again, not much about Storey is very romantic. I mean, can you even imagine someone setting a novel in this pokey old place?"

"Now who's lacking imagination?" Ann said. She splashed her friend, and Corrie splashed her back with a laugh.

"Whatever. Listen, I'm going to run up to the house and get some more sunblock and a snack. I'm famished. I'll be back in a sec. Want anything?" said Corrie.

"I'm good."

Corrie splashed off her innertube and left it on a nearby flat rock. She waded downstream to where she could easily climb the opposite bank. Ann had already put her newly won poison ivy identification skills to use by determining the path leading in was free and clear of the hated vine. She wanted no repeats of her earlier catastrophe.

Ann shoved off the rock with one foot and relaxed back on her innertube as it drifted into the current, allowing the slow-flowing waters of this stretch of the creek to pull her along. As soon as she heard the gurgle of the riffle and felt her feet touch the shallower depths, she hopped off and waded back up to the rocks. She climbed on her innertube, dangling her feet over the edge, and lodged it against the rock to hold herself in place in the half-shade cast by the rustling cottonwoods above.

"The Lily Maid," Ann said with a laugh. "Leave it to Corrie to make a connection between the romance of Avonlea and the muddy banks of Storey Creek. But she's right: My imagination is better than that. If I can't imagine I'm Anne Shirley playing at the Lily Maid with only an old innertube as my vessel, I'll never be much of a writer. And I do love that poem, especially the part that says, 'There surely I shall speak for mine own self, and none of you can speak for me so well.'"

She had unearthed a dusty anthology of Tennyson at the library, a volume so old it smelled of yellowed pages and hadn't been checked out for decades. Reading "Lancelot and Elaine," the poem that had so inspired Anne Shirley, gave Ann a thrill as she suffered with Elaine in her silent, unrequited love and reveled in the symbolic romance of dying of a broken heart.

"Storey Creek isn't exactly romantic, but I can imagine I'm Anne Shirley playing Elaine in Avonlea while I wait on Corrie. It is pretty down here, even if it is a 'crick.'"

Ann glanced about at the pattern of sun and shadows cast by the cottonwoods lining the bank to the shimmery glistens of reflected light at the center of the creek. A pair of dragonflies danced by, the light glinting off their transparent wings like the hint of a dream. The soft ripple of the flowing waters was a cradle song, lulling Ann as she rocked on their current. She relaxed on her innertube and began to envision Anne Shirley's Lily Maid-inspired shipwreck. She imagined herself as Anne in all the crucial scenes, playing out the dialogue in her mind. There went the leak, then Ann Alwyn as Anne Shirley gathered her pall and coverlet as she watched the flat fill with water. Without a moment to spare, she sprang to the bridge pile. Just as Gilbert Blythe arrived in Harmon Andrews's dory, Ann dozed off. She furrowed her brow in her sleep, aggravated to find that this particular Gilbert did not look like the one she had conjured from the novel's description, nor even the one of the miniseries she and Corrie had watched on public television. Instead, this Gilbert had a strong resemblance to the teasing hazel eyes and wavy hair of one Cameron Addair.

"Ann," she heard Gilbert's voice call, and she smiled. There he was: the hero of the moment. "Ann," he repeated loudly.

Ann started awake and sat up quickly, disoriented. The innertube wobbled, then capsized. She stood, dripping and indignant, her innertube corralled in one hand and the other on her hip. Cameron Addair came splashing across the creek in swim trunks, a ratty T-shirt, and rubber wading boots. He wore a smirk on his self-satisfied face. Ann felt her cheeks burn.

"You could have killed me," she said.

"The water's only four feet deep."

"I'm well aware of that, but what if I'd hit my head on that rock and knocked myself unconscious?" Ann glared.

"Why the melodrama?" he asked.

Ann ignored the question. "What do you want?" she said.

"I came to tell you that Dad called, and Corrie's still on the phone with him. She didn't want you to think your bosom buddy . . . "

"It's 'bosom friend.'"

"Whatever. That your bosom buddy forgot all about you. And she said to bring you this sunblock so you wouldn't fry."

"You know, a gentleman wouldn't have snuck up on me like that."

"First, I didn't know you didn't hear me yelling at you from the bank. Second, I'm not your Gilbert What's-His-Name."

"Blythe. It's Gilbert Blythe."

"Whatever. He's not here."

"That is certainly apparent," said Ann.

Cameron gave her a strange look.

"What?" she asked.

"How long have you been down here?"

"I don't know. Think about it: I didn't wear a watch because I was going swimming." She tapped her head. She was pleased to see that her sarcasm was not lost on Cameron when he rolled his eyes.

"Well, did you wear sunblock? Because you're really red," he said.

Ann raised her hands to her face and winced. She glanced at her arms and saw that Cameron was right.

"Oh, no! I must have been there a lot longer than I realized. I'd better go."

"Chill a minute. I want to talk with you."

Ann imagined Grandma having spies everywhere to spot her alone with a boy. No doubt the Misses Page were hiding in the weeds growing along the banks. She had to get out of there.

"I need to leave," she said.

"I promise I don't bite."

"Yes, but Acacia might. I doubt she wants you hanging out here with me," Ann said. She retrieved Corrie's innertube from the rock.

"I don't care what Acacia thinks," said Cameron.

Ann stopped, an innertube in each hand. "You sure seemed to at Corrie's barbecue."

"What's it to you?"

"Absolutely nothing, other than you were consorting with the enemy."

"The enemy?"

"You heard what she said about me and about my mother." Ann's voice cracked on the last word and tears stung her eyes. Why had she chosen this precise moment to revisit that scene, not to mention lose it? She refused to cry in front of Cameron Addair. She grasped the two innertubes more firmly and waded noisily downstream. After only a few steps, she slipped on the mossy rocks of the creek bed and fell in the water again. She heard Cameron's splashing steps behind her as she struggled to stand.

"Here, let me help you," he said.

"I'm quite capable."

"Hand me the dang innertubes, and let me help you," Cameron said in exasperation. He tossed the tubes onto the rock before helping Ann to her feet.

Ann crossed her arms and glowered.

"Look, I can't stand Acacia Thorne any more than you can. I spent that whole evening talking to her so she'd leave you alone."

"What? Why?"

"Because she was being a jerk, and I know what it's like to have a parent you can't explain. My dad's never going to be Father of the Year, trust me. I did the first thing I could think of to get Acacia to shut up. Now I have to put up with her calling me all the time, and that's a real sacrifice, let me tell you."

A dragonfly lit on his nose, and he jumped. Ann smiled a little in spite of herself.

Cameron ran his hand over his head. "Look, I don't know, and I don't care what your parents did or didn't do or might have done."

"I don't even know what they did or didn't do, and I don't want to imagine what they might have done," Ann said, the tears coming despite her efforts. "My father never told me anything, and no one here will talk about my mom. It's driving me crazy. But I don't even know if I want to hear what they have to say."

"Hey, it's OK. Come here," Cameron said, wrapping her in his arms.

For a breath, Ann let him hold her, comfort her. Then, the image of Grandma flashed across her mind. She shoved him away.

"I have to go," Ann said. She hurried noisily to the bank and scrambled up to the path. At the top, she glanced back at Cameron standing in the middle of the creek.

"Thanks," she called.

He flashed a crooked grin. "You're welcome."

"And just so you know—Gilbert Blythe wouldn't be caught dead in that outfit."

12

Her Mother's Trunk

"Careful on that last step," Grandpa said. He and Uncle Edward were hefting a large trunk down from the shadows of the garret.

"Where do you want this?" asked Uncle Edward.

"In my room, please," said Ann.

Uncle Edward and Grandpa lugged the trunk into Ann's room where Grandma and Aunt Janis were sitting on her bed, talking.

"It does my heart good to see Amelia's desk back in this room. It was one of her most prized possessions," Aunt Janis was saying. "And now you'll have her trunk, too."

"What'd she store in that thing, bricks?" asked Uncle Edward. He mopped his brow in the farmhouse's sweltering upstairs.

"Edward, surely you knew my daughter better than that. It's full of books," said Grandpa.

"Of course," Uncle Edward said.

"Let's go down and have some iced tea while the ladies go through this trunk," said Grandpa.

Uncle Edward didn't argue.

Ann ran her hands over the worn wood and tarnished hardware. "Where did Mom get this? It looks really old," she said.

"It is. It belonged to your great-great grandmother. Amelia found it up in the garret and decided it looked like something out of a book. She wasn't happy until we cleaned it out and brought it down. It used to sit right there along the wall," said Grandma.

"How come it ended up back in the garret?" asked Ann. She tried to sound casual, but it was a question she'd had since coming to Sunflower Lane. Other than the photographs on the walls downstairs, there was little trace of her mother left in the house, and nothing in what had been her bedroom. Why had they tried to erase her very presence from her childhood home? Had she done something truly horrible?

"Wasn't that because of the rain?" asked Aunt Janis.

"Yes. We had a bad storm several years ago. It blew some shingles off, and we had water damage in that room. We had to repaint everything, so we cleaned it out and stored the furniture in the garret," said Grandma.

That doesn't sound terribly mysterious, thought Ann. "How come you never brought it back down?"

Grandma looked at her hands. "We just didn't."

"Your Uncle Edward helped haul everything up; he wasn't real interested in hauling it back down again that soon. He's needed this many years to forget how much that trunk weighs," said Aunt Janis with a laugh.

Ann smiled. Aunt Janis always knew how to make everyone feel comfortable.

"Well, go ahead and open it. Let's see what's inside," said Grandma.

Ann undid the clasp and raised the lid. The hinges protested with a shriek but held firm. Carefully, Ann set out stacks of books, reading their spines.

"These are all classics," she said.

"Your mother loved to read, just like you do," said Aunt Janis.

"What's this?" asked Ann. She held out a plaque and read the inscription. "Mom was valedictorian?"

"She sure was. She got all the brains, and I'm not too proud to say it. You take after her that way, I can tell," said Aunt Janis.

"I hope so. Let's see, here's another award: State Cherry Pie Champion."

"She was also an outstanding cook," said Grandma.

"I do *not* take after her that way," said Ann.

"Give it time. Remember: 'Practice makes perfect.' You're getting better slowly but surely," said Grandma.

Ann nearly dropped the plaque at Grandma's unexpected compliment.

"These look like old yearbooks." Ann paged through one, looking for her mother's picture in the class composite. "Here she is. Some of the girls had short hair, but hers was long, just like mine. Wow, look at the beehives on some of these girls. I'm glad that's gone out of style."

"Oh, it was beehives for that generation, and it's mall bangs for yours," said Aunt Janis.

"Someday you'll look back and wonder what you young girls were thinking," said Grandma.

"Maybe, but until then I'll wear them proudly. As it says in *Little Women*, we must 'be elegant or die,'" said Ann as she continued to page through the yearbook. "Here's another picture of Mom. She was a Homecoming Queen candidate?"

Aunt Janis glanced over her shoulder. "Yes, she was. Oh, I'd forgotten that dress. My, wasn't it pretty?"

Ann turned to the senior class in their graduation gowns. "Is that Arthur? Whoa, he had hair once. And that's Molly's mom. She told me she and Mom were friends. Is this the guy who owns the grocery store?"

Grandma adjusted her bifocals. "Yes, that's Rich Richards."

Ann lifted the yearbook and studied the picture. "That almost looks like Corrie's stepdad."

"Yes, he and your mother were in the same grade," said Aunt Janis.

"Really? He always seems older somehow. And he's smiling. I haven't seen him smile all that much. Corrie says he's pretty grumpy."

"Now, don't be mean. John's always been a real nice young man. He'd have been a real catch a long time ago if he'd ever let himself be caught," said Grandma.

Ann stared at her grandmother. She of so few and such guarded words had been almost chatty this evening.

"Is there anything else in there?" asked Aunt Janis.

"Yes, this jar. It looks like it's full of dried flowers."

"That's a rose jar. Your mom made it. She dried roses from the garden and wild roses and any roses she could find," said Aunt Janis.

Ann opened the lid and breathed deeply of the rich scent. "It smells heavenly. Is there something other than roses in here?"

"Yes. She layered roses and spices and a spritz of her perfume," Aunt Janis said.

Ann closed her eyes and imagined the delicacy of a mother who had loved that scent. It was like the ghost of her embrace across the years.

"Is that all that's in the trunk?" asked Grandma.

Ann put the lid back on the rose jar and set it aside. "The only other thing are some blank books."

"Oh, yes. Your mom loved to write. She dreamed of being a writer someday," said Aunt Janis.

"Really? I do, too."

"She wrote poems and stories and kept a journal in those books. She always had some of them around."

"I like to journal, too. Or I did. I quit when Sabrina found it and read it. I paid for that dearly, considering there were several sections dedicated to my opinion of how she treated me. I destroyed my own journal, so she'd never be able to look at it again."

"You could start keeping one again. Use one of your mother's blank books. No one will read it here," said Grandma.

"That's a great idea. Are Mom's journals still around somewhere?"

"No," said Grandma.

"She had me bring them to her when she and your dad were living in Kansas City," Aunt Janis said.

"Oh." Dad had probably gotten rid of them when he destroyed Mom's pictures. Ann didn't know if she felt disappointed or relieved.

"I'm going to go check on dinner. Put these things away and then come down," said Grandma.

"I'll help," said Aunt Janis.

Together, they began to refill the trunk.

"Ann, honey, are you close to your half-sister?" Aunt Janis asked as they worked.

Ann snorted. "Hardly. I honestly think she hates me. She babysat me for as long as I can remember, and she was a dictator about it."

"But she's only five years older than you."

"Yeah, but Dad said she was old enough to watch me when he was gone. She ordered me around and made me do all the chores while she sat and ate potato chips and watched TV."

Aunt Janis handed Ann another stack of books. "Was she nice to you?"

"Nice is not in Sabrina's vocabulary. I think she wishes I'd never been born."

"Do you mean she hurt you?"

Ann glanced at the discolored skin on her hand where Sabrina had dumped scalding hot chocolate on her when she was four. And the scar where she'd been cut picking up the broken shards of her favorite cartoon character glass after Sabrina purposefully shattered it. And the jagged scar on her knee from the shove down the stairs.

"Maybe I'd better plead the Fifth on that one," said Ann.

"You know she probably acts that way because of what her mother did."

"Huh?"

"You know—your dad's first wife decided she didn't want to be married or deal with a child anymore, so she just left."

"You mean she walked out on them?" asked Ann.

"You didn't know? Oh, dear, I've said too much. Just forget I ever opened my big mouth."

"No, it's OK. That explains so much about Sabrina. I honestly kind of feel bad for her now."

"But it doesn't give her the right to mistreat you," said Aunt Janis.

Ann said nothing.

Aunt Janis wrapped Ann in a tight embrace. "You're safe here at Sunflower Lane—you know that, right? You're with us. And your grandparents and Uncle Edward and even your Great-Uncle Pete, and especially me—we're all so glad you're finally here."

Ann nodded. "I know. Thanks."

Aunt Janis kissed the top of her head. "Let's head down and see if your grandma is ready for supper."

"I'll be right there. I'm going to put these blank books away."

Ann arranged the books in her desk drawer. She turned to her mirror and traced the outline of her reflection thoughtfully.

"What other secrets do you suppose are buried around here in old trunks and old memories?" she asked.

13

Ann's Imagination Goes Wrong

"Why young girls have ever wanted to go to someone else's house and stay up all night when they could sleep in their own beds I'll never know," Grandma said when Ann asked permission to go to Corrie's for a slumber party. "In my time, we were happy if we didn't have to share a bed with our siblings after a long day of work on the farm."

"Well, I've never been to a slumber party, so I can't really tell you much about them yet. But I suppose it's because it's something out of the ordinary. It will give us that much more time to talk. And you know, sometimes the best thoughts and ideas come when no one else is up."

"Do you mean to tell me you're staying up late to have those 'thoughts and ideas'?"

"No, but sometimes I wake up, and if I have a fantastic idea for a story or poem, I have to get up and write it down. At the very least I have to get up to think about it at my window. I like to sit there in the darkness and listen to the wind in the trees and the sound of tires on the highway. I love to watch the fireflies below mirror the sparkle of the stars above. It's peaceful."

"I didn't know you were having trouble sleeping," Grandma said.

"Oh, I'm not really, but if I wake up with an amazing idea, I don't want to forget it. I've learned the hard way that ideas that come to you in the middle of the night are never there the next morning. And there's something kind of thrilling about thinking I can 'stare into the night while others take rest' at my own window. I've never had such a lovely window before."

Grandma looked at her granddaughter distrustfully. "Amazing ideas in the middle of the night are not something I'm used to having. But to each his own, I suppose."

"So sleepover: yes or no?"

"Yes," said Grandma. "As long as . . ."

". . . I behave myself. I know."

It took every ounce of willpower for Ann not to roll her eyes.

"Do you think it's going to rain?" Ann asked Corrie as they frosted cupcakes and awaited the arrival of the other girls.

"Maybe. But a little thunder and lightning would add to the ghost stories."

"Ghost stories, huh? That sounds lame." Cameron smirked and swiped a cupcake before they could protest.

"We take our literary efforts seriously," Corrie said.

"Well, just because you do doesn't mean anyone else does," Cameron said. He leaned against the refrigerator with the practiced nonchalance of an adolescent boy.

Ann glared. Cameron Addair was truly aggravating. Oh, not Gilbert Blythe-level aggravating, but close. He had a knack for getting a rise out of her with his teasing. He'd made fun of her and Corrie constantly. He'd mocked their two-person book club, complained about their nonstop chatter, and mimicked the way they talked when they emulated the speech of their favorite literary heroines. But criticize her writing efforts? That was the type of thing that would get a slate cracked over his head if there were only a slate nearby for the cracking.

"I'll have you know, *Mr.* Addair," she said, making purposeful use of italics, "that I shall welcome the feedback of any *qualified* individual. However, I regret to inform you that *you* are far from qualified to comment on the merits of *anything* I write."

Ann's italics were not lost on Cameron, although they only seemed to amuse him, much to her dismay.

"Oh, really? Anything you write?" he asked. He leaned over and stared into Ann's clear, blue eyes.

"Anything. Not even a grocery list," Ann said with a stubborn tilt to her chin.

"Ouch," said Corrie.

"Chill. I was just teasing." Cameron helped himself to another cupcake and left.

"Your brother is so annoying," said Ann.

"That's just Cam's normal, everyday personality. You get used to it."

"Maybe you do, but I'm positive I won't."

"Really? You know Anne hated Gilbert at first. Maybe Cam will be your Gil."

"Cordelia Addair! How dare you even hint such a thing? Who are you, Jane Andrews proposing on behalf of her brother?"

"It's not a bad idea. If you married Cam, we'd be sisters."

"Corrie, I have no intention of marrying your annoying brother just so we can be sisters. Trust me, I already have a half-sister, and she is more than enough."

"OK, OK. I wouldn't really wish my brother on anyone, especially my bosom friend."

Ann was spared any further discomfort on the subject by the arrival of the other girls, this time, without the grating presence of Acacia Thorne.

"I swore everyone to secrecy about our slumber party so we wouldn't have to put up with her," Corrie had said when Ann asked.

In short time, the girls were gathered around the table enjoying pizza and ice cream as they chatted nonstop about Ginny's latest crush, Molly's work on her father's farm, and Laura's trip to Wichita to visit her aunt. Then, they adjourned to the basement to watch a romantic comedy on Corrie's VCR. As they laughed together, Ann realized she'd never had this many people she could consider friends before.

I should probably thank Dad for getting me sent here, she thought sarcastically. *Of course, he'd have to be there to answer the phone or return a call sometime so I* could *thank him.*

"Time for the ghost stories," Ginny said when the movie was over. "I'll go first."

She switched off the lights and flicked on a flashlight, shining it on her face as she regaled them with a story featuring more blood and gore than Ann was prone to like. She regretted having read the copy of *In Cold Blood* she discovered among her mother's books earlier that week.

"Molly, you go," said Ann when Laura had finished. She was certain Molly would share something equivalent to a children's story—which she did.

After Corrie and Laura told their stories, it was Ann's turn. She had opened her mouth to begin her tale when Molly asked, "Did you hear something?"

"No, scaredy-cat," said Ginny. She gave Molly a good-natured poke.

"I think it was just thunder," Laura said.

Ann, too, thought she'd heard a dull thump, but she wasn't about to admit it. She turned the flashlight on her face and looked around at her expectant audience. She had written her story out and practiced it in her room for dramatic effect, and she was ready.

"Valancy lived in an old farmhouse in the Flint Hills," Ann said.

A clap of thunder sounded, dull and distant.

"See, Molly? We told you it was thunder," said Ginny.

Ann continued, "Valancy's family had lived in the house for generations, and family legend told that her great-great-grandfather hid a chest full of gold somewhere on the land, but no one ever found it. Then, one summer, a terrible drought struck the land,"

"Oh, no," said Laura. "Droughts are bad news on a farm."

"Crops withered in the fields and wide cracks split open the parched earth like so many canyons."

"Nice line," Ginny complimented her.

"Did you hear that?" asked Molly.

"It's just the rain. Go on," said Corrie.

"Valancy's father had made some ill-informed business decisions, and the farm was in danger of failing. Many a night, Valancy sat by her open window, wishing she could find the long-lost treasure. Then, one stormy night, Valancy was awakened by a strange noise. She rose from her bed and crept quietly downstairs."

"Don't go, Valancy," whispered Molly.

"Has this girl never watched a horror movie?" asked Ginny.

"Once on the ground floor, she realized the sound was coming from the cave."

"Oh, I don't like caves," said Molly with a shiver.

"Valancy slipped to the cave door where a weird blue light shone up the steps. Slowly, she descended, drawn as if against her will. It was pitch dark, but at the bottom, something white and silvery and all-together spectral glowed."

"Awesome description," said Corrie.

"Valancy recognized the ghostly face of her great-great-grandfather. He extended an icy hand, grasped her by the elbow, and led her to the far end of the cave where he pointed a bony finger at the wall. She reached out a shaky hand and pressed the wall firmly. A sound of rock on rock shattered the silence as it moved. There, inside, was a great wooden box, the lost treasure chest, filled to overflowing with gold."

"Whew! I thought there might be a snake down there. You never can tell with caves," said Laura.

"And so Valancy saved the farm, although some of her relatives never believed a ghost led her to the treasure that dark night."

"Nice," said Corrie. She led the others in a round of applause.

"OK, let's talk about boys," Ginny said.

Ann sighed. "I'm going to go get some water."

She climbed the dark stairs to the kitchen where she could hear the storm clearly. As she filled her glass at the sink, she thought, for the first time, that she heard something creak nearby. *Maybe Molly was right*, Ann thought. She shut off the faucet and listened. *Why didn't I turn on the overhead light when I came up? And what if there are ghosts in this house?*

"Boo," whispered a voice in her ear as a crack of lightning split the night and a peal of thunder shook the dishes in the cabinets.

Ann had never been a screamer, although in the split second she realized she was not alone in Corrie's kitchen, she would have given anything to be able to call for help. She spun around, the water from her glass sloshing out on her ghostly attacker. When the white blob in front of her didn't dissolve, Ann realized whoever was with her was human.

Frantic, Ann tried to sidestep the intruder. If it wasn't a ghost, then someone must have chosen that very night to break into the Alexander home to kill them all, just like *In Cold Blood.* She slipped on the wet linoleum, but two strong hands reached out to keep her from falling. Ann had never thrown a punch in her life, but she did then.

"Ow!" cried the attacker, stumbling backwards and into a chair. "Dang it, Ann, what'd you do that for?"

Ann caught her breath. She reached for the refrigerator door and opened it a crack for more light. There, one hand to his eye, stood Cameron. Another bolt of lightning outlined his tall frame.

"You grabbed me," Ann said in a harsh whisper.

"Because you were going to fall. That's the last time I try to do anything chivalrous for you."

"You wouldn't know chivalry if it smacked you in the face," Ann said with no regard for word choice. "Besides, you tried to scare me."

"It's not my fault you were telling your stupid stories. Did you think I was the ghost of your great-great-grandfather?"

"You spied on us," Ann said with a hiss.

By now, lights had come on all over the house. The girls ran up from the basement, and John and Ellen hurried down from their bedroom upstairs.

"What on earth is going on down here? Did I or did I not tell you not to make a racket?" asked John.

"I came up for some water," said Ann in an attempt to head off a retort from her bosom friend.

"And I came down for a drink and tripped and smacked my eye," Cameron said. He pointed at the chair. "The noise scared Ann, and she spilled her water."

Corrie tried and failed not to laugh at the sight of her brother's puffy eye, for "not even fear of punishment can stop the giggle in a girl."

"It's no laughing matter. That looks pretty bad," John said with a growl.

Corrie glared at her stepfather, and Ann cringed with embarrassment. Cameron's eye did look terrible.

"Put some ice on it and go to bed," Ellen said.

"I'll clean up the water," Ann said.

"And Cameron will help you since he frightened you. You girls go back to your slumber party. Everyone, off to bed," said Ellen.

Cameron handed Ann several paper towels and they mopped up the floor in silence. When they'd finished, they looked warily at each other.

"If you ever . . . " they began in unison.

"Ladies first," said Cameron.

Ann did not miss the dangerous reference to chivalry, but she didn't waste time pointing it out to him. "If you ever tell anyone I thought you were a ghost or a murderer, I'll tell them it was a girl who gave you that black eye," Ann said, arms crossed and a defiant lift to her chin.

"And if you ever tell anyone you gave me a black eye, I'll tell them you were mad at me because I wouldn't go out with you."

"What? That's preposterous."

Cameron shrugged. "Those are the terms. Unless," he said, leaning one hand over Ann's shoulder and onto the refrigerator, "you would agree to go out with me."

Ann's heart gave a strange little thump as they stood there in the semidarkness. Was he serious? Of course not. He was trying to bait her. All he ever did was tease. And anyway, Grandma had meant it when she said, "no boys." Ann had no intention of getting on Grandma's bad side by breaking her number one rule. She had enough trouble as it was without being locked in her room at Sunflower Farm until she was thirty. Besides, romance was fine in books, but she had no interest in going on a date with Cameron Addair—no interest, whatsoever. Oh, he was every bit as aggravating as Gilbert Blythe after all.

"Your secret's safe with me," said Ann. She slipped under his arm and back to the safety of the slumber party below.

14

Grandpa Keeps a Secret

"I had my doubts about lilac at first, but this color is real pretty," Grandma said. She stepped back to survey the walls of Ann's room.

"I'm glad you like it. It's my favorite color. I've always wanted my dreamroom to be lilac," Ann said with an appraising look around her.

"'Dreamroom?'"

"That's what I always called the room of my dreams when I imagined what it would be like. It's changed over the years, but it always had windows, and it was always this color."

"Well, you do seem to have a good eye for color, and your hand's real steady around the trim."

Ann turned from where she was edging in around the closet doors. Had Grandma just paid her a compliment?

"Thanks. I've never painted before in my life, so the credit is all yours for teaching me."

Grandma smiled. "Maybe we just make a good team."

"Maybe we do." Ann smiled. "Aunt Janis said the white curtains she made are done. They're going to look awesome at my windows."

"All you need now is a new quilt to match."

Ann shot Grandma a worried look. "Uh, do you mean I should make one? Because I don't know anything about sewing, much less quilting."

"No, I mean I think we need to look through the cedar chest in the cold room. I made a Sunbonnet Sue quilt years ago using scraps from some of your mom's and Janis's childhood dresses. I found some lavender fabric on sale, so I used it for the solid blocks in between. I probably wouldn't have picked that color, but waste not, want not. I guess it was a blessing, because now you're here, and you like purple."

"That was fortuitous," said Ann.

They painted for several minutes in silence.

"I suppose we'd better start thinking about doing some back-to-school shopping. You didn't bring a lot of clothes," said Grandma.

"That's because I don't have a lot of clothes. I brought everything I own," Ann said. Her tone was matter of fact, but her limited wardrobe, collected from thrift stores and clearance racks, had always embarrassed her.

"We'd better start so we can find some sales. Is there anything in particular you need?"

"Probably some new jeans and tops for now. Maybe a sweater or two when it turns colder."

"Yes, I noticed your jeans are getting frayed. They'll do for chores around the farm, but you should have some nicer things for school."

"If I'm getting jeans, is there any chance I could have just one pair of pleated jeans?

"Pleated jeans? What's that?"

"They're really cute. Some have one pleat on each side of the button, and some have two. Others have a whole series of pleats. Everyone's wearing them."

"If everyone was wearing a sack over their heads, would you want to do that, too?" Grandma asked in an adaptation of her more standard, "if everyone jumped off a cliff" moral.

"To quote Anne Shirley when she wanted a dress with puffed sleeves, 'I'd rather look ridiculous when everyone else does,' even with a sack over my head. I only have a few clothes from the secondhand shop and some of Sabrina's hand-me-downs that don't fit well. That's why I always look like a fashion magazine collided with a nightmare. And you don't know what it's like to be teased by the mean girls for not being in style."

"Oh, don't I? I'll never forget what the mean girls around here said about me having to wear my brother's old boots. They were the only ones that fit, and we couldn't afford anything else. So yes, I understand, and yes, you can have the jeans. We'll shop around to get the best deal we can, of course."

"Thank you. I am grateful to have new clothes, and I'll be 'ever so much gratefuller' with pleated jeans for my first day of school."

"Just remember: 'Pretty is as pretty does.'"

"Be that as it may, I agree with the philosophy that it's easier to be good if your clothes are in style."

"Where on earth do you come up with these things, Ann?" Grandma asked. She shook her head as she returned to her painting.

Ann didn't answer because she had stopped to listen to the sound of something coming in the lane with a loud racket. "I think I hear the grain truck," she said.

She stepped to the window and watched the vehicle roar the last few feet in a swirl of dust. It lurched to a halt, and Grandpa hopped out as if he were several decades younger. Wheat harvest was in full swing, and he was helping Arthur by driving the truck to the grain elevator. He came in the front door, whistling a cheery tune.

"You two still painting?" he called up the stairs.

"Yes," Ann said over the banister. "And it looks perfect."

"I'm glad you like it. I've come to see if you'd like to ride along with me to take this load to the grain elevator. You can see what wheat harvest is like first-hand," he said.

"That sounds awesome. Is it OK with you, Grandma?"

"Of course. I wouldn't want to deprive you of the adventure of a ride into town with your grandpa driving a full grain truck during wheat harvest."

"Do I need to change?" Ann gestured to the old yellow T-shirt and cutoffs she was wearing. She had learned that there were chore clothes and town clothes.

"Not to go to the elevator," Grandma said. "You'd better hurry—your grandpa might leave without you."

Ann wrapped her brush in a plastic bag and hurried out to the truck. Grandpa had backed around and was waiting for takeoff.

"Hold on," Grandpa said. "Things can get a little rough in this old truck."

He adjusted his cap and gripped the wheel as if preparing for the Indianapolis 500. He put the truck in gear, and they were off, churning up a dusty cloud behind them. Ann reached to steady herself against the frame as they bounced onto the county road and over the railroad crossing.

"I think I know why Grandma said this would be an adventure," she said. Ann surmised that the grain truck, like most of the farm implements still in use at Sunflower Lane, was held together more by her grandfather's ingenuity than by genuine mechanics. Some of them, like the truck in question, seemed to defy the laws of physics.

"Yeah, it's great. I always kind of enjoyed driving the truck into town during harvest," Grandpa said over the din.

"Why?" asked Ann.

"After puttering along on the combine, it's gives you a shot of adrenaline."

"I can see that," Ann said with complete honesty. She bounced and slid along the seat, the wind whipping her hair around her face. "Are you sure you shouldn't take it easy—for your heart, you know?"

"Not at all. I take my medication and watch myself," Grandpa said, whistling a spirited song.

Grandpa tended to drive fast—"one mile per hour for each year old he is," Grandma once said. Ann glanced at the speedometer, positive they must be going well over Grandpa's age, but the faithful vehicle was rumbling along at 55.

They clanked and banged into town and up to a line of waiting trucks at the grain elevator.

"Busy day," Grandpa said. He leaned his elbow out the window.

"You really seem to be in your element," said Ann as she watched the pageant performed in front of her. Trucks of every color snaked along the elevator waiting their turn to be weighed, have a sample taken to test for moisture, and dump their load of grain.

"Sure am. Look—that's John Alexander in front of us," Grandpa said.

"How do you know?"

"I know all the old trucks around here. Only time I wouldn't know someone is if they got a new truck, and that's not likely with the price of wheat these days."

Grandpa honked his horn and reached his hand out the window. John returned the greeting. Then, a second hand, followed by a face with the remnants of a black eye, poked out of the passenger window. It was Cameron. Ann closed her eyes and sighed. Why did he seem to have perfected the knack of showing up everywhere she was?

"Isn't that Corrie's brother?" asked Grandpa.

"Yes." Anne's tone was terse.

"Looks like he got a black eye."

"He probably deserved it."

She turned her head to the side, feigning complete absorption in the grain elevator until Cameron's smirk disappeared back inside the truck.

After they had emptied their load, Grandpa pointed the truck in the direction of Main Street.

"Let's stop at the café and see what the news is," he said.

"You mean your 'office,'" said Ann. She had never accompanied him to catch up on the news with all the other farmers at the café before, but she decided it would be an interesting study in local color. She would be sure to recreate the scene in her journal later.

When they entered, the animated conversations rolled out the door and into the warm air. Ann saw every age, height, and build of farmer wearing overalls, jeans, Western shirts, boots, and caps. They were talking about harvest and worrying over the weather as they sipped coffee and devoured plates of homestyle food. Grandpa led Ann through the maze of people and toward the back in search of an empty table, introducing her along the way.

"Herman, this is my granddaughter, Ann. Rich, my granddaughter Ann . . . Why, hello, John, Cameron."

Ann's heart sank as Grandpa parted the last wave of the sea of farmers. *I really cannot catch a break!* she thought.

"Bernard, Ann. Have a seat," John said.

"Why, thank you," said Grandpa. He sat next to John, and Ann slipped into the booth next to Cameron with a sigh.

"Hey, Ann," Cameron said.

Ann nodded.

"What happened to your eye?" Grandpa asked Cameron after he'd ordered coffee for himself and a pop for Ann.

Ann cringed.

"I fell. Isn't that right, Ann?" Cameron's elbow jostled hers ever so slightly.

"What, into some other boy's fist?" said Grandpa.

"Not exactly."

Ann could hear the taunting in his voice.

"Chair," John said.

"Yeah. It was the other night when Corrie had her slumber party," said Cameron.

Ann's cheeks burned. Grandpa looked at her with a furrowed brow. "That so," he said.

Grandpa and John compared the ups and downs of that year's harvest over coffee while Ann sat sipping her pop and actively ignoring Cameron's grin and his very existence.

After what seemed like an eternity, John looked at his watch. "Well, we'd best get back after it. That wheat won't cut itself," he said.

They all stood and left their cash directly on the table. Grandpa shook John's hand. "Take care of that eye," he said as he shook Cameron's. Then, he turned, and Ann followed, repeating the same performance as they worked their way to the door.

"Roger, this is my granddaughter, Ann. Charlie, my granddaughter, Ann," he said to the oldest man in the room.

The wrinkles on the elderly farmer's face and his stooped back spoke of many a previous harvest. Unbeknownst to Ann, Charlie Richards was a prankster and permanent fixture at the café where he sat most days to listen to the gossip and swap stories with anyone who wandered in. He was also every bit as deaf as Great-Uncle Pete.

"What's that?" He cupped his ear.

"My granddaughter, Ann," Grandpa repeated loudly enough to quiet the din around them.

"Nice to meet you," Ann said, taking the arthritic hand the old farmer offered.

Charlie shook Ann's hand slowly. "And she's dressed in yella. Must be lookin' for a fella," he said.

A hush fell around them, the chatter suspended at Charlie's loud proclamation. Ann heard Cameron snicker behind her; it was time to teach him a lesson.

"Well, if I were lookin' for a fella, I certainly wouldn't look here," she said, shouting but leaning in as if sharing a secret with Charlie. She gave Cameron a pointed look. "I don't see a single eligible candidate."

Charlie cackled, and Grandpa ushered Ann to the door.

As Grandpa herded the grain truck back onto the highway, he looked sideways at Ann.

"So are you going to tell me the real story behind that boy's black eye?"

Ann stared intently out the window. "Didn't he tell you?"

"He did, but I don't buy it. Especially with those pink cheeks of yours and the way he kept looking at you."

"I don't know what you mean."

"Ann, I might be old, but I'm not blind. What happened?"

Ann told him the whole story, although she left out the part about Cameron asking her out.

"Please don't tell Grandma. He was just trying to scare me. That's all. You know how he teases Corrie and me all the time. I feel like Grandma was finally starting to like me a little bit, and I don't want her to get the wrong idea."

"A little bit? Of course, she likes you. She's not real demonstrative, but she cares about you."

"But if she thought I wasn't following her rules, she wouldn't be happy. Please?"

Grandpa drove in silence for a few moments. "I don't usually have secrets from your grandma, but I think this time it might be best to keep this between us."

"Thank you." Ann breathed a sigh of relief.

"That really was quite the shiner you gave him." Grandpa sounded almost impressed.

Ann enjoyed the rest of the drive in the rattletrap of a grain truck. By the time she arrived back home, she felt as if every bone in her body had been shaken out of her skin, dusted off, and reintroduced into the wrong place.

"How was your trip?" asked Grandma with an innocent lift of her eyebrows.

"You could have warned me," said Ann.

"Oh, I didn't want to ruin it for you."

"If today is any indication, I'm not cut out for farm life, and I never will be."

"You will be. Just give it time."

"You really think so?" asked Ann.

Grandma smiled and patted her hand. "I really do."

As long as I don't mess it up, thought Ann.

15

The County Fair

August had come to Sunflower Lane, and the farm's namesake flowers bloomed in wild profusion along the dusty roads.

"Now I understand why Kansas is called the Sunflower State and why your grandfather named this land Sunflower Lane," Ann said to Grandpa one afternoon. She had come walking in the laneway carrying a spontaneously picked bouquet of the bright, yellow flowers. "I never knew sunflowers could be so lovely. And they smell delightful—almost as nice as lilacs. I imagine the streets of heaven must be lined with lilacs and sunflowers. I think they don't bloom at the same time on Earth because then we'd have nothing to look forward to in heaven. I'm going to put these in a vase on my dresser, and when they dry, I'll make a sunflower jar to set beside my rose jar. That way I'll have a glimpse of summer all year round."

Ann's room had transformed into the dreamroom of her heart. It breathed back her own essence in the pale lilac walls, books, pictures clipped from old calendars discovered in the garret, and the wild rose petals she'd dried and stored lovingly in her mother's rose jar. A stack of new school supplies and Ann's recently confirmed schedule at Storey High sat on the desk, and several more books filled a bookcase rescued from the garret. Ann's personality perfumed the space about her and adorned its every corner with her vibrant energy.

Ann hummed along to the song on the country radio station as she arranged her flowers at the kitchen table. A hint of baby's breath from Grandma's garden was the final touch, and Ann sat admiring her bouquet when Grandma came in.

"That's real pretty, Ann. You seem to have a knack for arranging flowers," Grandma said.

"I think the beauty is in the flowers themselves. I didn't improve on it."

"You should enter an arrangement at the county fair next week in the wildflower category. I'm taking up my oatmeal bread and a few things from the garden. You might as well take an arrangement. You're real good at it."

Ann was not used to such open praise from her grandmother. "OK. That sounds fun," she said.

She spent the next week watching the weather with a worried eye, certain a violent hailstorm would appear on the horizon and destroy the flowers she had in mind for her arrangement. On the opening day of the fair, Ann rose with the first streaks of dawn and gathered sunflowers along the lane, snowy Queen Anne's lace beside the field, and purple gayfeather along the county road. She spent little time fussing with her arrangement, instead embracing the wild essence of her material as she placed the blooms in an old crock. She added a simple lavender bow as a finishing touch. After breakfast, Ann carried her bouquet carefully to the car and held it in a cautious embrace as Grandma drove to the county fairgrounds in nearby Bergendale.

Ann and Grandma entered their items in the open class and then spent the morning looking at the exhibits. It was the first time Ann had ever gone to a county fair. She discovered beautiful quilts, crocheted afghans and doilies, knitted sweaters, painted landscapes, handcrafted wooden dressers, and photographs that captured the beauty of the open prairies and their horizons as she wandered through the buildings. Then, she and Grandma went through the barns, and Ann oohed and aahed over the bucket calves and sheep. By midafternoon, they had seen Grandma's oatmeal bread take first in yeast breads and her watermelon dominate gardening. Then, it was time for the flower judging.

"I can't watch," Ann said as the judge carried three ribbons to the display area. She closed her eyes.

"Well, I can, and I can tell you that you won a ribbon."

"I did?" Ann's eyes popped open.

"You got third place."

"I can't believe it!"

"I can. Far be it for me to disagree with the judge, but in my opinion, yours is the prettiest arrangement up there," said Grandma.

"I'm so glad you suggested I enter. I've never won anything in my life."

"I only wish I'd thought to bring the Polaroid," said Grandma.

"I'm sure Corrie's mom would take a picture when I come back with them for the carnival tonight."

"Mind you don't forget. I want to commemorate this," Grandma said. She wrapped her arm around Ann's shoulders and gave them a gentle squeeze.

"Me, too," said Ann. But she wasn't referring to the ribbon.

That evening, Ann and Corrie chattered like the proverbial magpies all the way to the fairgrounds. John Alexander sat stoically at the wheel, glancing in the rearview mirror at them whenever their laughter erupted in the backseat. Ellen listened with a good-humored smile, and Cameron rolled his eyes with aggravating frequency. Ann was less than pleased when John instructed them all to stay together after they'd taken the required picture of her with her winning bouquet. She didn't want Corrie to get into trouble with her stepfather again, so she said nothing about having to roam the fair with Cameron in tow.

The evening was a blur of lights, rides, and games, of cotton candy and funnel cakes, the latter a favorite of Corrie's who insisted on a return trip to the stand. Darkness had settled in by the time the group of three waited in line for the Ferris wheel.

"I was really nervous about starting school when I found out I was staying here, but now that I have my schedule, I think I'm ready," said Ann.

"Speak for yourself. I could always use more of summer break," Cameron said.

"Enough school talk. We'll be up soon," Corrie said, an eye on the line as she finished her second funnel cake. "I'm really stuffed, but it would be unforgiveable to waste this."

"Because you couldn't share with your big brother," Cameron said.

Corrie ignored him. "My big brother is going to have to sit by himself."

"Fine by me. It's the only way I'll get any peace and quiet," he said, tucking the Teddy bear he'd won at the shooting gallery under his arm.

"Or we could go look for Acacia Thorne," Ann said sweetly. "It's a pity she and Jeff Sands got back together. Otherwise, I'm sure she'd love to ride the Ferris wheel with you."

Cameron stepped all six feet of himself toward Ann and towered over her. "Well, she might make better company than some people I know."

"I'd have to agree," said Ann. "And I really don't like her."

"Next," called the carnie.

Ann slipped into the seat, readying herself for her first-ever ride on a Ferris wheel. Corrie was stepping to join her when she suddenly clutched her stomach.

"Ooo. I don't feel so great," said Corrie. "I think that last bite of funnel cake was one bite too many."

"Or it could be the two funnel cakes along with the ice cream, peanuts, and cotton candy," Cameron said.

"Whatever," said Corrie as she glared at her brother. "But I feel a little queasy, so I think I'd better sit this one out.

"I'll stay with you," Ann said. She remembered how Anne Shirley imagined nursing Diana Barry through the smallpox, even if it meant she caught it herself and died. That, right there, was true friendship for you.

"No, I'll be fine. I just don't want to go on any more rides for a while. You two go ahead."

"Keep it moving up there," yelled someone behind them in the line.

"Go on," Corrie said, shoving Cameron in the direction of the ride.

Ann looked hopelessly on as Cameron shrugged and stepped into the waiting car. What would Grandma say if she knew Ann went on the Ferris Wheel alone with a boy?

"What's the matter? You afraid of heights?" Cameron said.

"Hardly," Ann said. She crossed her arms over her chest and stared straight ahead. Everything would be fine, as long as Grandma didn't find out. And how could she? Besides, she was in the middle of a carnival, not sneaking off somewhere. Maybe if she didn't speak to Cameron, he'd take the hint and leave her alone forever, or at the very least, during the ride.

"Nice view," said Cameron as they rose above the fairway.

Ann nodded.

"Aren't you going to speak to me, Ann?"

Ann shook her head.

"You really need to take things less seriously."

Cameron's last comment was met with silence, so he shrugged and watched the lights of the fairway below as the great wheel spun round and round before slowing to a stop.

"Great," muttered Ann. Of all the times for them to stop the Ferris wheel, it would be when she was stuck at its pinnacle with Cameron Addair.

"You do realize I'm not the one who bailed on this ride. If you want to be mad at someone, be mad at my sister. I don't know what game she's playing."

"She's not playing at any game. She didn't feel well. I should have stayed with her instead of letting myself get stuck here with you."

"You know, most people think I'm a pretty decent guy."

"I am not most people."

"I thought you and I were getting along pretty well these days. Why the change?"

"Change? What change? There's been no change. Oh, wait. You mean because I gave you a black eye? That hardly seems like 'getting along,'" Ann said.

"The creek?"

"Oh, you mean your unchivalrous attempt to terrorize me. The one that preceded the time you attempted to terrorize me in the middle of the night at Corrie's slumber party."

"Terrorize you? That's one way to put it, I guess. Don't you ever talk like ordinary girls?"

"No," said Ann. "Because I am extraordinary."

"True enough."

"What do you mean by that?"

"Look," said Cameron, slipping his arm along the back of the seat. "I'm sorry I scared you at the slumber party, and I'm sorry I made you fall in the creek. Can we please just let it go?"

Ann looked up into Cameron's eyes. The lights from the fairway reflected in their dark pools under the night sky. She swallowed.

"You know, if you'd try even a little bit, you might enjoy the view from up here. Come on, have a little fun," said Cameron.

"I can assure you that 'I am excessively diverted,'" Ann said.

"Tell your face that," Cameron suggested. He leaned closer.

Ann's palms broke out in a cold sweat. "Look, I will forgive your past transgressions if you'll remove your arm from the back of this seat," she said.

Cameron opened his mouth. He exhaled a frustrated sigh and lowered his arm. "Fine," he said.

"Thank you," Ann replied softly, looking out across the lights below. The ride lurched back into motion, and Ann blamed it for the strange, fluttery feeling in her stomach.

16

Ann's Birthday Surprise

Ann awoke before her alarm to the early rays of August sunshine on her sixteenth birthday. She lay for a moment, watching the pattern of shadow and light created by the dance of the oak branches outside. Those trees were so solid they seemed eternal. Had they painted a similar scene on this same wall on the morning of her mother's sixteenth birthday? What had her mother seen sixteen years ago on the last day of her life, the day Ann was born?

Ann sat up and looked around. "Wish you were here to celebrate my birthday with me, Mom," she said to the room. Her mother had always been an image in her mind's eye, but since coming to Sunflower Lane, she had started to become more real. Even though Ann didn't know much about her mom, she felt a connection to her for the first time.

She slipped out of bed and knelt beside her mother's old trunk. She'd lost count of the number of times she'd looked through the books and yearbooks and mementos her mother had stored lovingly in it. She ran her hands over the dry covers as she stacked them beside her.

"I should read something of hers in her honor," said Ann. She considered each book, finally selecting a slim volume of collected poems.

Ann glanced at the clock. She still had ten minutes before her alarm went off.

"Just one," she said, paging through the book. "Wait, what's this?"

Ann withdrew a single sheet of paper. Brittle rose petals fell out of it as she unfolded it.

"It's a letter to Mom," her eyes scanned the page. She squinted, trying to make out the words written in the sloppy handwriting.

Dear Amelia,

By now you've guessed how I feel, but I have to tell you anyway. I love you. Please tell me you feel the same way.

R.J.

"Mom had a boyfriend before Dad? I wonder if he knew? For that matter, I wonder if Grandma knew, considering how adamant she is about me not even thinking about boys. I'd better not ask. And who is R.J. anyway? I wonder why they broke up. Was it a disagreement or something more tragic, like what happened with Clarence and Lily?"

Ann's alarm interrupted her imaginings. She carefully folded the letter and added the few petals to her mother's rose jar that now adorned her dresser.

The tantalizing scent of Grandma's buttermilk blueberry muffins greeted Ann as she descended the stairs.

"Good morning, sweet sixteen!" called Grandpa when she entered the kitchen. He broke into a rousing chorus of "Happy Birthday," and Grandma sang along.

"Now, sit down and eat your breakfast. I made the muffins you like so well," Grandma said. She rested a hand for a breath on Ann's shoulder.

Ann smiled up at her grandmother. She was starting to learn the little gestures she used to express what she didn't say.

"Thanks, Grandma. I really appreciate it."

"This is the big day. Are you ready for your driving test?" asked Grandpa.

"As ready as I'll ever be. And I feel confident knowing I had the best teacher out there."

"Goes without saying," said Grandpa.

They devoured their meal of scrambled eggs, ham, and the sweetness of the muffins made with fresh blueberries from a bush in a sunny corner of Grandma's garden. They seemed to hold all the goodness of the summer sun in their burst of flavor. When they'd finished, Ann rose to clear the table and help with dishes.

"Sit back down for a minute," said Grandma.

Ann dutifully sat, worry gnawing at her. "What did I do or forget to do now? It's just my luck to get into trouble on my own birthday."

"You're not in trouble. We want to give you our gift," said Grandma.

Grandpa slid a small box wrapped in purple paper across the table to her. "For our Ann."

He offered her his pocketknife. Grandma was a firm believer in reusing any scrap of wrapping paper and woe to all who did not slit each taped seam of any gift with surgical precision.

"A locket! I've always wanted one. And it even has my initial on it."

"It was your mother's. We gave it to her on her sixteenth birthday," Grandma said.

"The chain broke, and she stored it in her trunk until she could afford to fix it. I suppose over the years she just forgot. I slipped it out before Edward and I brought the trunk down so we could get it cleaned up and repaired. We wanted to surprise you. We put her picture in it," said Grandpa.

Ann opened the locket, and there was her mother's smiling face, so like her own. Tears formed at the corner of her eyes.

"Thank you. It's like she's here with me, in a way."

"And having you here is like she's here with us, too," said Grandpa.

Grandma swiped at her eyes. "Enough of this sentimental mush. Day's a wastin', and we have chores to do before you go for your driving test this afternoon."

Ann laughed. Some things would probably never change.

"Grandma?" Ann called when she came in the front door following her driver's license exam.

The house was dark and eerily quiet. Ann felt fear clutch at her chest. Had something happened to Grandma? She hurried to the kitchen.

"Surprise!"

The shout ricocheted off the narrow walls of the kitchen as Ann's friends jumped up from behind the table. It had been moved to the center of the room, and a cake, beautifully decorated with a miniature white house with green shutters and gables, sat at its center.

"Happy birthday," said Corrie. She hugged Ann tightly.

"Did you plan this?" Ann asked.

"Nope. It was all your grandma's idea. I just helped her organize it."

"Really? Grandma, I never knew you to be so sneaky."

Grandma smiled innocently. "I just had the idea. Corrie invited everyone, and Ellen made the cake so we could keep it a surprise. And Janis dropped off some of her homemade ice cream."

"Thanks, everyone. I'm so glad I can spend my birthday with you."

"So did you get your license?" asked Ginny after Grandma had taken several pictures and Ann was cutting and serving cake.

"Yes. You surprised me so much, I forgot all about it."

"She's a legal driver in the state of Kansas," Grandpa said.

"It's all thanks to you," Ann said. She handed him a large slice of cake, and Corrie added a generous dip of ice cream.

"It's thanks to the fact that you tried real hard and practiced," said Grandpa. "Now, if you ladies will excuse me, I think I'll take my cake to the front porch and let you talk in peace."

"I'll join you," said Grandma.

The girls chatted and joked and ingested far more ice cream and cake than was healthy in anyone other than a teen. Then, they gave Ann her gifts: a Storey High T-shirt from Laura, earrings from Ginny, a beaded bracelet from Molly, and her very own, eight-volume set of the Anne books from Corrie.

"You guys are awesome. This is the best birthday I've ever had," said Ann.

They chatted and laughed and told stories until the afternoon had passed. Then, the other girls left, but Corrie was allowed to stay for supper and for the night.

She and Ann talked for several hours in Ann's dreamroom after Grandma and Grandpa went to bed. Ann thought about showing Corrie the letter she'd found that morning among her mother's books, but something held her back. It was as if that bit of information were something just between them, a link to the mother she'd never known. She didn't want to share it.

As they rolled out Corrie's sleeping bag next to the twin bed, Ann suddenly realized it: Dad hadn't called. He hadn't sent a gift or even a measly card. Her own father had completely forgotten her birthday . . . again. She should be used to it by now, but it still stung, even after all these years.

"What's the matter?" asked Corrie.

"I just realized my father did absolutely nothing for my birthday. I don't know why I was dumb enough to think he would. It's not like he ever did anything when I lived with him," Ann said. She pressed her lips together tightly.

"I'm sorry," said Corrie. She sat by Ann and hugged her.

"It's time I just admitted it: My father is a colossal jerk!"

"I'm not going to argue with you, but don't let him ruin your birthday. Think of how your grandma planned a party, and your grandpa taught you to drive so you could get your license today. And hey, all of us girls came to make sure you had the best sweet sixteen ever."

Ann nodded. "You're right. I am grateful for all of that."

Corrie slapped her head. "I can't believe I forgot. There's one more gift."

"But you already gave me a gift. And you helped Grandma organize my party."

"This isn't from me." Corrie reached in her duffel bag and pulled out a Teddy bear. Ann recognized it as the one Cameron had won at the fair.

"Your brother sent this?"

"Yes. I think he likes you," said Corrie.

"No, he doesn't. He just doesn't have any use for a stuffed animal."

"Why wouldn't he like you? You're smart and pretty and all spirit and fire and dew. Besides, you are probably the first girl ever who didn't flirt with him nonstop."

"Well, he *can't* like me," said Ann.

"Why not?"

"Because Grandma will ground me for life if she thinks I'm encouraging any boys. That is her number one rule for me: no boys. And she's made it very clear she means it."

"Really? How come you didn't tell me before?"

"Because I didn't think it'd be a problem. It's not like I've ever had Ruby Gillis's string of beaux lining up. Besides, it's kind of embarrassing. It's like she doesn't trust me."

"Maybe she'll change her mind?" said Corrie.

"Maybe. But honestly, I don't think I even care. I'd probably make a mess of dating, since I have no experience, and my father is such a shining example of what to look for in a boy. The only thing I know about love and relationships is from books. I only wish I didn't feel like Grandma was always watching to catch me doing something wrong."

"I don't think she is. I've spent the last week talking with her to organize your party, and she seemed like she genuinely wants you to be happy at Sunflower Lane. One thing I've learned after moving to Podunk Storey is that people around here are very guarded with their emotions."

"Tell me about it," said Ann.

"So you'll keep the Teddy bear? Please do. If I go home with that thing, I'll have to deal with Cam, and that is such a drag."

"I don't know. It's kind of risky. You'd better take it back."

Corrie took the bear and thought for a moment. "Ann, I'd like you to have this bear someone gave me. It's mine, but I want you to have it. There—will that work? Now I'm technically the one who put it in your hands and gave it to you. Besides, it's awfully cute, don't you think?"

Ann smiled. "All right, I'll keep the bear. But don't tell your brother about my grandma's rule. He would tease me mercilessly, and that would make it that much worse."

"I promise. Now, let's get some shut-eye so we're not falling asleep over breakfast. I think that really would get us in trouble with your grandma."

Ann switched off the light and lay back against her pillows. In no time, she heard Corrie's deep breathing, but Ann couldn't sleep. She watched the shadows the oaks cast on her room in the moonlight and thought back over the day. It had been an eventful one, what with the letter, the locket, her license, the party, and what Corrie had said about Grandma. Maybe she was right; maybe Grandma did care for her, but she just showed it differently.

And maybe her father never had cared. Maybe she'd been fooling herself all along, thinking there would be a happy ending to her story with him.

She hugged the Teddy bear tightly to her chest and shut her eyes against the tears.

17

The Wings of Anticipation

"I'm home," Ann called as she returned on the first day of school.

"How'd it go?" asked Grandpa.

"Fine. But I have homework already."

"Sit down and have a cookie first. Then, you can do your homework," Grandma said.

Ann smiled. She was starting to learn how to read between the lines of what Grandma said and did. She might not say it directly, but the cookies were her way of saying she was interested in Ann's day.

"I started off the day by learning lockers are assigned first by class, and then alphabetically. Unfortunately, Corrie's is on the floor below mine, but mine is straight across from the senior lockers. So that means I'm across from Cameron and his best friend, Lee Ambrose. Oh, joy. But, on the bright side, it puts me at the opposite end of the hall from Larry Zima." Ann took a ferocious bite of her cookie.

"Who's Larry Zima? Do you know any Zimas, Thelma?" asked Grandpa.

"No, they must be new to the area," Grandma said.

"Larry Zima is a football player who walks around with his shirt half untucked, his hair sticking out in every direction from under a dirty cap, and speaks most of the time in monosyllables. He's in my

Spanish class. I made the mistake of introducing myself, and he wouldn't leave me alone after that. It's only the first day, and he's already trying my patience."

"You know patience is a virtue," said Grandma.

Ann wrinkled her nose. "You've told me that a thousand times, Grandma, but I'm not convinced it's a virtue I possess much of."

"What about the rest of your day?" asked Grandpa.

"I have Advanced Placement History first hour. It's mostly juniors, but it's the first year they've offered it, so there are some seniors, like Cameron, taking it to try to get college credit. I think I'm going to like geometry. I guess I'm not much like Anne Shirley in that regard. I detest chemistry, but I love English and creative writing. I have Mrs. Chapman for both of those classes, and she is undoubtedly a kindred spirit."

"Did you find any activities you want to do?" said Grandpa.

"Yes. Auditions for the play are this week. They'll announce which one they're doing tomorrow. I wish Mrs. Chapman were directing it, but it's Mr. Weaver. I don't know him. I hope he's as nice as she is."

"I'm sure he will be," said Grandpa.

"All in all, it was a good day, other than having to deal with Larry Zima. I fear he is going to be my Charlie Sloane," Ann said with resignation.

"Who's Charlie Sloane? Thelma, do you know any Sloanes?" asked Grandpa.

"No, I don't. Are they new to the area?"

"Charlie Sloane is the goggle-eyed boy who has a crush on Anne Shirley and drives her crazy," explained Ann.

"Oh, your book. Sometimes I don't follow your jumps between reality and fiction," said Grandma.

"It's OK. Sometimes I'm not sure I do either."

Ann's excitement at her first day of school in no way matched that of her second.

"I have the most thrilling news," she told her grandparents as soon as she walked in the door. "They announced the play today. It's *Anne of Green Gables*! Can you imagine if I could be Anne Shirley? No one other than Corrie could possibly know Anne as I do, and she's not interested in the lead. I simply *have* to be Anne," Ann concluded, subscribing to the notion that whosoever most closely imitated her literary heroine was closest to achieving Green Gables perfection.

"Don't count your chickens before they're hatched," Grandma cautioned.

"I know, Grandma, and I am worried. Everyone says Acacia Thorne gets whatever she wants at that school. I'll just have to give it my best shot."

The next evening confirmed Ann's worst fears. Acacia was front and center for auditions when she arrived.

"I hope she doesn't try out for the lead," Ann whispered to Corrie and Ginny.

"If she does, she'll get it," said Ginny whose acceptance of Acacia's stranglehold on school activities was based on years of experience.

"If that man gives her the lead, I refuse to be in this play, no matter how much I love *Green Gables*," Corrie said.

"I'm not sure my convictions can take me that far," said Ann.

"Break a leg, Ann." Cameron Addair—of course.

"You're auditioning?" she asked.

"Yeah. I figured, why not?"

A vision of him as Gilbert flitted through her mind, but she pushed it aside as Mr. Weaver began the auditions.

"We are here to choose the best among you for this theatrical adaptation of a children's classic," Mr. Weaver said, striking a dramatic pose. He was a rotund man with an impressive combover. He was wearing a red button-up with a stain on it, brown polyester pants that were an inch too short, a scarred black belt that was half a hitch to the side of center, white tube socks, and grimy gray tennis shoes. To Ann's eyes, he looked anything but dramatic, and she immediately took offense at his description of her beloved book.

"'Children's?'" she said in a harsh whisper to Corrie. "Why, it's a classic, right up there with any other. I can already tell Mr. Weaver doesn't have a single hair of a kindred spirit among the few hairs he has left."

"We shall begin with Acacia reading the part of Anne and Kristin reading the part of Diana on page thirty."

Ann's heart sank, but she would show she *was* Anne Shirley. After only a few lines, it was clear Acacia Thorne as the lead would make L.M. Montgomery roll over in her grave. Ann fidgeted as Mr. Weaver asked one after another of those present to read. At last, he called her name.

"Let's see, Ann . . . Well, isn't that an unfortunate coincidence? Ann Alwyn, you read the part of Miss Josephine, and Corrie Addair, Diana. We'll continue with Acacia as Anne."

Ann read her lines, certain they would all switch roles and repeat the scene. But when they'd finished, Mr. Weaver thanked them and told them to take a seat.

"That concludes our auditions," said Mr. Weaver. "Unless there is anyone who didn't have the chance to read for a part they wanted to?"

Ann raised her hand.

"Yes? Ann, isn't it? The unfortunate coincidence."

Ann's lips tightened. Sabrina had called her many names in her life, but even she hadn't thought to call her an "unfortunate coincidence."

"I'd like to read for the part of Anne Shirley," she said.

"Well, isn't that sweet. Ann reading for Anne," Mr. Weaver said with a smile that was anything but sweet. "I could let you, but I can assure you it would be a waste of your time."

Ann felt her face flush and her nose go up. How dare this man insult her and judge her talents without cause!

"I would enjoy the opportunity nonetheless," Ann said, eyes sparking. Something deep within Ann was beginning to stir, some remote corner of her spirit that had sprouted at Sunflower Lane, far from her father's criticism and her half-sister's bullying. Ann knew down to her toes that Acacia would be handed the role of Anne Shirley, but she refused to cow before the arrogant Mr. Weaver.

"Fine."

Ann climbed to the stage in high dudgeon and took her place as two other girls were assigned roles.

"Wait," said Mr. Weaver. "Ann, take off your shoes. You're far too tall."

Too tall? thought Ann. *Why, I'm shorter than Acacia by at least two inches.*

But she slipped off her shoes, tossed them roughly out of the way with a thunk, and raised her chin that much higher. When the scene was over, she strode from the stage and to the waiting Bessie outside. She slammed the old truck's door, started the engine, and left.

Back home, a still-angry Ann recounted the whole scene for her grandparents.

"I know in my bones I am not getting the role of Anne Shirley or any role at all, even though I read very well. I don't know what came over me when I stood up to that nasty man, but I refused to let him attack my dignity. Well, I had flown 'up on the wings of anticipation' over this, and now I've thudded back to earth."

Regardless of her words, Ann's heart still harbored some glimmer of hope the next morning as she sat awaiting the cast list in the daily announcements. She was not surprised, although she was still hurt, to hear Acacia's name announced for the role of Anne Shirley, and neither she nor Corrie were included at all. Oh, Acacia would gloat, and she'd fling herself at Cameron as Gilbert, despite her boyfriend. It was almost enough to make Ann feel sorry for him.

"Oh, Ann," sympathized Molly as Ann turned resolutely to her textbook.

"Ann, I'm not taking that role," Cameron said from the desk behind her.

"I don't need you to fight my battles for me."

"I'm well aware of that, but I don't want to be in a play with that dictator."

"You should've told him before they announced it," said Ann.

"Oh, he'll find out soon enough."

Ann thought she couldn't have borne Acacia's smug smile in second period if not for the knowledge that Cameron wasn't going to play Gilbert.

That evening, as Ann sat listlessly doing homework after supper, the phone rang.

"Ann, you're never going to believe it," Corrie said by way of greeting.

"Believe what?"

"The play is without a cast."

"What?"

"Cameron went to the first practice tonight, and he informed Mr. Weaver in front of everyone that he refused to play any role after the way he treated you. Weaver started screaming like a maniac. The others decided they didn't want to spend their time getting yelled at either, and they quit. Only Acacia and two others were left."

"Weaver will just replace them," Ann said.

"I don't think so. Word has gotten around about what happened, and everyone thinks that man is a tyrant."

"Won't Cameron get in trouble for leading an anti-Weaver insurrection?"

"For what? Changing his mind about a role? Besides, Theo Larsen and Lee Ambrose said they canceled the play one other time when Weaver tried to direct. No, I think his play is toast."

"I hope you're right," Ann said, knowing Grandma would have scolded her for being uncharitable if she'd heard both sides of the conversation.

"And there's something else I have to tell you. When John overheard me telling Mom about how you stood up to Weaver at the auditions, he started chuckling. I asked him what was so funny, and he said, 'Not only does your friend look like her mother, it sounds like she has her temperament.' I asked him what he meant, and he said, 'No one ever got the better of Amelia Holmberg. No one could convince her to do something she didn't want to do.'"

"I forgot they were in the same grade. I saw John's picture in my mom's yearbook. I wonder why he never said anything about her before."

"Who knows? Maybe it's because he doesn't even know how to talk to me. Or he didn't know what to say. It can be hard for people to talk about someone who's passed away, you know."

"Yeah, I've noticed. That's probably it. Thanks for calling me, Corrie. I can't wait to see what happens with Weaver and his play."

The next morning, the halls were alive with the excitement that only a Friday can produce among high schoolers. Even the chattering in Ann's small first hour class threatened to drown out the daily announcements and the juicy tidbit Ann was waiting to hear.

"The school play has been canceled due to a lack of interest. Instead, Miss Harper will be directing *Brigadoon*."

"All of this has made me certain of two things, Corrie," Ann said on the bus ride home. "One, I'm not auditioning for anything else here. With Acacia Thorne around, all efforts are futile. And two, I will not participate in any activities involving Mr. Weaver."

"And three," added Cameron from across the aisle where he sat, casually reclined with his cap tipped over his eyes, "Cameron Addair is a decent guy. And he might know a thing or two about chivalry after all." He sat up, slipped his cap back, and leaned forward with a grin. "Wouldn't you agree, Ann?"

"He has his moments," was all she would admit.

She turned from Cameron's roguish smile and watched the countryside as it rolled by the open bus window, the warm afternoon breeze whipping her hair. She had to keep him at a distance or risk losing all the ground she'd gained with her grandmother.

18

The Storm

"That's us," Ann said. She watched a smiling meteorologist on TV announce a band of severe weather that could last well into the night.

"Calm down. A tornado watch means the conditions are right for a tornado, not that one's been spotted," said Grandma.

"But I've never been in a tornado, and there aren't any sirens out here."

"Not to worry. We've seen one or two," said Grandpa.

The storm rolled through, followed by another that knocked out the power.

"Oh, no. I have my first history exam tomorrow," said Ann.

"Hold on a minute. I got out the kerosene lamps in case this happened. Here—I used this one when I was a boy," Grandpa said. He lit the wick and placed the glass shade on the antique lamp. "Set it on the end table beside you."

Ann complied, waving her face with her notebook in a vain attempt to alleviate the stuffiness of the closed-up house while she squinted at the tiny print in her textbook, sweat beading on her face. Ann tried to focus, but the flickering lamplight coupled with interludes of wind, thunder, rain, and hail were unnerving.

An hour later, the storm had subsided, but the lights remained off. Ann was the unfortunate sufferer of a raging headache and case of nerves before her first exam. Grandma declared it was time they all tried to get some sleep. Grandpa helped Ann fold out the sleeper sofa so she could stay closer to the cave, and Grandma cracked open one of the windows with a reminder to shut it if the rain returned. The sweet smell of fresh, rain-washed air filtered in, although Ann found it incongruous with the raging winds of the previous hours.

"I'll never sleep a wink," Ann assured her grandparents. But as the fragrant breeze drifted over her, she relaxed. Ann was resting pleasantly when the next storm struck with a crash of thunder so loud the dishes in the china cabinet rattled. Ann sat upright in bed, disoriented and frightened.

"Move," called Grandma as she rushed into the living room and opened the cave door.

Ann heard what sounded like a train rushing toward them, and the air around her tasted and smelled strange. She untangled herself from the sheet and leaped to the floor. She followed Grandma without hesitation down the steep steps to the cave, the last morsels of her fear of it disappearing in the face of a greater danger. Once below, Ann sank to the cold, stone floor, her legs weak. Total blackness surrounded them, and the air in the cave was eerily cool after the stuffiness.

"Come sit on the bench at the back," said Grandpa. He helped Ann to her feet, and she dropped, trembling to the bench.

"Lots of your ancestors have waited out storms here," said Grandpa.

"That's right. This house has stood for over a century. It can withstand another storm," Grandma said.

"But what if this is the one it doesn't survive? Oh, this is every bit as terrifying as the storm Uncle Abe didn't predict in *Anne of Avonlea*," said Ann.

"Another book?" asked Grandma.

Ann nodded.

Grandpa took her hand and patted it reassuringly.

After some time, Grandpa rose and listened at the door.

"I don't hear the wind. I'll go take a look," he said.

"Are you sure it's safe to go up?" asked Ann.

"I'll be careful."

Several moments later, Grandpa returned with a flashlight and their shoes.

"Put these on before you come up. The window in the living room shattered," Grandpa said.

Ann swallowed. "What if I had still been asleep beneath that window?"

Grandma drew in her breath sharply but didn't answer. "Was it a tornado?" she asked.

"Looks like it might have been. There'll be limbs down. We'll know more when it's light out. For now, let's all try to sleep as best as we can."

Ann spent a restless night sandwiched between her grandparents in their bed, for even Grandma was shaken enough to be hesitant to send her upstairs. When the first gray streaks of dawn began to show, they all rose, dressed, and went outside.

"It's freakishly still out here now. It's just as creepy as the storm was," said Ann.

Everywhere, plants were flattened, limbs carpeted the lawn, and leaves and debris stuck to the side of the house. Ann turned, stupidly looking around the strange scene.

"Oh, no!" she cried. "The Rose Queen."

The beautiful tree that had greeted Ann on her first morning at Sunflower Lane had been wrenched from the earth whole, spun out across the yard, and deposited on the other side of the house upside down with its entire root system snaking out through the air. Ann had not shed a tear during the whole frightening ordeal, but the sight of the beautiful tree tossed aside like a piece of kindling was too much. Her lip trembled, and teardrops streamed down her face.

"Don't cry. I know it was a beautiful tree, but we can plant another one, together. It will be your tree at Sunflower Lane. Besides, it's better than if something happened to one of us," said Grandma. She wrapped Ann in an uncustomary embrace.

Ann nodded, sniffling.

"Grandma and I will look things over, and you go get ready for school," said Grandpa.

"We still don't have power. You'll have to make yourself a peanut butter and jelly sandwich for breakfast, I suppose," said Grandma.

"I can't let you do all the work. Look at this mess, and what about your heart, Grandpa?" Ann said.

"I promise not to overdo, and I'll call Arthur and Uncle Edward. There will still be plenty of work to do when you get home. Besides, you have your exam," Grandpa said.

"I'll probably fail now."

"You'll do fine. You've done your homework every day and studied for a week, so just imagine the best instead of the worst," Grandpa said.

By the time Ann boarded the bus, she was feeling somewhat better, although the sight of damaged trees and scattered limbs and litter along the road painted the broader extent of the storm's path. When Corrie and Cameron got on, they looked as fresh as ever.

"What's the matter?" asked Corrie after one look at the dark circles under her bosom friend's eyes.

Ann recounted the events of the previous night. "I did my final studying for the history exam by the light of a kerosene lamp last night, and I still have a raging headache."

"That sounds romantic—like something right out of Green Gables," said Corrie.

Ann rubbed her temples. "Romantic is not the word I'd use for it. Between the lamp and the tornado and the stress of this exam, I could do with a little less romance."

They said little for the rest of the way, and Ann sat staring listlessly at her open textbook. She would do her best, but her best might not be good enough, she thought, as she climbed wearily to the classroom. She was so tired she no longer felt nervous. She pulled out two pre-sharpened pencils and her favorite eraser and placed them neatly on her desk. Ann was staring insensibly into space, waiting for the bell to ring and the torture of the exam to begin when a hand appeared in front of her bearing a cold can of cola.

"Drink that before Mr. Williams gets here. The caffeine will help with your headache," said Cameron.

She wanted to say that her grandmother would have a conniption if she knew Ann had a pop first thing in the morning, but then again, Grandma had told her to eat peanut butter and jelly for breakfast. Clearly, in this post-tornadic world, all bets were off.

"Thanks," she said. She sipped the cold beverage. As much as she hated to admit it, Cameron was right. She already felt better.

"Good luck on the exam," Cameron said.

Ann drank her pop, feeling the caffeine begin to dispel some of the fogginess in her mind.

The exam hour passed quickly, and Ann's arm ached after furiously writing her answers. She trudged to her locker, exhausted. Corrie was waiting for her. "How'd it go?" she asked.

"Hard, but not as bad as I expected. You know how it is when you face the unknown. Now I just have to stay awake through the rest of the day."

"Good luck," called Corrie before dashing to her next class.

Ann was retrieving her books from her locker at the end of the day when Corrie came running again. "Come with me. We have the truck," she said.

"Didn't you ride the bus this morning, or was I hallucinating?" asked Ann as they walked to the parking lot.

"Yes, but we called Mom and explained what happened at your grandparents' place. She and John dropped off the truck so we could go home with you and help clean up."

"That was nice of them. See, maybe John isn't such an ogre after all," Ann said.

"Oh, not all the time. Or maybe he's just an ogre to me. Let's go. Molly and Ginny are going to meet us there, too, and so are Lee and Theo and Laura and her boyfriend, Chris. Let's go home and get to work."

Home, thought Ann. *Sunflower Lane really* is *my home.*

"Cordelia Addair, you are the best bosom friend ever. Thank you,"

"Don't thank me," Corrie said. She slid to the middle of the bench seat next to Cameron. "It was Cam's idea."

Ann climbed in and shut the door. She turned grateful eyes to Cameron. "Thank you."

He shrugged. "It's nothing."

As they rolled through the golden autumn afternoon, Ann wondered what Grandma would say when she came driving in the laneway with Cameron Addair. Corrie was there, too, so she'd probably be OK. And as long as he didn't do or say anything stupid, there'd be no reason for Grandma to doubt he'd only come along to help with the clean-up.

"I can't mess this up now," she said to herself.

"What?" asked Corrie.

"Nothing. Nothing at all."

19

Doors

“It will be a Golden Picnic, just like Anne Shirley had, only mine will be golden because of the autumn palette,” Ann said as she packed a lunch. It was a perfect fall Saturday, the danger of poison ivy had passed with an early frost, and she was planning a walk and picnic in the Enchanted Forest.

“Of course,” Grandpa said.

“Do you know what she means?” Grandma asked him in a whisper.

“Not the faintest idea, but it’s probably from a book.”

Ann heard them, but she was in a mood that matched the sunny day. She continued her preparations as if they hadn’t said a thing.

“My only regret is that Corrie can’t join me, but she’s in Kansas City visiting her father. Sometimes I feel sad for her because she misses her dad and KC a lot. But it’s nice she can go visit as often as she does. Well, I’m off on my walk.”

“Be careful,” said Grandma.

Ann set out down the lane and lifted her face to the warmth of the sun. She breathed deeply of the autumn perfume on the air as she “roam’d from field to field.”

“‘I’m so glad I live in a world where there are Octobers,’” she quoted Anne Shirley as she wound along the path in the Enchanted Forest.

The sunshine filtered through the dappled canopy above, gilding the path and the undergrowth. Autumn had stitched of the hillside a patchwork of color one leaf at a time, and its filigreed beauty mirrored Ann's outlook on the day. She sat on one of the large, limestone rocks tossed from the fields above during the oilfield days of the 1920s, according to Grandpa. Ann had christened the line of rocks twisting up the hillside "Mending Wall," an appropriately poetic name, she thought. Here she now sat listening to the distant growl of Arthur's combine as it crept across the nearby soybean field as she dreamed, somewhere between the past of the hillside and the uncertainty of her future. She pulled her journal—what she now called her "Jimmy book" after another Montgomery heroine named Emily Starr—from her backpack and looked thoughtfully around before writing.

This truly is an Enchanted Forest. I've never felt this free and at peace before. I can almost forget my own father didn't care enough to get a job to get me back. I'm starting to love Sunflower Lane. It's the first place that's ever felt like home. But I suppose I really should want to be with my father. The question is, does he want me with him? And would I even want to go back to Denver if he did?

Ann gazed thoughtfully up for a moment, unsure of the answer. She sighed and continued writing, documenting the trials and tribulations of the life of a sixteen-year-old high schooler living in rural Kansas. Not a small amount of space was dedicated to Larry Zima's not-so-subtle hints at an invitation to Homecoming.

But I won't dedicate so much as another drop of ink to Larry Zima. None of my news is particularly thrilling, and I'm sure no one else would find any of it very interesting. But it is the story of my little corner of the world. Perhaps one day, in thirty years or so, I'll look back on it and use it to inspire me and to write something others will find quaint or clever or even romantic.

Finally, when she felt she had sufficiently written herself out, Ann closed her journal and sat a while a longer, at peace with the sights and sounds and scents of the mellow autumn day. The light reflected off the heart-shaped leaves of the redbuds above her, rustling like tiny golden lockets in the autumn afternoon. She soaked in the perfect tranquility of that place, certain it must exist somewhere on the pages of *Green Gables*. After a time, she followed Mending Wall up to the pasture where she dropped among the warm blades of whispering tallgrass. She lay there, searching for the shape of her future in the clouds. Then, she stood and looked out across the tops of the trees she had left behind in The Enchanted Forest and to the fields beyond. In the distance, Ann could see the Storey water tower, but her eyes could see yet farther. She closed her eyes and filled her lungs with the freshness of that perfect afternoon. Somewhere, deep within her, she felt the call of something infinite, a breath of liberty, and like the free bird, she claimed that vast sky for her own.

"All this space used to really freak me out," Ann said as she looked down on Sunflower Lane. "But now, I don't mind it so much. I'm starting to appreciate these expansive vistas because you never know what is just beyond the horizon. I think that's where Stafford's other door is. It's like the horizon is full of doors waiting to be opened, just like Anne Shirley's bend in the road."

Ann glanced at her watch. "I'd better go. I need to study at least some today."

She wound down the deer trail through the Enchanted Forest, enjoying the solitude under its interwoven branches. When she stepped onto the county road, she saw Bubba Joe Ramsey's decrepit pickup pull away from the mailbox at the end of Sunflower Lane. Bubba Joe was the reclusive rural mail carrier who was so shy he could barely stand to raise his hand in a half wave from inside the truck, but to Ann, he was a Hermes delivering messages from the outside world on winged tires. Ann had yet to receive any mail, but hope still welled up within her each time she lowered the mailbox door on its creaking hinges.

Ann continued to the lane and opened the box. There was nothing but Grandpa's farm paper and a single postcard from Nashville. She turned it over. It was from her father.

Ann,

Howdy from Nashville! The band is going places.

Dad

She turned the card over again, as if somewhere she might find more than those few impersonal lines.

"Stupid. What, you think some text is going to magically appear and that he'll tell you how much he loves you and wants to bring you back? It's not like he ever said that when you were right there under his nose, so why now? He totally forgot my birthday, and he can't even bother to call. Get real, Ann," she said to herself.

She shoved the mail in her backpack and crossed to the laneway, tears forming in her eyes. But instead of going home, she turned into Lover's Lane. She followed the path to a circle of large, limestone rocks along the creek that she had christened Idlewild after the ring of birch trees where Anne Shirley and her friend Diana had their playhouse. It was where Grandpa's brother Clarence and Lily Bellerose used to sit and talk. The sturdy oak bearing their initials and a heart still shaded the quiet space.

Ann dropped to one of the stones and let the tears fall.

"That stupid postcard was so impersonal that it was worse than him not sending anything at all. Why do I think he'll ever change? I'm an idiot."

"Only sometimes."

Ann jumped. It was Cameron. She wiped the tears from her face.

"Why do you enjoy terrorizing me?" she asked.

"Sorry. I really didn't mean to scare you."

"What are you doing here?"

"I saw you turn in, so I thought I'd say 'hi'," he said.

"What, are you stalking me now?"

"No, I was going home after I helped Arthur with the soybeans in the field across the road. I do have to make money to pay for college next year, and I am allowed to be on a public road."

"I need to go," Ann said. What if Grandma saw his truck at the end of Lover's Lane and knew they were here together? Horrific images filled her imagination.

"What's the rush?"

"I need to study for our history exam on Monday."

"Don't you want to tell me why you were crying?"

"No," Ann said shortly. "And I really need to leave."

She brushed past him and started down Lover's Lane at a fast clip. He caught up with her in a few strides.

"Say, Ann. You know Homecoming is coming up . . ."

"That's nice."

"And I was wondering . . ."

"Oh, look at that pretty bird," said Ann. She was almost running.

"Could I ask you something?" Cameron said as they reached the laneway where his truck sat.

Ann stopped and turned to look directly at him. "Don't," she said.

Cameron studied her upturned face, pale and tear-stained, and her big, pleading eyes.

"I was only going to ask if you could help me fill in some spaces I have in my history notes. You take way better notes than I do," he said.

Ann let out a breath of relief. "OK. Call me at five o'clock sharp tonight. I'll be helping Grandma make supper, so I know I'll hear the phone." *And Grandma will be able hear the entire conversation and know I'm not doing anything wrong.*

"Sure. Yeah, I'll do that. Happy studying."

"You, too," she said. She gave a half wave and hurried down the lane.

"Cameron Addair, please leave me alone," she said when she heard his truck back out and turn onto the county road. "I can't mess things up at Sunflower Lane. I clearly don't have anywhere else to go."

But that night, the phone never rang.

20

Romance in Storey

"I'm not surprised we didn't get invited to Homecoming. Even though I've been here a year, I'm still a new girl, too. But it's not like I could've gone. John is such a grouch he probably wouldn't have let me go anyway," said Corrie.

"I *know* my grandma wouldn't let me go. But considering all the awkward ways Larry Zima has hinted at an invitation, I think I'm fine without being asked to the dance. You know, there are times I wonder if even the creative genius of L.M. Montgomery could have produced a character as odious as Larry Zima to torment her heroine. He is entirely beyond words and belief."

"I guess we can't expect things to be as they are at Green Gables. John is no Matthew Cuthbert, that's for sure."

"I can't believe you two are talking about that book again," said Cameron through the screen patio door, interrupting their conversation on Corrie's deck. "I thought surely you'd be gabbing about the dance and dresses and bows and stuff like that."

"Bows? Have you ever seen me wear a bow?" Corrie was disgusted.

"Never noticed," Cameron said. "I thought you'd want to go because it might be 'romantic.'" Cameron mimicked his sister's voice.

"It's one thing to talk about romance in books and another to stare romance cold in the face in the middle-of-nowhere Kansas where no one will invite me and my stepfather would say 'no' anyway," Corrie said.

"You going, Ann?" asked Cameron.

"Nope. I'm like Jo March in that respect—I tend to scorn romance other than in books, and I want to achieve something truly splendid before I settle down. Even then, I don't intend to give up my dreams."

"Why won't you go? Don't you know how to dance?" Cameron taunted.

His challenge hit its mark, and Ann poked her pert nose in the air, eyes flashing. His teasing still annoyed her. So often the brunt of Sabrina's snide remarks, she never suffered teasing well.

"I'll have you know that I am an excellent dancer," Ann said. Sparks of anger flashed in her blue eyes.

"Oh, really?" Cameron said.

"Yes. In Denver, I had the choice of classes for my P.E. credits, and I took dance."

"Like ballet? That won't get you far at a Kansas high school dance."

"No, not ballet. I learned a variety of styles—Latin dances, waltz, the jitterbug, the Charleston, and," here Ann flashed a triumphant, smile, "country swing and two-step."

Cameron crossed his arms. "I don't believe you."

"Oh, don't you?" said Ann recklessly.

"Nope," Cameron leaned forward, only inches from Ann's face. "Prove it."

"Prove it?"

"Yeah. Let's put on some music."

Ann shook her head as if dealing with an impertinent child. "I can't dance without a partner," she said.

"You're in luck because I happen to be an 'excellent dancer' myself."

"What . . . You . . . I'm not dancing with you," she said.

"See, you don't know."

Ann pushed her chair back with a shrieking scrape across the defenseless planks of the deck.

"Fine. But then, you'll leave me alone. Deal?" She extended her hand.

"Just for the rest of the day." He said, shaking her hand.

"The rest of the week," Ann countered.

"Deal. Corrie, go grab my boombox. It has a mix tape in it," said Cameron.

Corrie scurried inside for the requested boombox and returned shortly. "I can't wait to see this," she said.

"Ready?" Cameron asked. He pushed the last of the chairs to the side of the deck for a makeshift dancefloor.

"I was born ready," said Ann.

"Just hit play," he told Corrie.

As Alabama spilled out on the evening air, Cameron reached for Ann's hand. Almost before she had her footing, she was spinning and twisting and pretzeling on her bosom friend's deck. When the song ended, Corrie hit pause, and Ann stepped calmly back to the table for a sip of her pop.

"Not bad. Now, show me you can two-step, and I'll eat my words," said Cameron.

"You really are aggravating. You know that, don't you?"

Corrie cued up the next song, and Cameron reached for Ann's hand as George Strait's "It Ain't Cool" began to play. Ann stared resolutely past his shoulder as they danced, finding herself too short to look over it, although she refused to make eye contact. When the song reached the chorus, Cameron sang along. Ann was surprised that someone so irritating could have such a good voice. She regretted her mental compliment when Cameron changed the lyrics, inserting her name into them. She glared at him, but Cameron only grinned.

"Just teasing, Ann. Surely you know that by now," he said.

Oh, she knew it, but she didn't like it. She returned her gaze to the fields beyond, willing the song to end. When it did, Cameron still held her hand.

"You win, Ann. You're right: you're a good dancer."

Corrie let the tape continue to play, and Anne Murray's "Could I Have this Dance" drifted out on the evening air.

"It's the last song on this side. We might as well finish it off," said Cameron.

Ann's mouth opened to decline, but Cameron challenged her again. "What's the matter? Afraid?"

"Fine," Ann said through clenched teeth.

Cameron held her hand close to his chest in a closed position and led Ann in a gentle sway to the music; none of the adolescent hands on shoulders for him. Ann hated to admit it, even to herself, but Cameron Addair was every bit the excellent dancer he claimed to be. But she would not acknowledge it to his face, oh, no. She continued to stare stonily past his arm to the sunset beyond. The last glowing embers of the day were slipping below the horizon, painting the western sky in a brilliant prairie collage. Ann tried to lose herself in the twilight's beauty and ignore the closeness of the insufferable Cameron Addair, but he was having none of it.

"The least you could do is look at me. Or are you afraid of that, too?" he said.

Ann turned a piercing gaze on her dance partner.

"I've never been afraid of anything in my life," she informed him, a proud tilt to her golden head. She waited for Cameron's response, but this time, he said nothing. He gazed into the blue depths of her eyes where they reflected the dusky light. Ann's gaze faltered under Cameron's frank look, and she stared back past his arm.

"Fine, then," said Cameron. He dropped Ann's hands and walked nonchalantly to the patio door. He turned with an incorrigible grin and added, "You win this bet. But don't expect me to dance with you at Homecoming if you won't even look at me."

Ann stood in the evening birdsong and sighing wind, feeling oddly exposed outside the embrace of the dance. She regained her wits just as Cameron opened the door and stepped inside.

"That won't be a problem, since I'm not going to that stupid dance," she shouted after him.

"Keep the tape," he said before shutting the door.

Ann dropped with a huff into the chair next to Corrie. "Between your brother's nonsense and being hounded by Larry Zima, I'm glad I can't go to Homecoming," she said.

"Are you sure your grandma wouldn't let you go? I mean, you haven't asked her. Maybe we could go together and watch everyone else, even if no one asked us to dance."

"And have Larry Zima corner me? Thanks, but no thanks. Besides, it's not worth the risk of asking her. We're getting along pretty well these days, and I don't want to mess it up. Honestly, I think I'd rather stay home. If I've said it once, I've said it a hundred times: 'there is no use trying to be romantic in' Storey, because romance certainly is not appreciated here."

21

A Talk with Aunt Janis

"I'm so proud of you, honey," said Aunt Janis around the bobby pins she held in her mouth.

"This is the first time I've ever been allowed to join anything," said Ann. She watched in the mirror as Aunt Janis twisted her hair into an elegant updo. Ann was being inducted into the National Honor Society that evening, and Aunt Janis insisted she come to her house so she could style her hair for the special event.

"Tell me all about what's going on in school," said Aunt Janis. She poked the bobby pins into Ann's thick mane of wavy hair and reached for more.

"Let's see. Well, Foreign Language Club made an altar for Day of the Dead. It was really cool—we had photos and candles and bread. Anyone who wanted could bring a photo of a loved one who's died, so I put Mom's picture on it. Fortunately, it didn't go up in flames."

"Flames? What on earth happened?"

"Larry Zima, that's what happened. He was looking over his shoulder at me as we left class—I was glaring at him, of course—and he walked into the altar. He knocked the candles over and some of the tissue paper flowers caught on fire. Thankfully, Mrs. White had a water bottle on her desk, and she doused it."

"That sounds scary."

"It was a mess. But that wasn't the only Larry Zima trauma that week. There was also the poem."

"What poem?" asked Aunt Janis.

"We're working on a chapbook of stories and poems in my creative writing class. Anyone in school can submit, and then we read them, but we don't know who submitted them. It's called a blind read. Some of the submissions were really good, and others were horrid. The worst one in the history of the world was 'Ode to Ann.' Only Larry Zima could be responsible for something that atrocious. Let me quote:

'She smiles like no one else can.
She's awful sweet, her name is Ann.'"

Aunt Janis shook her head. "I'm no poet, but I even think that sounds pretty awful."

"I will never forget my humiliation when I read that poem, even if I live to be a hundred."

"Did you have anything accepted for the book?"

"Yes—two stories and three poems," said Ann, unable to hide the pride in her voice.

"Congratulations! That's real exciting, honey."

"It is. I can't wait to see my name in print."

"Make sure you tell me when it comes out. I want to buy a copy."

"It will be out around Thanksgiving," said Ann.

"Are you excited for the holidays? I'll be glad to have the kids home for a few days. Thanksgiving with your grandmother is always a big affair. We have turkey and mashed potatoes and stuffing and cranberries and pumpkin pie with homemade whipped cream. And of course, your grandmother's famous crescent rolls. As your great-uncle Pete likes to tell her afterwards, 'Thelma, I'm full as a tick.'"

Ann laughed. "I've never had a real Thanksgiving dinner before. It should be fun—as long as Grandma doesn't expect me to make the pies. She's trying to teach me to cook, but, as Anne Shirley would say, 'I can assure you, it is uphill work.'"

"You're making progress, from what I hear. Mom says you're learning real fast."

"Really?"

"Yes, and Pete said those cookies you took him were 'right tasty.'" Aunt Janis imitated Great-Uncle Pete's tone and expression.

"I'm glad Great-Uncle Pete didn't hold a grudge after our first meeting. I guess that proves that 'after a good dinner, one can forgive anybody, even one's own relations.' Or, in this case, after a pan of blonde brownies."

"Is that your class ring?" asked Aunt Janis.

"Yes. It came in this week." Ann held her hand out and admired her ring.

"That's real pretty. You didn't get your birthstone, though."

"No, I didn't. I've always liked amethysts because they're my favorite color. Then I read *Green Gables,* and Anne Shirley says amethysts are the 'souls of good violets,' and that made me love them even more. I wasn't going to get a class ring—most kids get them when they're sophomores, and besides, I don't even know if I'll be here next year. But Grandpa told me I should get one, even if I don't do my senior year at SHS. He said it would be a souvenir of my time in Kansas. Grandpa still has his class ring from 1931, can you believe it? He said to get whatever I liked best, so I picked an amethyst."

"That was your mom's birthstone, you know," said Aunt Janis.

"I guess I hadn't thought of that." Ann gazed thoughtfully at her ring.

"There. All done." Aunt Janis applied a liberal amount of hair spray over Ann's hair and handed her a mirror.

"Oh, Aunt Janis!" said Ann as she studied the style from all angles.

"Is that what you had in mind?"

"Yes. It's perfect. It looks so elegant—just exactly how Anne Shirley would wear her hair."

"You'll be the prettiest girl there, and the smartest. My, you do have a lot of hair—just like your mother," Aunt Janis said.

"Did you do Mom's hair for special occasions, too?"

Aunt Janis smiled. "Of course. We played dress-up and styled each other's hair from the time we were little. She did my hair when I married Edward."

"Did you do hers when she married Dad?"

Aunt Janet flushed. She applied more spray to Ann's hair before answering. "No, she had a simple wedding and did her own."

"Really? I've never seen any pictures of their wedding. Grandma only has up her senior picture and some from when she was little. Sabrina told me Dad destroyed all Mom's pictures after she died because he couldn't bear to see her. Not that he was around much."

Aunt Janet paused. "Do you think that's true?"

"I don't know. Probably. I guess I never questioned it. He sure isn't very affectionate. Sabrina's always hinted he blames me for her death, and he probably does."

"That would be very small-minded of him if he did," said Aunt Janis.

Ann pursed her lips and raised her eyebrows. "Dad and Sabrina specialize in small-mindedness. Did you know he didn't even send a card on my birthday? He's sent one measly postcard since I came, and it was weeks late and didn't even mention my birthday."

"I'm sorry, honey. There's no excuse for that."

"I suppose I shouldn't talk about him that way. I mean, I think he tries."

Aunt Janis sat beside Ann and took her hand. She looked directly into her niece's eyes. "Never, never give anyone the benefit of the doubt if they hurt you."

Ann had never heard Aunt Janis sound so serious before. She nodded.

Aunt Janis hugged her tightly. "I'm just so glad you're here. It's like having a part of my sister back. I still miss her, you know."

"Why doesn't anyone talk about her? I mean, they say bits and pieces, and I always hear how much I look like her. But there's still so much I don't know."

Aunt Janis wiped her eyes. "Amelia's death was completely unexpected. She was so young, and she'd had a very normal pregnancy. No one expected her to have complications. It hit us all real hard, but especially Mom. She was devastated."

"Do you think Grandma blames me, too?"

"No, not even a little bit. Don't think that for an instant. I think she was surprised at how much you resemble your mom, but she's so happy you've come to Sunflower Lane."

"You're sure she's not just putting up with me?" asked Ann.

"Positive. Mom's not real demonstrative, but she cares about you. She's old-fashioned, but she has a heart of gold."

"Was she as strict with you as she is with me?"

"Strict? No. She has her expectations, but I wouldn't call her strict. Why do you think she is?"

"Did you have a 'no boys' rule?" asked Ann.

Aunt Janis laughed. "Goodness, no. I was a bit of a flirt in my time—you wouldn't know it to look at me now. Your uncle Edward and I were high school sweethearts."

"I know my parents met when Mom took her first job. Did she have any boyfriends here in Storey or in college?"

"She went out with some boys, but I don't think she ever went steady with anyone. Why do you ask?"

"Just curious. I thought maybe Grandma added the rule after you graduated and when Mom was still at home for some reason."

"No, your mom was never the social butterfly I was. She always had in her mind she was going to college. If there'd been a 'no boys' rule back in our day, it would've been directed at me. I'm not sure why Mom has that rule, but if you want me to, I could try to talk to her about it," said Aunt Janis.

"No, that's fine. We're getting along better now, and I don't want her to think I'm questioning her or complaining. Besides, it's not a big deal—the only guy trying to ask me out is Larry Zima, and gag me! But it freaks me out because I'm always afraid Grandma's going to see me talking to a boy or just standing next to one and get the wrong idea."

"You mean a boy like, say, Cameron Addair?"

Ann blushed. "Any boy."

"I think she trusts you, Ann. She just wants to keep you safe."

"But from what?"

Aunt Janis looked thoughtfully at Ann. "I think that's a question you'll have to ask her when you're ready and when you think she's ready to answer it. Now—let's get you in your dress. You don't want to be late for your ceremony."

Aunt Janis stepped to the sewing room to retrieve the new dress she'd made. Ann turned to admire her Gibson girl updo in the oval mirror. She propped her elbows on the vanity table and leaned her chin in her hands, studying the picture Aunt Janis kept there of her and Ann's mother when they were teens. She traced the outline of her mother's face, then searched the mirror for the resemblance in her own features.

"Not yet," she said to her reflection. "I'm just not ready to start asking those questions yet."

22

The Christmas Gift

"**G**randma, look! It's snowing," said Ann, nose pressed to the kitchen window. "I hope it lasts till the live Nativity this weekend. It would look just like we're in a Christmas card."

"You mean it would feel like it. When you get to be my age, the appeal of standing outside in the snow with arthritic joints seems like anything but a Christmas card," said Grandma.

"We can bundle up, and we'll have the cocoa and cookies to look forward to afterwards," said the optimistic Ann. She munched another of the delicate almond-flavored spritz cookies that were her undisputed favorite from among all the delicacies Grandma's Christmas baking had produced. Although Grandma grumbled about the time and mess it took to wrangle her well-used cookie press into making them, it did not go unnoticed by Ann that she had made a second batch once all the plates of sugar cookies, gingerbread men, peppernuts, and peanut brittle had been delivered to friends and neighbors.

"I'd have thought you'd seen enough snow in Denver to last a lifetime," Grandma said.

"It's not the same in a big city. It's all dirty and inconvenient, and I hated being trapped inside with Sabrina. But here, the snow is 'the poem of the air.' I couldn't believe how different it looked and felt the first time it snowed. I took a walk in the Enchanted Forest, and it was a winter wonderland. The snow was all drifted up in swirls around the trees, and I saw some deer near Mending Wall. It looked exactly like a print from Currier and Ives."

"You'll think it's a print if you ever hit a deer when you're driving," Grandma said.

"I hope I never do. I've never gotten over 'Traveling through the Dark.' It's a Stafford poem Ms. Miller had us read last year. I understood the symbolism of the dark, narrow road we travel, and the themes of acting responsibly for the greater good and making difficult decisions when no one is watching, but I wish he could have communicated that without killing an animal. It's the Matthew Cuthbert conundrum all over again. Anne Shirley said it's 'more romantic to end a story with a funeral than a wedding,' but I don't like to have anyone die in my literature. That's why when I write, my stories usually have an open ending."

"That's all real interesting, but don't you think you'd better finish up your homework so you'll be ready for supper?"

"You're right. I'm so sick of end-of-term exams. I already had two today, but there are more tests tomorrow."

Grandma gave an uncharacteristic sigh. "Oh, Ann. There are always more tests tomorrow."

"I guess if I have to study, I'll go snuggle up by the wood stove. I never dreamed it could be so warm and comforting. Besides, it's way more Green Gables than central heat and air."

Ann carried her books to the living room and curled up in a blanket next to the woodburning stove to study for her last exams before Christmas break. The past weeks had been busy ones for her. She had been involved in every tree-decorating, carol-singing, cookie-eating, gift-exchanging party that had presented itself to make up for all the years she had been told to go straight home to a dreary rental after school. Still, nothing could compare to her excitement at being part of the community live Nativity on Christmas Eve. Ann was to have her acting debut at last.

"It's real exciting you're going to be the Angel of the Lord," Grandpa said on the morning of the much-anticipated event.

"It's all thanks to Mabel. When she announced the auditions at Sunday School, I figured I'd be content with just being an ordinary angel. But she encouraged me to try for a speaking role. Mabel really is a kindred spirit. Of course, Acacia Thorne is Mary, but that's probably because she doesn't have to say anything. Can you imagine if the Angel of the Lord 'like' delivered the Good News? Cameron is Joseph, and I honestly feel sorry for him being cast opposite Acacia. Of course, that's not a very angelic thing to say. Maybe playing an angel is a bit of a stretch for me."

"I think you'll be able to pull it off. Just don't go looking for trouble on Christmas Eve," Grandma said.

"Don't worry. There's no poison ivy to be found, and there won't be any biscuits to burn up, so I'll be safe" Ann said.

"I only hope you don't catch your death standing out there without something on your head," Grandma said.

"Angels only wear halos, Grandma, not stocking hats. But I'll be up in the hayloft with the other girls, and I promise to bundle up with lots of layers underneath my robe and wings."

Ann's wish for a snowy stage was granted, as more snow fell throughout the day. Grandma fussed about her not wearing a hat, and Grandpa warned her not to lock her knees. But Ann's excitement at her first theatrical performance could not be mitigated in the slightest even by the potentialities of frostbite or fainting. She chattered excitedly with her friends in the corner of the machine shed that had been converted into a makeshift dressing room Acacia insisted on calling "the green room."

"Only thing green about this room is the John Deere tractor parked over there," grumbled Cameron.

Ann, much to her dismay, found herself laughing. She hid her amusement by turning to listen to Mrs. Jenkins, the harried woman who was making her own debut as pageant director for the church.

The outdoor living Nativity was her brainchild. Loretta Smith had written the script for the previous year's Christmas pageant herself, complete with a lighted star that guided the wise men from the back of the church to the front, and a camel on wheels. Ann had overheard Mrs. Jenkins tell Mabel that her blood still ran cold at the thought of living up to the expectations set by that camel. A live Nativity—complete with a rented camel from Wichita—was the answer, she'd said.

"All right, actors! Time to take your places. Let's make this pageant unforgettable. Ann, your halo's crooked." Mrs. Jenkins straightened the wire and tinsel headpiece.

"If you only knew," said Cameron.

"Would you like another black eye?" Ann asked sweetly.

"Stay on task," said Mrs. Jenkins, hands on her hips. "We cannot have the Angel of the Lord punching Joseph. Not on my watch. Let's get moving, people."

The Nativity stable was set up in front of the Jenkins' limestone barn to accommodate the spectators who came from the surrounding communities. As Ann stood in the hayloft awaiting her cue, she peeked out a crack at the silent night beyond. The sky had cleared following the day's snow, and the stars shone crisply against the depths of its blackness, like so many pinpricks in velvet. Below, an eager audience had gathered.

"Look at everyone," Ann said to herself, amazed at the crowd. "I see the Misses Page, and there's Arthur, too. Oh, and Aunt Janis and Uncle Edward—they brought Great-Uncle Pete, and doesn't he look dapper in his new coat. And there are Grandma and Grandpa, front and center. I think the entire Storey community turned out for this."

With a sudden rush, Ann realized she was part of that community now. A warmth of belonging rushed over her, defying even the glacial air in the barn.

"Ann Alwyn, you're almost up. Get in position," said Mrs. Jenkins. "And straighten your wings. Now they're crooked."

Ann adjusted her wings and took her place as the spotlight illuminated her, the Angel of the Lord come to bring the Good News from the hayloft of an old barn in Kansas. Her voice rang true and clear as she delivered her few lines. Corrie, Molly, Ginny, and Laura joined her for "Angels We Have Heard on High."

Ann and the heavenly host exited the hayloft door left and sat huddled together on the bales. Ann hated to admit it, but even with her layers, the unheated barn was chilly. She closed her eyes and imagined the steaming cup of cocoa that awaited her, and even sweeter this time, cocoa shared with family and friends.

"Come on—time for the big finish," Corrie said.

The angels stepped again to the open loft as the entire cast joined below to lead all present in singing "Joy to the World." Ann could hear Grandpa's strong tenor voice in the audience, and her eyes found him singing beside Grandma near the front of the crowd. She joined the chorus feeling for the first time a connection to a place she'd called home. A warmth settled over her, despite the frigid conditions.

She was still savoring the event afterwards when she gathered with her friends in a corner of the crowded machine shed, eating cookies and sipping hot chocolate.

"Did your Dad send you anything for Christmas, or did he mess up again like he did on your birthday?" asked Corrie after the others had left. She and Ann were seated by the decorated tree, soaking in the warmth of the nearby heater.

"What do you think?"

"I'm thinking that's a 'no.'"

"Bingo."

"What a jerk," said Corrie.

Ann shrugged. "You're not wrong. But there's not much I can do about it, is there?"

"Yes, there is. Eat more fudge!" said Corrie.

"Mabel does say it will cure about anything," said Ann.

"I'll go get some. Be right back."

Ann sipped her hot chocolate as she watched the soft, white lights on the Christmas tree reflecting their gentle glow in the gleaming balls. She saw Cameron approaching but pretended not to notice.

"Mind if I sit here?" he asked.

"Your sister will be back in a minute," Ann said.

"That's fine. I don't want to talk to her. I want to talk to you."

Ann fidgeted.

"Merry Christmas," Cameron said. He handed her a small, brightly wrapped package.

"Will this explode or something when I open it?" she asked, trying to keep her tone light.

"Just open it."

Ann slid her finger under the tape and peeled the paper back. Inside was an ornate wooden butterfly.

"Wow," she said.

"I made it."

"You did?"

Cameron grinned. "Don't sound so surprised."

Ann blushed. "Sorry. I didn't mean it that way."

"It's OK. John's been teaching me to use his scroll saw. It's just a beginner's pattern, but it made me think of you."

Ann admired the tiny cuts in the dark wood, the smoothness of the surface. "It's truly beautiful, but I can't accept it."

"Why not?" Cameron said.

Ann closed her eyes and exhaled. She'd have to tell him because this had to end. "Because I'll get in trouble with Grandma."

"For a gift?"

"It's not the gift."

"I thought she liked me."

"It's not even you. She has a 'no boys' rule, and she means it."

"It's just a Christmas gift. That's all. No strings. Unless you want strings?"

"Please don't make this so hard. Things are going well for me at Sunflower Lane, and I don't want to mess it up. Besides, that rule is embarrassing enough as it is."

"So how'd you get around my birthday gift?" asked Cameron.

"She never asked, thankfully. When I told Corrie I couldn't keep it, she took it back, and then she gave it to me."

Corrie returned carrying a plate laden with fudge. "Oh, Cam give you that?" she asked, spotting the butterfly.

"Nope, you did. Just like that nice Teddy bear you gave her for her birthday. Isn't that right?" said Cameron.

"Sure, yeah, that's right," Corrie said. She took the gift from Ann's hands and immediately passed it back. "Here you go. Merry Christmas. My stupid brother made it so I could give it you."

"Keep it—please." He stood and went to join a group of friends.

"Man, my brother has it bad for you. But it sounds like you told him about your grandma's rule."

"Yeah. I didn't have much choice."

"I think he'll understand. He can be stupid, but he's not an ogre," said Corrie around a mouthful of fudge. "It's just good you kept that butterfly. You have no idea how many times he tried to make one until he got it right. John's workshop is littered with little pieces of his failed attempts."

"That's not making this any easier," Ann said.

"Sounds to me like you like him."

"I *can't* like him, or anyone for that matter. It's a moot point."

"Here: have a piece of fudge. Mabel might be onto something by saying it'll make anything better."

Ann bit into the chocolatey goodness of the fudge.

"Right?" asked Corrie.

Ann gave a slight smile. She watched as Cameron crossed the room to talk to a group that included Acacia Thorne. Ann closed her eyes, swallowed, and turned away.

23

In Which Something Thrilling Happens

"Winter days just zap the life out of me. I wish something thrilling would happen to break the monotony," Ann said one bitter afternoon in late January. She sat studying at the kitchen table with her chin in her hand while Grandma finished making supper. She had tried to call her father that afternoon again, only to have Sabrina answer and inform her to stop leaving messages, he'd call when he was good and ready. Her mood matched the weather outside.

"I don't suppose your sleepiness has anything to do with you staying up to read in bed," Grandma said.

"The books you gave me for Christmas are an irresistible temptation. You and Grandpa couldn't have thought of a more perfect gift, and I'm devouring them."

"There's a time and place for everything, and bedtime on a school night is not the time to stay up late reading," Grandma said.

"But I didn't stay up reading. I couldn't sleep because I was trying to figure out a different ending for *A Tale of Two Cities* so I could save Sydney Carton. I thought out so many options, but none of them was as satisfying. There really can't be another ending. Dying for love is the only one romantic enough. I still detest the thought of killing off a character, but I suppose sometimes you just have to send them to the guillotine."

"The guillotine? Are you sure you should be reading such things?" Grandma asked.

"Of course. Trust me, I read about worse stuff happening in the cities where I lived over the years. One thing you could always count on was a newspaper in the library."

"You probably shouldn't have been reading that either."

"And Dad and Sabrina probably shouldn't have used the library as a babysitter, but here we are," Ann said in a matter-of-fact tone.

"No, they most certainly should not," Grandma said. She continued stirring the chicken noodle soup simmering on the stove.

"Besides, the knowledge that there is a fugitive mouse at large somewhere in this house is not conducive to a good night's sleep. I've been hiding under my blankets ever since we heard it scurrying around in the cold room."

"It's real common for a mouse to find a way inside when it gets this cold," Grandma said.

"Common or not, I am not inclined to feel empathetic where rodents are concerned. And I do not feel one iota of guilt about you setting a trap for it, although maybe we should have used pudding sauce for bait."

"Pudding sauce?"

A gust of winter wind blew in the back door with Grandpa, ending all thoughts of mice and guillotines.

"Got the sidewalk cleared off," he announced.

"I wish you wouldn't overdo it with the shoveling. I've told you I'd be happy to do it," said Ann.

"Nonsense. I'm fit as a fiddle. You just worry about your studies."

"Did you ever take chemistry, Grandpa?" asked Ann.

"Can't say as I did," Grandpa said. He peered over Ann's shoulder at the strange equations in her book.

"Count yourself lucky. You were spared the torment of a subject that 'harrows up my very soul.' Chemistry is to me what geometry was to Anne Shirley."

"Torment and harrowing aside, you need to finish up your homework so you're ready for the basketball game," Grandma said.

"I still don't know why I let Corrie talk me into going. I should be reading over my paper for AP History one last time. But she wanted to go to get out of the house because she and John had an argument. So I'm only going for Corrie's sake," Ann said.

"A change will do you good, too," said Grandma.

"I suppose. You're sure you're OK with Cameron driving us? I don't want to get in trouble."

"That's fine. You're going with Corrie, not him," Grandma said.

"Exactly," Ann said. She closed her chemistry book with a relieved sigh. "Whew! I'm glad I'm done with this wretched chemistry. I guess I can read over my paper again now."

She reached for her backpack and pulled out her history binder. She riffled through it, then pulled out one folder after another.

"Oh, no! I must've forgotten my paper in my locker."

"I thought you already finished it," Grandpa said.

"Yes, but I always read over my papers one last time the night before they're due. I don't think I should mess with a formula that has worked so well this far," Ann said.

"I'm sure it's fine," Grandma said.

But Ann was not convinced.

"I'm sure it's fine," Corrie said as they sat at the basketball game.

"Are you and Grandma consulting on this? That's exactly what she told me," said Ann.

"No, but we both know what we're talking about."

"The image of my paper tucked away in my locker is positively plaguing me. I can just see it up there mocking me," Ann said at halftime.

"So go get it," said Acacia Thorne. She had overheard their conversation despite her obnoxious cheering for her boyfriend, Jeff Sands.

"She can't. The school is locked after hours," said Corrie.

"No, it's not. The back door's open so the pep band can get into the band room, and from there, you go up the back stairs because that door doesn't lock. Like, everyone knows that," Acacia said.

"But it's off limits," said Ann.

"I suppose you're too much of a goody-two-shoes to run up and get your stupid paper."

"I am not," said Ann, cheeks flushed.

"What, not enough lights for you? Is our little Miss City Slicker afraid of the dark?" Acacia's face wore a taunting sneer.

"Of course not."

"Then I dare you to go get your paper," Acacia said.

"All right. I'll go after the game," Ann said

"No, now. When no one else is there."

"Fine."

"Ann, it's Diana Barry's ridgepole all over again. Something is bound to go wrong," said Corrie.

But Ann was already donning her coat.

"Then we're going with you," Ginny said.

"No, you go by yourself. We'll wait outside to totally make sure you get your stupid paper," Acacia said.

"Oh, I don't think this is a good idea," said Molly.

"Ignore her, Ann," Cameron said.

But Ann was already off. She led the way out of the gym and across the snowy parking lot to the main school building, her temper still aflame. She would make Acacia Thorne swallow her words, or "perish in the attempt."

"Ann, slow down! It's slick out here," called Corrie.

But Ann marched resolutely onward to the high school's back door. She yanked it open and strode down the stairs to the brightly lit band room without a second thought. No one was there to see Ann as she continued across the room and out the other door. When it clicked shut behind her, the darkness of the back stairwell settled around her. She didn't dare turn on a light and draw attention.

"I would never admit it to Acacia Thorne, but I *am* afraid—of getting in trouble, not of the dark. Grandma will ground me for life if I get caught."

Only her voice kept her company as she climbed the first flight of stairs. She steadied herself with a hand on the wall, using the light of the exit signs to guide her. She stopped on the first floor and listened. The 1920s-era brick building creaked an occasional arthritic joint, but she heard nothing else, and continued to the second floor. Ann paused outside her locker, but only inky silence met her ears as she began the challenge of opening her combination lock by the feeble light of the signs. After two failed attempts, a wan beam of moonlight broke through the clouds and fell through the window in the stairwell. She opened her locker, rummaged through it for her paper, and shut the door quietly.

Ann turned to begin the odyssey back to her waiting friends when a wobbling flashlight beam and voices drifted up the stairwell at the opposite end of the hall.

Ann pressed herself into the miniscule space between her locker and the doorframe.

"Oh, no," she whispered. "I *am* going to get into trouble, and all because of a stupid dare."

"Dude, relax. I just gotta get my 'study guide.'"

Ann heard the quotation marks around the words spoken in the unmistakable voice of Damian Vance. Considering Damian had already been suspended once for having beer in his locker, Ann was positive he was not retrieving a conventional study guide. What if someone caught them all there together? She would be labeled as a co-conspirator in any and all of Damian Vance's misdeeds. Fear at that image propelled Ann forward, and she scurried to the stairs before Damian and whoever was with him reached the second floor. Once on the first floor, Ann took to her heels and ran like one inspired.

"Got it," Ann cried as she burst out the back door, waving her paper triumphantly.

Ann's warm shoes met the cold snowpack of the sidewalk. She wobbled in a crazy dance for a breath before crashing to the ground.

"Ann!" shrieked Molly.

"Are you OK?" asked Corrie, kneeling beside her.

"Well, I'm neither killed nor rendered unconscious. But I think I sprained my ankle." She winced.

"Here, let me help you up," Cameron said. He reached a strong arm around Ann's shoulders.

Ann thought she ought to decline, but after her fright at nearly being caught breaking a rule and her nasty fall, she discovered she didn't have the energy to argue.

"This is all your fault," Laura told Acacia.

Acacia, like Josie Pye before her, had enough imagination to envision herself implicated in Ann's injury and rule-breaking, and her defense was to be that much nastier.

"I don't see what Ann has to complain about. She got her stupid paper, and she gets to have your brother throw himself all over her."

"Shut up," Ginny said.

"Whatever. I'm going back to the game. I have to support my boyfriend. But little Miss Bookworm wouldn't know anything about that."

A hot answer rose to Ann's lips, but she clamped them shut. She'd had enough trouble for one evening, and she would still have to tell Grandma what had happened. She swallowed her words and her pride as she limped on Cameron's arm to his truck.

"Acacia Thorne dared me to go get my paper, and I needed it. What could I do?" Ann asked Grandma the next afternoon from the couch where she lay with an icepack on her swollen ankle. She had missed school for the first time that year because of the previous evening's caper.

"You could have given her a soft answer to turn away her wrath," was Grandma's unsympathetic reply. "I'm very disappointed with your behavior. Sneaking around like that in the school after dark when it's off limits!"

"But Grandma, I wasn't sneaking. It was unlocked."

"It's still deceitful. If you'll do that . . ." Grandma let the sentence hang.

"But I wasn't deceitful. I told you exactly what happened, and I could have lied and told you I slipped on the sidewalk. Don't I get a little credit for being honest?"

"You're going to be the death of me. I worry about you constantly, and then you take it into your head to go sneaking around and looking for trouble."

"Yes, well, you're right. Is that what you wanted to hear? I sprained my ankle, and it's incredibly painful. I didn't sleep a wink last night. Trust me, I have learned my lesson, and this is one mistake I will not repeat," Ann assured her.

"Good," Grandma said, retreating to the kitchen.

Ann burrowed under the quilt with a heavy heart, watching the snow fall through the picture window beside her. "I've lost any ground I ever gained with getting Grandma to trust me," she said.

She closed her eyes against the tears. The warmth of the woodstove embraced her, and it fought back the mournful bitterness of the winter wind howling outside. Grandma was baking bread, and its aroma wrapped Ann in the comfort of its scent. She hadn't slept well the night before, and she was so drowsy. Oh, how her ankle throbbed, and her forehead itched, too. She reached up a heavy hand to scratch it and felt something warm under her fingers. Her eyes popped open, and she jerked upright

"The mouse!" shrieked Ann, flinging the rodent from her bangs.

Grandpa had come in the front door just in time to see a mouse fly across the living room, bounce off the wall, and dash helter-skelter down the short hall and out the door he still held open.

"What's all the commotion?" Grandma said, hurrying from the kitchen.

"Mouse is gone," Grandpa said calmly.

"It was in my bangs," Ann said. She gave her hair a thorough rubbing. "I'll never forget the feeling of its cold little tail between my fingers. It will be my lifelong nightmare. I'll probably die from some mouse-borne illness."

Grandma actually giggled. "I thought your hair looked a little ratty."

"Very funny," Ann said. She tried to sound miffed, but she was relieved that Grandma was already less angry with her. "You know, you shouldn't laugh at me, Grandma. You should count yourself lucky the Page sisters weren't here when this happened, because that's exactly how it would have gone in a book. And they'd have told everyone in town, the county, and the entire state we had a mouse."

"You said you wanted something 'thrilling' to happen. If a sprained ankle and a mouse in your hair isn't thrilling, I don't know what is," said Grandma. She returned to the kitchen and her baking, and Grandpa chuckled as he followed her.

Ann leaned her forehead against the window. Fully awake now, she watched the snow swirl as it picked up in intensity. She sighed across her reflection in the pane, then wrote her initials on the fog left by her breath.

"I wonder how long it will take me to get Grandma to trust me again?" she asked.

But the silently falling snowflakes had no answer.

24

Cupid Unswerving

"**I** am positively dreading this day," Ann said to Corrie as they walked into school on Valentine's Day.

"Larry Zima?"

"Yes. I've had Larry-inspired nightmares for the past two nights. In one, he showed up at my locker dressed in a tux and dropped to one knee to ask me out. In another, he came as his own singing telegram dressed as Cupid. That one still makes me shudder."

"Gross. That one makes *me* shudder," said Corrie.

"The only good news is Grandma knows I have no interest in him, so I won't get in trouble if he does try to give me a card. Or show up as Cupid. I'll only 'sink through the floor with mortification.'"

"Good luck," said Corrie as she turned into the first-floor hall of lockers.

Ann climbed the last flight of stairs to her locker in silent dread of what she might find. At the top of the stairs, she peeked around the corner to get a lay of the hallway land. The coast was clear, but something was hanging over the combination lock on her locker.

"What's this?" she said.

"Looks like a gift bag," said Cameron from across the hall. He sauntered over.

"You amaze me with your keen powers of observation," Ann said. She slipped the pink and red gift bag off the lock and peeked cautiously inside.

"What is it?" said Cameron.

"Aren't you nosey? It's chocolates. Oh, no. Surely Larry didn't buy me candy."

"I doubt it was Larry. He wouldn't leave a gift hanging off your locker. He'd want to see the look on your face when he gave it to you."

"For once, you might be right. One of the girls probably left them for me as a surprise. I'll figure it out," Ann said.

Ann asked Molly and Laura about the provenance of the gift bag, but they were as surprised as she. She was still no closer to discovering the identity of her mysterious Valentine after her first class.

"Hey there, Nancy Drew. Any luck figuring out who left you that candy?" asked Cameron when she approached her locker between classes.

"Not yet," said Ann.

He leaned against the locker next to hers. "What if I told you I knew who it was?"

Ann kept her gaze focused on finding her book and binder for her next class.

"Don't you want to know?"

She looked up at him pointedly. "Only if it's not going to get me in trouble with my grandmother. She's still hot with me for coming in here for my history paper."

Cameron grinned. "I put the bag on your locker."

"What did I just tell you?" She reached into her locker, grabbed the chocolates, and shoved them into his chest. "I can't keep these."

She slammed the door and took a step to get around him and make her escape, but he stuck his arm out in front of her and stopped her.

"Chill. They're from Corrie. She wanted to surprise you, so she asked me to hang the bag on your door before you got here." He handed the bag back to Ann.

"Oh." She took the bag and stood in awkward silence. Then, the bell rang, and she slid around him and to her next class.

Corrie stopped by Ann's locker before third period.

"Thanks for the chocolates," Ann said.

"Huh?" said Corrie.

"You don't have to play dumb. Cameron spilled your secret. He said you asked him to leave the bag on my locker as a surprise."

"Oh. Yeah, that was me. Stupid brother." Corrie raised her voice as she left for class. She smacked him for good measure as she walked by his locker.

"That's me," he said. He shut his locker and crossed the hall. "Told you. But I'll bet you thought they were from some dashing secret admirer.'"

"Ha, ha. Very funny. But you know, I'm having a terrific day celebrating with my friends. So terrific, in fact, that even you cannot ruin it."

Cameron glanced over Ann's shoulder. "Maybe not, but I bet he can."

Ann spun around, her heart sinking to her very toes. Larry Zima was fast approaching. She grabbed frantically for her books for her next class but only succeeded in dropping them all over the hallway floor. Papers spilled out of her binder, and Ann reached desperately for them in big handfuls. She kicked her locker door closed and turned to make her escape, but Larry had beaten her and planted himself in her path.

"Happy Valentine's Day, Ann," he said, shoving a bouquet of something large, red, and definitely artificial toward Ann's face.

Instinctively, Ann took a step back.

"Roses. They're fake so they'll last forever. Here." Larry took a step toward Ann and waved the flowers under her nose. They were so tacky they even had glue drops on the petals to simulate dew.

"No, thank you," Ann said, finding her voice and taking another step back. She bumped into Cameron. She could tell he had a smirk on his face without even looking.

"They're for you. Today's Valentine's Day," said Larry.

Ann stood straighter, attempting to look as dignified as possible with papers, books, and binders sticking every which way in her hands and Larry Zima parked in front of her with those ridiculous flowers.

"I am well aware of that, but I cannot and will not accept flowers from you."

Ann turned on her heel, dodged around Cameron, and strode down the hall with a befuddled Larry Zima watching her escape, artificial roses in hand.

"I'll just leave 'em here," he bellowed after her.

"And there they were, sticking out of the slats in my locker when I snuck back after class," Ann told Grandma that afternoon. "Why does he torment me?"

"I'm afraid you might have to tell him you're not interested," Grandma said.

"Please don't think I'm trying to encourage him, because I can assure you, I'm not. He's only hinted around that he likes me, but this! I swear the image of Larry Zima standing in the middle of the hall with those fake flowers makes my blood run cold every time I think of it. I'm sure I'll remember it until the day I die. I was so angry! I ripped those stupid flowers out of my locker door and left them on top of the trash can at Larry's end of the hall. If that doesn't get the message across, nothing will. I mean, I don't want to hurt his feelings. I know what it feels like not to be wanted. But this is getting ridiculous. Surely he'll get the picture."

"You'd be surprised," said Grandma.

"Did you ever have some lovestruck swain losing his head over you, Grandma?" Ann asked.

"One or two," said Grandma with a soft smile.

"Why, Grandma! You heart-breaker."

"Oh, go on," Grandma said, laughing.

Ann grinned. It was moments like this she enjoyed spending time with her grandmother. "Chocolate? Corrie gave them to me."

"That was real nice of her." Grandma selected a plump bonbon.

Ann heard the thumps of Grandpa knocking the snow off his boots on the back step. Then, the door opened, letting in a gust of wintry wind. Grandpa peeked around it.

"How are my two Valentines?" he asked.

"Fine," said Ann. "Come have one of the chocolates Corrie gave me."

Grandpa stepped through and bowed. He handed a red rose to Grandma and a white one to Ann.

"Happy Valentine's Day," he said. He gave each of them a kiss on the cheek.

Ann breathed deeply of the rich perfume of the delicate petals. "Thank you. I've never had flowers before," she said.

"Sorry your first one had to be from your old grandpa," he said.

Ann stood and wrapped her arms around him in a tight embrace.

"Don't apologize. I honestly wouldn't want it any other way."

25

Controlled Burn

"March has felt like one long slog," Ann told Grandpa as they bounced through the pasture in Bessie. It was spring break, and while Corrie spent that week of freedom with her father in Kansas City, Ann had stayed at home nursing a spring cold and reading. An ever-present mug of tea with honey and a box of tissues had accompanied her for the first half of the week. Yesterday, she had ventured out to sit on the swing and absorb the spring sun while Grandma readied her garden to plant potatoes. Now, on Friday, she was feeling well enough to accompany Grandpa as his renter, Arthur, burned pasture.

"I'm sure glad you're on the mend. You got run-down with all your studying," Grandpa said.

"I hope it pays off. Midterms were hard, and I want to get good grades and do well on my AP History exam in May. But today, I'm not going to think about books or studies or even the fact that I haven't heard from Dad in weeks. I'm here to see honest-to-goodness cowboys burn pasture. I'm sure it will inspire me to write something."

"It is kind of beautiful, but it can get pretty exciting sometimes," Grandpa said.

"Have you always burned pasture?"

"It's been a practice since long before I was born. Why, even the Native Americans burned the grass here to make better grazing for the bison."

　　　　　Julie A. Sellers

Ann's imagination conjured up herds of the solid, brown animals that populated the plains before they were obliterated.

"Pasture burning is as much a part of this land as the limestone under these fields," Grandpa said in one of his more poetic moments, which was not lost on Ann. "It gets rid of all the invasive species."

Ann and Grandpa were part of a small crew helping Arthur do a controlled burn in the pasture at the top of the hill. The wind had been too strong earlier in the week, but that day, Arthur had called to say he was ready to begin. Grandma had fussed at both of them for being part of the activities, claiming Ann's inexperience and Grandpa's heart as good reasons to stay home. Only Grandpa's assurances that they would be driving the truck with the water tank and staying out of the way mollified her. So when Grandpa got out of the pickup to help the others get started, Ann raised a brow.

"I thought you told Grandma you wouldn't be anywhere near the flames," she said.

"I'm just checking in with them. I'll come right back so I'm ready to report for duty if they need water," he said.

Ann watched him walk across to the group of men, among them John Alexander and Cameron. He caught her watching and raised a hand in a subtle wave. Ann turned her head and pretended not to see him.

True to his word, Grandpa returned to the truck after a few minutes, and he narrated the scene they watched through the windshield.

"That's a firestick," he said.

"It looks like a pipe bomb," Ann said. She watched Arthur attach a length of pipe to his four-wheeler. She had seen him fill it with gasoline and cap it, so she could imagine its possibilities for danger.

"There's a hole in that plug that lets the gas drip out as he drags it along. It sets the line to be burned. They'll burn a fireguard first, and then the real show will start."

"What will we do?"

"Be ready to roll if something gets out of hand. They have the small tank on the other four-wheeler Cameron's driving, but if a fire jumps a line and gets rolling, they'll need more water than that. If that happens, you stay in this truck, no matter what, OK?"

Ann nodded. She had no desire to be in the middle of a prairie fire. There were limits to feeling a part of Sunflower Lane or getting material for stories, and being burned to a crisp was where she drew the line.

Ann and Grandpa watched the flames begin to crackle across the pasture, growing in height as they devoured the dry grass. A headwind was coming up, and the fire marched in a feverish line across the plains. Cameron monitored any stray sparks as the fire passed, leaving a black, pungent path in its wake. Ann sat breathless, watching the age-old pageant of the prairie.

"It's good we're about done with this smaller pasture," Grandpa said after some time. "That wind is picking up again. I'll go see if Arthur plans to do any more, or call it quits for today. You sit tight."

Ann continued to watch as the last flames danced, the scent of fire strong in her nose. She sat with her elbow on the window, trying to select the perfect words to describe the stunning display of nature she had witnessed. She was checking off a list of adjectives in her mind when a shout shattered her thoughts. Ann turned to find that the rising wind had whipped up the last of the flames, and a fire now raged across the sidelines and into the ditch along the road. She saw Cameron race toward them on his four-wheel, and Grandpa began to run toward the truck.

"No, your heart," Ann said.

She slid across to the driver's side, cranked the ignition, and threw the pickup into drive. She coaxed Bessie across the pasture faster than she'd ever driven her there. Grandpa stopped and bent over to catch his breath, waving Ann on to where Cameron and the others had begun to beat at the errant flames with gunnysacks. John clambered into the bed of the truck almost before Ann brought it to a halt. She leaped out, and Arthur took the wheel. Ann glanced at the billowing smoke and flames for only a moment before running to where Grandpa was slowly walking back toward the group.

"Grandpa! Is it your heart? Are you all right? Do you need a doctor?" She shouted as she ran, and tears streaked her face.

"I'm fine," Grandpa said when Ann reached him. She threw herself into his arms, coughing herself.

"Oh, I was sure it was Matthew Cuthbert all over again. He had heart trouble, too, you know, and it was a terrible fright that killed him. I know I always say I wish things would happen 'just as if I was a heroine in a book,' but I don't want you to have a heart attack." The words spilled out of Ann in a rush. Her legs gave out, and she dropped to the grass, coughing.

"Calm down, Ann. It's not my heart, it's my age. I forget I can't run as fast as I used to."

"Are you sure?" Ann asked, her tears turning into hiccups. She continued to cough.

"Positive. You're not rid of your old grandpa yet. But you look like you saw a ghost, and it sounds like you got a lungful of smoke."

"It's just this stupid cold," Ann said.

"I'll take you home."

"I'm fine. They need the tank. I can wait."

Grandpa turned and glanced back to watch as the others began to gain control over the fire.

"I think your friend might have gotten hurt," he said.

Ann scrambled to her feet and looked across the pasture. John was studying Cameron's arm.

"Oh, no." She took a step toward them, but Grandpa stopped her.

"You don't need to breathe any more of that smoke. I'll check on him."

Ann dropped back to the ground, still coughing. She watched Grandpa as he talked with John and Cameron. He looked at Cam's arm, then motioned to Ann. Cameron shook his head, but Grandpa slapped his back and pointed her way again. Cameron nodded and strode across the pasture to where Ann waited. She could see his blackened shirt sleeve from a distance.

"Are you OK?" she asked, jumping to her feet. She still coughed.

"Yeah, it got me, but not bad," he said.

"It looks pretty bad to me," said Ann.

"Your grandpa told me to take you down to the house. He doesn't want you breathing any more of this smoke, and he wants your grandma to tend this burn."

Ann hesitated.

"Come on, Ann—those are your grandpa's orders. I think the sight of this will convince your grandmother I'm not up to anything." He raised his arm.

"Maybe I should drive," Ann said as they walked to John's truck.

"You know how to drive stick?"

"*Touché.* You drive."

Cameron flinched as he put the truck in drive and maneuvered it onto the county road. The spring breeze, laced with the smell of burned grass, filtered in the window. An old country song played on the radio as they drove in silence down the hill to Sunflower Lane. Ann thought the lack of conversation should be unnerving, but she was surprised to find it wasn't.

Grandma saw them from where she was weeding her flower garden out front. She rose stiffly and watched as Ann climbed out of the truck coughing and Cameron held his arm.

"What on earth has happened?" asked Grandma. She went first to Ann and placed a hand on her back, patting it lightly.

"I just got a lungful of smoke. Please go look at Cameron's arm. He got burned."

Grandma took one look at the blackened sleeve and shooed them into the house. "Both of you, sit," she said.

Cameron caught Ann's eye and smiled, but they sat dutifully, one at each end of the kitchen table. Grandma placed a pitcher of water on the table.

"You, drink," she said to Ann. "And you, let me see that burn."

She gingerly lifted Cameron's arm and surveyed the damage.

"It's not the worst I've seen," she said.

"But it would've been better if I hadn't tried to barbecue myself, right?" he said.

Grandma smiled. "I doubt you tried. Prairie fires are real dangerous, whether they're a controlled burn or not. You'll need to get that shirt off and rinse your arm with cold water."

"Yes, ma'am." Cameron said. He followed Grandma to the bathroom.

"Here's a clean towel and one of Bernard's old shirts," Ann heard Grandma say.

Grandma returned to the kitchen and put her hands on her hips. "Your Grandpa didn't do anything to himself, did he?" she asked.

Ann shook her head.

"How'd you get close enough to breathe in that smoke?"

Ann related the incident truthfully. That was always the best policy with Grandma.

"Ann saved the day. She drove the truck right up to where the guys needed it like she'd been doing it her whole life," said

Cameron as he came back. He patted his arm gingerly with the towel. He was wearing a Storey Senior Center T-shirt.

"I just reacted," Ann said.

"And it sounds like you did so in a level-headed way," said Grandma. She began applying petroleum jelly to Cam's wound.

Ann stared. Had Grandma just said she was level-headed? As Grandma herself would say, "would wonders never cease."

"You feeling better?" Cameron asked as Ann drained her glass of water.

"Yeah, thanks. You?"

"I'll live."

"Nice T-shirt," she joked.

"You laugh, but I think this makes me an honorary member of the Senior Center, and their monthly dinners are the best. I still remember the ham balls you made when the FFA did the program there last year, Mrs. Holmberg. One of the best things I've ever eaten."

"You are such a kiss-up," said Ann.

Cameron grinned.

"All right, you two—enough of your silliness. Cameron, I've covered your burn with this bandage to get you home. We'll take you," said Grandma.

"Thanks, but I need to take the truck back up for John."

"Nonsense. I'll drive it to the pasture, and Ann can follow in our car with you. If they're done burning, then you can go home with John. But if they're not, we're driving you."

Later, after they had dropped Cameron off, Grandma said, "Cameron seems like a nice boy."

Ann wondered what she meant. She looked at Grandma sitting serenely at the wheel after she'd ordered Ann to take it easy in the passenger seat. Ann opened her mouth to ask, but she wasn't even sure of the question. What if she said something that gave Grandma the wrong idea? She leaned her forehead against the window and watched the patchwork of burned pasture, dusty roads, and the first blades of tender, green grass peeking through in places as the blurred image flew by. In that split second up in the pasture when she saw Grandpa in danger, she had realized just how much both her grandparents had come to mean to her. Now, Grandma had said she was level-headed and trusted her to drive up to the pasture alone with Cameron. Nothing was worth jeopardizing that hard-earned trust, and she would do anything within her power to keep it.

26

Tea with the Misses Page

"Thank you for helping us with our newsletter," said Miss Genevieve.

"You do have a way with words." Miss Winifred nodded her approval.

"You're welcome," said Ann. She sat in their parlor in a stiff, chintz armchair awash in pink and lavender roses. It was the first time she had visited the Misses Page. They had called to ask for her "writerly assistance" with the historical society newsletter, and Ann thought it wise to stay on their good side. Accordingly, Ann drove Bessie to the Page home one afternoon after school where she was graciously welcomed as if she were royalty. The sisters wore freshly ironed dresses and buffed pumps, although their signature hats were missing inside. Ann had spent the next two hours crafting the sisters' ideas into a narrative for their newsletter. It was a process that involved a good deal of patience and waiting as the two bickered—always politely—back and forth.

"Now, let's have some tea," said Miss Winifred when they had finished.

"I'll go with you. You always make it too weak," said Miss Genevieve.

Ann pulled her notebook out and jotted down a description of their living room as she waited among the figurines, tatted doilies, African violets, and general bric-a-brac. The place was a story in and of itself, she decided as she glanced at the dark wood trim polished to an impeccable gleam. In fact, the entire episode smacked of Green Gables. An antique grandfather clock chimed the hour, reminding Ann, along with the half-light filtering through the lacy curtains, that the afternoon was slipping away. But she wasn't about to rush out on tea with the Page sisters. The possibilities for their disapproval were too great.

"Here we go. I hope you like gingersnaps and cucumber sandwiches," Miss Winifred said as she bustled into the parlor. She placed a silver tray complete with a china teapot, cups, saucers, plates, and linen napkins, on the coffee table.

"Yes, thank you," said Ann, though she'd never eaten a cucumber sandwich before in her life.

Miss Genevieve poured the tea, and Miss Winifred passed the refreshments.

"We saw you made the honor roll again," said Miss Genevieve as they sat sipping their tea.

"Congratulations," said Miss Winifred, clapping her hands.

"Thank you." Ann smiled, making every effort not to spill anything on the pristine hardwood floors. She envisioned herself being banned forever from this home where time seemed to have stood still if she dropped so much as a crumb.

"We always follow all the local happenings," said Miss Genevieve.

Miss Winifred nodded. "It's important to know what's going on in one's community."

"Of course." Ann managed not to crack a smile, although she knew there wasn't much chance of the sisters missing anything in the community, or the entire county, for that matter.

"That's why we wanted to take such great pains with our newsletter this time. We're embarking on a fundraising campaign for the museum, and we want to make a good impression." Miss

Genevieve spoke as if the fate of Storey's history rested solely in her hands.

"Mabel Walsh said you like to write, so we checked with your grandmother," Miss Genevieve said.

"And your grandmother said you're an excellent writer." Miss Winifred nodded emphatically.

"She did?"

"Oh, yes. Thelma Holmberg's not one to brag, but we could tell she's real proud of you. Isn't she, Genevieve?"

"Indeed."

Ann pondered the unexpected compliment while she nibbled her dainty sandwich. The sisters continued chatting.

"We saw Acacia Thorne in town yesterday. Are you girls the same age?" asked Miss Genevieve.

"Yes," Ann said flatly.

"Are you friends with her?" Miss Winifred asked.

"Not really." Ann was trying her level best to abide by Grandma's rule of thumb of not saying anything at all if it wasn't something nice.

"Come now, Winifred. What would Ann have in common with that Thorne girl? She is rude and impertinent and spoiled rotten." Miss Genevieve sniffed.

Ann laughed. "You won't get any arguments from me."

Miss Winifred shook her head sadly. "She mocked us once, and I'm afraid we've never gotten over it."

"That was rude of her. But then again, she mocks me, too, so I guess now I know I'm in good company," said Ann.

"You're friends with Ellen Alexander's daughter, aren't you?" said Miss Winifred.

"Yes, Corrie is my best friend."

"She seems to go back to Kansas City a lot to visit her father." Miss Genevieve's look showed disapproval for anyone whose actions indicated Storey was somehow insufficient.

"Yeah, she misses him. They're pretty close."

"Genevieve and I heard her brother is going to study to be a veterinarian."

"That's what I heard, too," Ann said. She reached for another finger sandwich and tried to change the topic. "These are delicious."

"He seems like a nice boy," said Miss Genevieve fixing her piercing gaze on Ann.

"And these cookies are sublime," Ann said, helping herself to another one.

"Oh, would you like the recipes? I'd be happy to share them with you," said Miss Winifred.

Ann smiled in relief. "Oh, yes, please. I'm getting a lot better at cooking than I used to be."

"I can hardly believe it's been almost a year since you came to live with your grandparents," said Miss Winifred.

"What are your plans for this summer?" asked Miss Genevieve.

Ann smiled wryly. It was a nice way for them to ask if she was staying. She assumed she was. Dad had finally returned her call last week. In the grand total of five minutes he'd talked with her, it was clear he was still more invested in his new band than in finding a steady job. Besides, Ann really didn't want to leave Sunflower Lane, a fact that made her feel guilty anytime she admitted it to herself. She knew it was ridiculous to feel disloyal to a father who had never been loyal to her.

"I think I'm going to work for Uncle Edward. He said he could use some help in his shop. I don't know anything about farm implements, but he said he'll teach me to take orders. And he said he really needs me to help him clean up his supply shelves."

"A job! That would be very enterprising of you," said Miss Winifred.

"A good use of your time. And a good way to earn money for college. I assume you're planning on going to college?" said Miss

Genevieve. Her tone signaled that to think anything else would be severely frowned upon.

"Oh, yes. Definitely," said Ann.

"What do you want to study?" asked Miss Winifred.

"I think English. I love to read and write. I think I might like to be an English teacher and write on the side."

"A teacher! Just like us! Oh, that would be so lovely, wouldn't it, Genevieve?"

"It is a noble profession. A challenging one, but very worthwhile," said Miss Genevieve.

"And you'd be following in your mother's footsteps. She was an English teacher, you know."

Ann nodded. It was one of the few things she'd always known about her mother.

"I hope you just don't throw it all away like she did by eloping with some . . ."

"Genevieve, be nice." Miss Winifred interrupted her.

The last bite of cookie stuck in Ann's throat.

"Winifred, please do not interrupt me. As I was saying, make sure you have your priorities straight. And when the time comes to choose a life partner, if you choose one at all, which we certainly didn't find necessary, be sure he is responsible."

The mix of tea and cookies and cucumber sandwiches swam in Ann's stomach. Great-Uncle Pete's words from last summer came back with astounding clarity. She had ignored them, pushed them down, but now the same tale had been flung back at her. She wanted to escape the confines of the room, but she knew better than to flee and give the sisters more grist for their gossip mill.

"Of course," she said. Her tongue felt like lead in her mouth.

"See? I told you Ann was sensible, just like her grandmother," said Miss Winifred.

"Thelma is a sterling example to follow." Miss Genevieve punctuated the pronouncement with a tap of her hand on the arm of her chair.

"More tea, Ann?"

"No, thank you Miss Winifred. I'd probably better head home. I have some homework to do for tomorrow."

"Thank you for your assistance with our newsletter," said Miss Genevieve.

"Come back anytime. It's always so lovely to talk with you," Miss Winifred said.

They accompanied her to the door and stood side by side as she backed out, waving. Ann kept the smile pasted on her face until she was out on the county road.

"Eloped? They eloped? But why?" Ann said. And then the realization struck her. She slammed on the brakes and gripped the wheel. "Did they have to get married? Was it because of me?"

She gazed down the dusty section road through the green blades of tallgrass in the pastures on both sides. She searched for the answer somewhere in the distance, on the horizon, but always came up short. Ann felt she stood at the edge of a black abyss, and every rosy image she'd crafted of her mother over the years teetered on its brink.

"It would explain so much—why no one talks about Mom, Grandma's rules. But is it true? I *need* to find out the truth." Her breath caught as another possibility wiggled its way into her thoughts. "What if I'm the reason Mom married him and not R.J.? What if she really didn't want to, but she had to? I not only killed her, I made her miserable before that."

A cloud of dust on the horizon alerted Ann to an approaching vehicle. She swiped the tears from her eyes and put Bessie in gear, focusing her eyes on the skyline as she tried to forget the past she'd just imagined.

27

The Invitation

Ann was genuinely beginning to wish the concept of prom had never been invented.

"Whose ridiculous idea was it anyway?" she demanded of Corrie one rainy afternoon when they were discussing the event in Ann's dreamroom. Ann sighed and looked out the window at the gray afternoon that had spoiled their plans for a picnic supper in the Enchanted Forest in the cruelest of April jokes. She agreed wholeheartedly with Anne Shirley that "it's easier to be cheerful and bear up under affliction on a sunshiny day." As it was, the damp chill only added to the dismal mood in which Ann now sat discussing the social event of the school year at Storey High with her bosom friend.

"But you like the theme of 'When I'm With You.' I'd go if I were an upperclassman," Corrie said.

"I wish you were, so I would at least have someone to talk to. If I even go, that is. I haven't asked Grandma." Ann sighed, regretting that something so silly as prom could elicit so many sighs from her in the same day.

"Who's to say someone won't ask you to go?"

"It wouldn't matter if they did. You know all about Grandma's 'no boys' rule. Besides, who's going to ask me? Larry Zima? Gag me! I'll pass."

"You know he's going to try."

"Yes, and it will be the skating party all over again," Ann said. Images of Larry Zima careening toward Ann on roller skates and shouting an invitation to couple skate while the rest of the Foreign Language Club watched played across her mind like a horror movie on slow motion.

"Maybe my brother will ask you," Corrie said.

"Ha," scoffed Ann.

"Why not?"

Ann sighed—noting it was the third time in this short conversation. "It doesn't really matter, does it? Grandma wouldn't let me go even if someone did invite me. Let's not talk about it anymore, because it's just as depressing as this lousy weather."

The rain lasted until Thursday afternoon. By then, Ann thought she would lose the last threads of her sanity if she didn't get outside and away from all thoughts of prom.

"Be home before dark," Grandma told Ann as she put on her jacket and set out on an evening walk with Sam at her heels.

"I feel almost optimistic again," she confided to Sam. "It's hard to feel glum on the first day after a rainy spell, especially when it's a Thursday. I love Thursdays—there's such a sense of anticipation wrapped up in them."

With a wag of his short tail, Sam turned down Lover's Lane to follow the trail of some scent his keen nose detected, but Ann continued down the road. She felt a sense of peaceful contentment as she walked through the cool April air to the Enchanted Forest. She turned into the pasture entrance and slipped through the barbed wire fence, as she had been doing regularly since the poison ivy threat diminished last fall. She felt a sense of urgency to enjoy all the walks she could before the itchy vine returned. Tonight, she felt the peace of the timber wrap her in its embrace. She stood and breathed under the shelter of the purple dome formed by the redbud trees populating the hillside, feeling in her very soul that the Enchanted Forest was her kindred space. The shadows of approaching twilight were already filtering through the delicate, hummingbird-shaped blooms above as Ann slowed her pace and walked lightly under them.

"It's just like the White Way of Delight," she said reverently. "Only, purple, of course. I'll have to write a description when I get home, full of juicy adjectives. Even though I've learned to slash them mercilessly from my compositions, I grant myself the freedom to use the purplest of prose in my journal."

Ann followed the path still discernible through the shoots of young grass to the clearing where the aged lilac stood in its green blush of new leaves.

"I can almost imagine some dashing hero could step out and find me here at this lilac bush, just like in *Kilmeny of the Orchard*," Ann said. She leaned against the bush. "Of course, I'd have to tell him he needed to wait until I'm thirty for Grandma to allow me to go on a date, but any hero worth his salt would do that, wouldn't he?"

Ann glanced about, in spite of herself, but no literary leading man was to be found. She continued to Mending Wall, brushing her fingers over the roughness of the stones as she followed their serpentine line to the top of the hill. She paused in the open pasture above, the tallgrass rustling around her at the sweetness of the threshold between day and night. She gazed out to the hint of green poking through the burned pastures to the east, the gray ribbon of highway to the north, the brilliant flame of the sun inching toward the western horizon. Ann's breath caught at the beauty of the scene before her, an impressionist painting brought to life by the magic of an early spring dusk. She dropped to the ground and watched, transfixed, as the sun slipped toward the distant line between earth and sky, pulling the curtain slowly closed on the day. One by one, the stars sparkled against the backdrop of violet and sapphire. Up above, two birds circled, inky vees in silent flight. The uninterrupted vista seemed too beautiful to be real, a "dream the world was having about itself" that evening. Ann imagined herself with the birds, gliding on strong wings over the vastness of the rolling Flint Hills, this land of endless horizons, watching a girl full of dreams watch the sunset below. She felt herself very small in that moment, her dreams so grand yet so trivial under the expansive firmament, her tribulations so miniscule when compared to the heavens.

Ann rose, reluctant to leave the beauty of the evening. She'd need to hurry, or she wouldn't be home before dark, and Grandma would scold her. She climbed between the strands of barbed wire, through the ditch, and onto the road. She had just crossed the bridge at the foot of the hill when she heard the sound of an approaching vehicle behind her. It honked, and she glanced back. For some reason, she wasn't surprised to find Cameron there. She stopped, and he parked beside her and got out.

"Pretty, isn't it?" he said, motioning to the last colors of the sunset.

"So are you stalking me now?"

"No, I was at Arthur's doing some work and happened to see you on my way home. Call it fate."

"Whatever. I'd better go. Grandma will have a fit if I'm not back by dark."

"Ann, wait. I want to ask you something."

"Cameron, it's not OK for me to be here alone with you. I'll get in really deep trouble with my grandma."

"Would you please just let me talk?"

Ann sighed. "Fine. But hurry up."

"All right then, straight to the point. Will you go to prom with me?"

Ann stared. "Excuse me?"

"I'm asking you to be my date to prom."

"Why are you doing this? I told you what my grandma said about boys."

"But she knows me, and I'll go and talk with her and tell her I asked you and . . ."

"No. Please. Don't do that. Don't say anything," Ann said.

"Why not?"

How to explain? Ann hadn't even had the nerve to tell Corrie what the Misses Page had said about her parents eloping. She just couldn't bring herself to voice the words and make them that much more real. If what she suspected was true, she kind of understood Grandma's rule. But this had to end. She couldn't keep dodging Cameron forever, and she didn't want to do anything to ruin what she had with her grandparents at Sunflower Lane. She didn't want to hurt Cameron either, but that might be the only way.

"Because I don't want to go with you, even if she said I could," Ann said.

Cameron's face looked first stricken, then angry. "Oh. Fine."

He climbed back in his truck and slammed the door. The truck lurched down the road as he sped away.

"I'm sorry," Ann said, but only the wind was there to hear her.

The final sliver of sun was sinking from view as Ann turned into Sunflower Lane. Tears burned the back of her eyes as she fixed her gaze on the lights twinkling out from the windows of home.

28

Prom

"Have you heard the latest news?" Corrie said as she skidded to a halt beside Ann's locker. It was the Monday before prom, and intrigue filled the halls of Storey High.

"What news is it this time?" asked Molly.

"Acacia and Jeff broke up."

"What? There's no way the two most popular people in school would break up right before prom," said Ann.

"It's confirmed. They did," said Corrie.

"It's really of no concern to me. I'll be glad when this whole prom craziness is over. My only regret is that Larry Zima continues to lurk around hinting at an invitation," Ann said.

The girls glanced down the hall, but no Larry was on the horizon.

"Wouldn't it be easier to tell him you're not interested?" asked Molly.

"She's sure good at that," said Cameron from across the hall. He slammed his locker and glared.

Ann pretended to ignore him. "If Larry would quit hinting and actually ask, I'd be happy to tell him I'm just going with my friends and that I'm not interested in going with him." She raised her voice and added, "*Or with anyone.*"

"Hey, Cam." Acacia Thorne's voice managed to pierce even the noise in the hallway.

"Hi, Acacia," said Cameron.

"Have you heard I totally dumped that loser I was dating? And I was, like, wondering if you'd wanna go to prom with me. I've wanted to go with you this whole time." Acacia gave Cameron a pouty look.

Ann's cheeks burned as she stacked her binders and books for first hour. She shut her locker more aggressively than necessary.

"Sure. That'd be awesome," he said.

Acacia squealed and draped her arms around Cameron's neck. Ann knew she had hurt Cameron, but badly enough that he'd go to prom with Acacia Thorne? But what choice did she have? Ann understood her grandmother's motives, and no boy, no matter how much she was starting to suspect she liked him, was worth messing up the first place she'd ever lived that felt like home.

"I totally can't wait for prom," said Acacia.

Cameron caught Ann's eye. Some small part of her wanted to pity the look on his face, but she clamped it down. There was no turning back now.

By Saturday night, Ann was starting to regret agreeing to go to prom at all. Grandma had given her permission to go with her friends, since the event was chaperoned, but Ann was still unsure. Molly had finally convinced her by loaning her a dress and matching heels and telling her in no uncertain terms she didn't want to miss her junior prom. She came and did Ann's hair in long, soft curls, then Molly's mom drove them to the banquet. Only SHS students could attend the meal, and Molly's boyfriend went to Coneville High. She would meet him afterwards while Ann walked with some other date-less friends to the gym for the dance.

Ann was miserable from the moment she entered the banquet hall. It was loud and hot, and Molly's shoes pinched her feet. The very first couple she saw was Acacia and Cameron. To top it all off, she discovered herself seated next to Jeff Sands, Acacia's ex. He had let it be known that he was going stag to prom to "spread the wealth." Even remembering that comment made Ann want to slap her forehead, and now, she found him monopolizing the conversation at her table. Jeff was a senior, and Ann had never really talked with him much. She knew he was a jock, but she'd underestimated his unparalleled ability to talk about himself. He prattled throughout dinner about his basketball scholarship to a small college the next year.

Ann's misery deepened as the meal wore on and Jeff leaned over and whispered banalities like "Pass the salt," glancing at Acacia to watch her reaction. For her part, Acacia laughed hysterically at everything Cameron said with sly looks at Jeff. One glimpse of Cameron's face as everyone left for the dance told Ann he was miserable.

Jeff followed Ann into the gym, still droning on about sports, and announced she'd have to dance first with him. She hoped the sheer volume of the music would end his pontifications, but no such luck; he merely talked all the louder as he dragged Ann awkwardly onto the dancefloor. Horror of horrors, Ann realized, the great and popular Jeff Sands couldn't dance. Saying he had two left feet would be an insult to left feet everywhere. She wondered if this "obscene travesty" known as prom would ever end. After two songs and at least ten bruised toes—Ann was sure she had sprouted more digits on her feet just for Jeff to step on—she excused herself from Jeff. She stood in the longest line for punch to get away from him.

"Go to prom, they said. You'll always regret it if you don't, they said. Yeah, right. I regret it, all right. I regret I'm here," said Ann to herself.

Whistles and hoots interrupted her grumblings. She turned to find Jeff in the center of the floor, lip-locked with Acacia. A wave of relief washed over Ann. No more flattened toes under Jeff's clumsy feet, no more thrown-out back with his awful spins, and thanks to the heavens above, no more listening to him.

"Looks like they made up. I thought you might have a sort-of date for the rest of the evening. I'm sorry," Molly said

"I'm not. In fact, I think I might call Grandpa and have him come pick me up."

"Stay. Sebastian and I will still give you a ride home just like we planned. Please? I promise you'll have fun," Molly said.

"Oh, all right. I hate to bother Grandpa, and I've already lost all feeling in my toes. What else do I have to lose at this point?"

Ann walked to the bleachers and slipped off her uncomfortable heels. She sat and people-watched, noticing Cameron sitting similarly alone on the other side of the gym. Ann danced some songs in groups with her friends. After a while, the lights stayed low, and the deejay played a series of slow songs.

"Looks like they made up." Cameron stood beside her with two cups of punch in his hand. He handed one to Ann and sat beside her.

"Yep."

"Can't say I'm sorry, though. Acacia is a terrible dancer," he said.

"So is Jeff. I feared for the safety of my toes, shins, back, and general physical and mental wellbeing."

"Think anyone will remember they dumped us as their prom back-ups?" asked Cameron.

"Ah, technically I was not Jeff's date," Ann reminded him.

"Thanks. I was trying to share the embarrassment."

"Don't worry. Based on some of the gossip about a clandestine afterparty, I'm not sure many of them will remember much of anything," she said.

"Good point."

Ann glanced at him out of the corner of her eye. The lie she'd told him had only made things worse. Grandma always said honesty was the best policy, but she'd tried to take the easy way out with Cameron. It hadn't worked.

"Cam, I need to tell you something. I lied. On the road that evening, I mean," she said.

"Why?"

"Because I'd just learned some stuff about my parents that I think explains why Grandma is so strict with me about boys."

"Like what?"

"I don't want to talk about it. I'm still trying to sort it out myself. I haven't even told Corrie, and she's my best friend. But I thought you deserved to know I didn't tell you the truth."

He took a sip of his punch before answering. "I know. I think I knew it all along, but I let my ego get in the way."

Ann smiled, and Cameron gave her a good-natured bump with his elbow. They sat in silence until George Strait's "It Ain't Cool," began to play. She remembered the autumn evening Cameron had dared her to dance to it.

"Wanna give Acacia and Jeff something to remember us by?" Cameron asked.

"What do you mean?"

Cameron stood and reached out his hand. "Ann Alwyn, may I have this dance?"

Ann hesitated for the briefest space of a moment. Grandma had said she could go to prom and that she could dance, just that she couldn't have a date.

"You may."

She slipped on her shoes, and Cameron led her onto the dancefloor. In the stuffy gym Ann's cheeks were suddenly warm and her palms were sweaty. They two-stepped smoothly across the floor, and Ann felt Acacia's eyes follow them. Ann had a spark of insight in that moment about people like Acacia who always want everything, especially what someone else has. Acacia was intolerable, and Cameron was right: this was undoubtedly enjoyable.

The last notes played, and the deejay announced the theme song as the final dance of the night.

"I suppose we might as well dance the last one," Cameron said.

Ann nodded, thankful he didn't remind her of how their previous efforts to dance one last song had ended in October. Cameron took her hand and held her, just as he had before, in that closed position that seemed so grown-up.

"Let's have some fun," Cameron said in her ear. "Give those two a taste of their own medicine. Follow my lead."

Cameron pulled Ann close, and she instinctively rested her head on his chest. His heart thudded loudly against her ear, and she felt him lean his cheek on her hair. The lights around them blinked against Ann's closed lids, but she refused to let herself think about what it all meant. She wouldn't go there; she couldn't.

The music faded to stillness, and Ann pushed gently away from Cameron. His hazel eyes reflected the soft smile on his lips. The moment was broken when Acacia shoved past them with an elbow and a glare, dragging Jeff behind her.

The lights came on, and Ann found Molly beside her. "Ann, we can take you home if you *still* need us to," she said with a smile.

Cam shrugged. "Sorry, I can't offer you a ride. Acacia insisted we come in her car. Apparently, my old beater wasn't good enough for her."

"We can take you home, too," said Molly. Sebastian nodded.

"Thanks," Cameron said. He offered Ann his arm, and she took it.

They exited into the sweet night air. The stars above were more authentically brilliant than the intensely blinking lights they left behind. They climbed into Sebastian's car, rolled down the windows, and drove pleasantly along listening to the radio. Molly and Sebastian chatted in the front seat, but Ann and Cameron sat quietly in the back. Finally, Cameron broke the silence as they left the town behind them.

"I'm a pretty smart guy. Why'd I agree to go to prom with Acacia Thorne?"

"I guess even smart people make mistakes. And I ought to know because I certainly make a lot," said Ann.

"What is it your Anne Shirley says? 'Tomorrow is a new day with no mistakes in it?'"

"Why, Cameron Addair, did you just quote *Anne of Green Gables* to me?"

"What can I say? You and Corrie have made me listen to your non-stop chatter about it forever. And I did watch that miniseries. I took some notes."

Ann laughed, finding herself completely at ease with Cameron. The rest of the ride home was every bit as enjoyable as sitting next to Jeff at the banquet had been disagreeable. When Sebastian pulled into the quiet yard at Sunflower Lane, Cameron hurried to open Ann's door for her. He offered her his hand.

"Milady. This is a full-service prom back-up date."

Ann stepped from the truck and took Cameron's arm. He escorted her to the front door where they stood in self-conscious silence.

"Thank you," Ann said at length. "You saved the evening from being an entire loss."

"You, too." Cameron said quietly. His unwavering eyes held hers.

Ann felt a strange, fluttery feeling in her stomach. Was he going to try to kiss her? She couldn't risk it. She extended her hand instead.

"Goodnight," Ann said lightly.

Cameron took her hand in both of his. Then, he leaned forward and brushed her cheek with a whisper. "Maybe you can save a dance or two for me when I'm home from college next year." He looked steadily at Ann, then raised her hand, held it for a breath, and gently kissed her palm. "Goodnight, Ann."

She slipped inside the house and up the stairs to her open window where the white eyelet curtains danced in the breeze and all the mysterious sounds and perfumes of the spring night filtered in. She saw the car's headlights stop at the highway and traced the pattern of Cameron's kiss written on her palm. A dance or two, she thought. That was all. Maybe someday she could grant him that.

29

Tea with Tragic Results

"I can't believe I let the Misses Page talk me into this," said Ann. It was Memorial Day weekend, and she and Corrie were sitting at the kitchen table helping Grandma peel potatoes and discussing the upcoming Community Talent Show.

"It'll be fun. Besides, it's for a worthy cause," Corrie said.

"I kind of feel like I already did my part for that 'worthy cause' when I helped write their Historical Society newsletter."

"Now, Ann. Where's your community spirit?" said Grandma.

"Grandpa's singing, and that should be enough to represent Sunflower Lane."

"Why don't you two girls do something together?" Grandma said.

"Trust me, Mrs. H., you don't want me to sing," said Corrie.

Ann slapped her forehead. "Why didn't I think of this sooner? I have the prefect idea. Let's do a skit together."

"A skit?" said Corrie.

"Yes. Let's do the raspberry cordial scene from *Anne.*"

"Now that is a truly brilliant idea."

"The what?" asked Grandma.

"Anne Shirley invites her friend Diana to tea, but she accidentally serves her red currant wine instead of cordial. She gets really drunk, and Anne gets in big trouble."

"I totally want to be Diana for that scene," said Corrie. "So you'll be Anne, but who should play Marilla? She's in that scene, too. We'd need someone older."

"Huh. I'm not sure."

They sat in silence, as they continued to peel potatoes.

"I could do it," said Grandma.

The girls stared at her, eyes wide, then at each other, then back at Grandma.

"Don't look so shocked," said Grandma, a smile playing at the corners of her mouth. "I used to do dramatics back when I was in school. I always kind of liked it."

"Really?" asked Ann.

"Sure." Grandma sat down her peeler and dried her hands. "Why don't you audition me?"

"Uh, OK."

Ann dashed up the stairs to her room and returned with her novel. She flipped through the pages to Chapter XVI.

"Here—read this part," Ann said, pointing.

Grandma glanced at the text, cleared her throat, and frowned. "'Anne, you certainly have a genius for getting into trouble.'"

"Whoa, that was perfect," said Corrie.

"Maybe a little too perfect," said Ann. "Have I given you that much practice getting after an Ann, Grandma?"

Grandma smiled. "Not that much. So do I have the part?"

"Yes!" the girls said in unison.

Sunflower Lane and the Alexander farm were a flurry of activity over the next two weeks as Ann, Corrie, and Grandma practiced and prepared for the talent show. Aunt Janis got caught up in the spirit and made a dress with honest-to-goodness puffed sleeves for Corrie, and a simple print dress for Ann. Grandma searched in the remote corners of her closet and produced a long skirt and white blouse she had worn for Storey's centennial celebration. An old tea set from the garret, a glass decanter filled with cranberry juice, and a plate of gingersnaps rounded out the props.

Grandma was as eager a participant as the two girls. "This is real fun," she told Ann one evening as she studied her lines.

"Have you ever read the book?" Ann asked.

"No, but this kind of makes me want to."

"We've made a few edits, so it works for the skit. We decided to end with the line about new days and no mistakes—because it closes the skit out so nicely. We know we're taking creative license with L.M. Montgomery's classic, but we aren't making up anything that isn't in the book and that couldn't just as easily have been said there."

"I'm sure L.M. Montgomery won't mind," Grandma said.

Ann smiled at her grandmother. "Thanks for doing this with me."

Grandma gently touched her hand. It was so uncharacteristic that Ann barely heard what she said. "We should do more things together."

Ann nodded. "Yeah. We should. Definitely."

The park was packed on the evening of the first-ever Storey Community Talent Show. Ann surveyed the large crowd seated in lawn chairs fanning out from the gazebo that would serve as their stage. They were up next.

"That's a lot of people. I hope they like our skit," she said.

"The Misses Page ought to be happy. Their fundraiser looks like it was a big success," said Corrie.

"It's our turn, girls. Break a leg," said Grandma.

They set up their props, and the show began. Marilla/Grandma called for Anne/Ann, and she came running, all nerves disappearing as she delivered her first lines. There, in the shade of the gazebo with birds twittering in the branches around them and the sweet gurgling of the fountain nearby, Ann Alwyn felt even more in touch with her inner Anne Shirley. The scene progressed beautifully, and as Diana/Corrie moaned about being sick and was clearly intoxicated, the audience chuckled appreciatively. Anne/Ann, fed by their energy, turned quickly on the smooth cement of the gazebo's floor to race back to Diana/Corrie with her hat and parasol. And that was when disaster struck.

Ann slipped and fell onto one knee with a thud she was sure must have ricocheted off the gazebo walls and across the entire park. Pain shot across her knee, but she sprang to her feet and kept going. A quick glance at Corrie revealed her friend's act was so good she hadn't even noticed. But Grandma, waiting in the wings, had a worried hand over her mouth.

They finished the skit without further incident, and when it was over, Grandma hurried Ann to a bench to survey the damage.

"Are you all right?" she asked.

Ann raised the hem of her dress to reveal a substantial floor burn on her knee.

"Oh, no," said Corrie. "How'd that happen?"

"I fell. And it throbs so hard I can feel every single heartbeat."

"You're not bleeding. Oh dear, do you want to go home?" asked Grandma.

"I'll live. I'm just embarrassed. I'm sorry I made a mess of this for you two."

"A mess? Why, that's the most fun I've had in years, and it's all thanks to you. I'm so glad you let me be a part of it," said Grandma.

Ann smiled, despite the pain. "Me, too."

"If you're sure you're OK, I'll go sit with Grandpa."

Ann nodded. "Go ahead."

"I'll go get you a glass of lemonade," said Corrie.

Ann sat glumly, looking at the oozing mess that was her knee and torn nylons, thinking that she would surely feel better if she could cry now. The tears she had bravely choked back during the skit refused to come, and she felt a sickening knot in her stomach.

"That looks nasty," Cameron said. He sat beside her.

"Yeah. It really hurts," said Ann.

"I take it that wasn't part of the original script?"

Ann shook her head. "No. I just slipped and made a fool of myself."

"Chill. No one even realized it wasn't planned."

"I finally get the chance to play Anne Shirley, and I mess it up. Why can't I ever get anything right?" The tears welled up at last in the wide, blue eyes she turned to Cameron.

"What do you mean?" he asked, elbowing her chummily. "Why, if slipping and falling during the middle of a performance isn't something your Anne Shirley would do, I don't know what is. Not that I'm an expert, but you and Corrie have tortured me with Anne-this and Anne-that forever. In fact, I think something like that should have been in the book. Why that author didn't think of it is beyond me."

"You're not just saying that because you're afraid I'll punch you again?" Ann asked with the hint of a smile.

"Nope," Cameron said. He looked kindly at her tear-stained face. "If anyone ever was like your Anne Shirley, it's you."

"Ann, here's your lemonade. They're getting ready to announce the winners," said Corrie.

Corrie stood beside the bench, and they listened expectantly as Miss Genevieve announced the third and second places. She adjusted her glasses before continuing. "And first place goes to the wonderful intergenerational skit, 'Tea With Tragic Results,' by Ann Alwyn, Cordelia Addair, and Thelma Holmberg."

"We won!" Corrie jumped up and down beside her. "Come on, Ann."

Cameron stood and offered Ann a hand to help her to her feet. "Your fans await," he said.

"Thank you," Ann replied as she arranged her dress over the remains of her nylons and the ugliness of her knee. Then, shoulder back and chin up, she walked without wincing to the stage.

And Cameron stood watching beside the bench.

30

What Ann Learns on the Job

"**E**dward, you should've hired your niece a long time ago," said the crusty farmer. Ann had just returned in what he claimed was record time with a part. She had been working part-time for one week in the farm implement store to help the perpetually unorganized Uncle Edward find some semblance of order in his inventory during the busy season.

"Don't I know it," said Uncle Edward.

Ann beamed. "Thank you for your purchase," she said as she rang up the sale.

Next in the door was Great-Uncle Pete. He didn't farm anymore, but he did enjoy sitting and talking with anyone who came in.

"Morning, Ann," he said. He shook her hand, slipping her a butterscotch as he always did.

"Good morning, Great-Uncle Pete. How are you?"

"Fair to middlin'. Arthur won't leave me alone these days."

"Arthur who rents Grandpa's land?" asked Ann.

The old codger grinned. "No, Arthur-itis."

Ann laughed.

"How's the job suit you?" he asked.

"I like it. I'm learning a lot about parts and crops and life here in general."

"You done good at the talent show. Could hardly believe my eyes when I saw Thelma up there."

"Grandma was amazing, wasn't she?"

"She used to do all kinds of things like that when she was little. She was real creative. Both her girls were, too."

"That's probably where I get my creative streak," said Ann.

"Course it is. You sure have brought her out of her shell, and I'm glad for it." He reached out a gnarled hand and patted Ann's shoulder. "Arthur and I are gonna go sit a spell and listen to the news."

"Can I get you anything?" asked Ann.

"Wouldn't mind some coffee. You seem to be able to make a decent cup."

Ann stepped to the coffeemaker. Keeping a fresh pot ready and waiting for the customers was another of her duties. After a thorough cleaning of the old appliance that would have met even Grandma's standards, Ann had been pleasantly surprised to discover that she could, indeed, make a decent cup of coffee.

"Here you go," she said.

Great-Uncle Pete stepped to a table to sit with two other farmers who were swapping their news. The bell at the door rang, and Molly came in dressed in jeans, an old T-shirt, and scuffed cowboy boots. She was working that summer, as she always did, on her parents' farm.

"Hi, Ann. I need this belt for the tractor." She handed Ann a slip of paper.

"Sure thing." Ann stepped to the back, located the belt, and returned.

"How's the job going?" Molly asked.

"Great. I can't believe how much I'm enjoying it. Don't get me wrong—I work hard, and there are still whole shelves I need to organize back there. But I like it."

"How's Corrie?"

"I had a nice, long letter from her yesterday. It sounds like she's having a great time with her dad in Kansas City. They've gone to museums and an amusement park and all kinds of restaurants."

"How long will she be there?" asked Molly.

"A couple of weeks. She wanted to spend her birthday there."

"I saw Cam yesterday at the Dairy Crème. He didn't go?"

"No, he was in yesterday for a part. He's helping John out and working for Grandpa's renter, Arthur, to earn money for college," Ann said.

"You seem to know all about his activities," Molly said with a grin.

"Just repeating what I heard," said Ann. She busied herself by neatly arranging the receipt book and pens beside the cash register.

"Whatever. I'd better get this back to Dad. Talk to you soon," said Molly.

Molly had reached the door when it opened, and John and Cameron walked in.

"Why, hello, Cameron. Ann and I were just talking about you," Molly said. She gave Ann an innocent smile as she left.

Ann blushed.

"Oh, really?" said Cameron. He and John leaned on the counter.

"Actually, we were talking about Corrie. I told her Corrie was in KC, and you were working," Ann said. She turned to John and asked, "How may I help you?"

"I need a hydraulic filter. Wrote the information down for you." He handed Ann a scrap of paper.

"I'll be right back," Ann said. She disappeared into the back and tried to read the scrawl on the note in the dim light between the tall shelves.

"Why is it that their notes are always on shreds of paper and in illegible handwriting?" Ann said to herself. She stepped to the window for a better look, and then located the filter.

                    Julie A. Sellers

"I think this is it. I apologize for the wait," Ann said. She handed the part to John.

"Couldn't read his handwriting?" Cameron asked.

"Yeah, yeah. I never got an A in penmanship," John said good-naturedly. "But you managed to decipher it, so no harm done. Could you put it on my account?"

"Of course."

"Thanks. I'm gonna get a cup of coffee before we leave."

Cameron leaned on the counter. "So how's life at your uncle's store?"

"More interesting than even I could have imagined."

"That's saying something."

Ann swatted him with the account book. "Aren't you funny."

"I think I am."

"Oops—I forgot to have John sign to put that filter on his account. Excuse me a minute."

Ann stepped to the table where John was listening to Great-Uncle Pete tell the story of the time he had been struck by lightning out in his hayfield.

"I'm sorry to interrupt. John, could you please sign so we can add that to your account?" said Ann.

"Oh, sure. Sorry—I always forget that step." John signed and returned the book to Ann.

"Thank you," she said. She glanced at the page as she walked back to the counter and frowned. She started to close the book and suddenly caught her breath.

"Something wrong?" asked Cameron.

Ann slammed the book shut. "What? Oh. No. Nothing's wrong."

"You sure? You went a little pale there for a sec."

"No. I just remembered I need to go place an order for Mr. Elliott. I'll talk to you later."

Ann rushed to the back office and dropped on the chair. She opened the book again to look at John's signature: R. John Alexander. It was the "R" that gave it away. It was the same as the one on the love letter she'd found in her mother's book of poetry.

"John Alexander was in love with my mother," she said. She ran her finger over his name. "Did she love him? If they were a couple, it was clearly a secret. Aunt Janis didn't know. And the Page sisters surely would've known if it hadn't been, and they can't keep a secret. But what happened?"

Ann stared out the window, wondering what her life would have been like if her mother had married John Alexander. How would things have been different if her mother had never left Storey? Would she have been happy without her college education? Would she have died anyway? What would Ann's own life have been like? And Grandma—would she have remained the smiling, creative woman Great-Uncle Pete remembered?

Ann looked back at the signature. "I guess I'll never know."

31

New Horizons

Ann drove home from work through the shimmery afternoon, finding a certain cathartic release from the heat in singing along with the country songs on the radio. As she bounced over the railroad tracks, she spied Bubba Joe Ramsey shutting the mailbox.

"He's late today. Must have had an extra-long nap." It was Grandpa's standing joke about the mail carrier's unpredictable schedule.

Ann turned into Sunflower Lane and left Bessie idling while she ran across the road for the mail.

"Farm paper, junk, junk, bill, and . . . Great. Another postcard from my father. Let's see—any bets on what it says this time?" She turned the card over and read the few lines.

> *What's shakin'? The band's down in Texas. Doing well.*
> *Stay cool.*
> *Dad.*

Ann tore the postcard in two.

"Why does he even bother?" she said. She continued her perusal of the mail. "Another bill, Kansas Landscapes Essay Contest . . ." Ann stopped. The novelty of her new job and the questions that still remained even after discovering the identity of R.J. had made her completely forget about the writing contest she'd entered. She shoved the rest of the mail back into the box and opened the envelope with shaking hands.

"Yes!" She jumped up and down in circles as she read.

A honking horn brought Ann's ecstatic dance to a halt. She looked up to see Cameron driving toward her. He pulled to the side of the road and got out.

"I take it your AP History score came today, too?" he asked.

"No, I just found out I won an essay contest. See?" Ann waved the letter and check in front of his amused face. Then she stopped short, realization registering. "Wait—your AP score came today?"

"Yes, everyone's did. So far, we've all gotten three hours of college credit."

Ann yanked the mail back out of the box and discovered one last letter in the folds of the farm paper.

"It's here," she said.

"Well, open it."

Accordingly, Ann tore open the envelope, read the contents, and thrust the paper in front of Cameron's eyes.

"Look!"

"I would if you'd hold still," he said.

"I got a five! That's six hours of college credit! I can't believe it!" Ann was fairly buzzing with excitement.

"That's fantastic," said Cameron. He grabbed Ann in a bear hug, lifted her off the ground, and spun her around on the edge of the dusty country road. Ann looked up at Cameron with smiling eyes. They stood and laughed, never hearing the slow-moving Cadillac coming down the hill.

"What's going on here?"

Ann and Cameron snapped to attention at the sound of Miss Genevieve's sharp question from the passenger's seat. She leaned across and looked out the open driver's side window, a blue straw hat accentuating her piercing gaze.

"Ann won an essay contest, and her Advanced Placement History results came in the mail. She got the highest score possible," Cameron said.

"Congratulations, Ann," Miss Winifred said. She was caught up in their excitement and clapped her hands.

"That's excellent news, Ann. However, you may wish to refrain from physical contact with a boy in public. Someone might get the wrong idea," said Miss Genevieve.

"Yes, of course," Ann said, cutting off Cameron's chuckle with a subtle elbow to the gut.

"Winifred, drive on. We'll be late to our church meeting."

Miss Winifred gave the two teenagers an impish wink as she rolled up the window and put the great white car in drive.

"Wonderful. Those two will probably tell the entire county what they saw or think they saw," said Ann.

"No, they'll be too busy talking about your accomplishments."

"I hope you're right. At least they didn't see me tear the postcard in two," Ann said.

"What postcard?"

Ann fished the pieces out of the mailbox and handed them to him. "From my father."

Cameron held them together and read. "Is he always this verbose?"

"That's been the story of this entire year. He doesn't call, and I've received a total of two postcards that might as well be addressed to a stranger."

"It sounds like he's still touring."

Ann sighed. "If you're trying to politely tell me that he's not going to get a real job and I'll be here for my senior year, there's no need to beat around the bush. I've known that for a long time."

"You OK with that?"

"Yeah. I mean, I have friends and a best friend and activities here. And my grandparents, of course. I never had any of that before."

"And a certain best friend's brother to tease you."

Ann rolled her eyes. "Yeah, him, too."

"So what's the problem?"

"Have you ever stopped to think what it feels like to know your own father doesn't care enough about you to give up his pipe dream and settle down?"

Cameron ran his hand through his hair. "Well, my dad's not going to win any awards for responsibility either, despite what Corrie says. He's fantastic at buying gifts but not at being there when you need him. You might've noticed I don't go to KC nearly as much as Corrie does. I didn't even go visit him much after my parents got divorced and we still lived there. We always ended up in a fight."

"I'm sorry. I noticed you didn't go, but I never asked why."

"It's OK. I'm over it. I always wanted to be a vet, so moving to Storey and working with John has been good for me. John's a good guy, and he makes Mom happy."

"I'm glad," Ann managed a smile. She wouldn't dream of telling him about the old letter she'd found among her mother's things.

"So I get it. Just remember what your dad does isn't your fault. Don't blame yourself," he said.

"I know you're right. If it's one thing I've learned, you can't make someone love you."

Cameron swallowed and put his hands in his pockets. "No," he said quietly, "you can't."

An uncomfortable silence settled between them for a breath.

"Well, I'd better go. I want to share my news with Grandma and Grandpa," Ann said.

"You'll have to hurry. The Page sisters probably already got word to them somehow."

Ann laughed and walked to Bessie. Despite the disappointing postcard from her father, she still felt happy with her achievements. Tomorrow was still a new day, with new horizons to follow, new dreams to dream, another door to pass through.

She put the truck in gear and gave one last wave to Cameron. He stood there a moment longer, leaning against the truck with his hands in his pockets, watching Ann drive away from him down the lane.

32

The Gate

Grandpa peeked his head in the back door just as Ann and Grandma finished doing the Sunday breakfast dishes.

"Ann, could you run up and check the water level in the tank in the pasture? Arthur hasn't fixed the pump yet, and it's too hot for the cattle to be without water. I'm trying to figure out what's wrong with the air conditioner in the car before we go to church," he said.

"Sure."

Sam bounded around her while she walked to the truck, his entire back end wagging a plea to go along. She opened Bessie's door, and Sam jumped in, his nose instantly raised to the partially opened window on the passenger side.

"I'm glad we can take a little drive, Sam. I need to edit an essay Miss Genevieve asked me to write for the Historical Society newsletter, but I'd rather be outside. Somehow, I've become an honorary member of the Society—the only one under sixty. I guess I don't mind, because I interviewed Grandpa, and I'm writing about Sunflower Lane, but revision is so tedious. It's one thing to sit down and let the words flow out onto a page, but it's quite another to revise. There is so little scope for the imagination in revision; it's just the nose-to-the-grindstone work of thinking about each word and phrase. And sometimes, you have to send your favorite ones to the guillotine. OK, Sam. You stay here."

Ann had arrived at the pasture entrance where she opened the gate, pulled through, and closed the gate after her as if she had been doing it her entire life. It was moments like this when Ann felt pleased with how well she had mastered some of the chores and tasks around the farm. She drove through the ruts across the pasture, chatting to Sam the whole way about her essay and her job, for he was an excellent listener.

Once at the windmill, Ann left the truck idling while she stepped cautiously around the cow patties to check the level in the tank. There was plenty of fresh water, so Ann allowed herself a moment to gaze off across the blowing grass to the horizon beyond, shimmery in the early morning warmth of the day. Ann leaned on the bed of the truck, her eyes tracing the swells of that "fitting floor for this magnificent temple of the sky."

"Just imagine what this must have looked like to the pioneers who first settled this area. That was thanks partly to the Homestead Act, as anyone earning six hours of credit on her AP History exam could tell you."

Sam barked and wagged his tail, running back and forth across the bench seat of the truck.

"You're right. Enough daydreaming. I'd better go home and get ready for church."

Ann circled Bessie back around. She bounced across the pasture and through the gate, singing along to the radio. She had changed into her dress and returned to the coolness of the living room to work on her essay when the phone rang.

"Who on earth could that be right before church?" said Grandma as she hurried to the phone. "Hello . . . Slow down, Herman . . . Yes, Arthur has a few head of cattle up there . . . What . . . ? Oh, dear . . . Yes, I'll tell Bernard, and he'll head up right away and meet you."

They all converged in the dining room where Grandma stood wringing her hands.

"The cattle are out. Herman Bentley saw them all across the road and went straight home to call us and get his horse. He said he'll meet you there and help you round them up. I'll call John and see if he can take his horse and come, too."

"But they were right there when I checked the water this morning," said Ann.

"Ann Alwyn, did you forget to shut that gate?" asked Grandma.

"No, I shut it. I distinctly remember shutting it."

"Well, it certainly didn't open itself," said Grandma.

"I'm positive I shut it," Ann said.

"You clearly can't be trusted to do even the simplest of tasks," said Grandma.

The comment cut to the quick.

Grandpa had gone to change his clothes, and he now appeared with such a serious look on her face that Ann's heart fell.

"Let me change, and I'll go with you and help," she said, as she rushed up the stairs.

But Grandpa was already out the door and jogging to the truck.

"He must be just as furious with me as Grandma is. But I was so sure I closed that gate. I must not have, or something happened, and I didn't get it closed right. I really messed up this time." Ann sank to the floor at her window and watched Grandpa roar out the lane, spewing gravel as he went.

Ann sat staring outside in agony without turning on a fan. It seemed as if she could only look hard enough, she'd be able to see if she'd closed the gate. She thought she had, but Grandma was right: how else could the cattle be out? Could she have been so careless as to fail to comply with the cardinal rule of pasture checking, closing the gate? It was thousands of times worse than accidentally selling the neighbor's Jersey cow like Anne Shirley did. Ann knew she'd never forgive herself if something happened to any of those cattle. She and Grandma were starting to really get along, and she'd thought she'd finally won her over. But now, she had gone and done something unutterably stupid.

Ann worried and thought out any number of unhappy endings to the calamity in which she found herself as she sat in her hot room. At last, Grandpa returned, and Ann's heart pounded so hard she felt weak. It would be better to rise, go downstairs, and learn the extent of the damage from the havoc her heedlessness had wrought, but she found she could not stand. Ann heard the door at the foot of the stairs open and steps ascend.

"Hop up here and dry those tears," Grandpa said.

"I can't. I made a terrible mistake, worse than any I ever made in my entire life, and trust me, that's saying something. I have colossally messed up."

"No, you did not colossally mess up."

"Yes, I did. I'm sure I must have forgotten to close the gate. I know you always say we all make mistakes, but it's a question of degree. This was not a mistake; this was a catastrophe! You told me to always remember to shut the gate, the very first day I was here. But could I remember that one, teeny, tiny instruction? No, I could not."

"You did shut the gate."

"What?"

"Arthur came just as we started rounding up the cattle off the road. He went in after you did this morning to work on that pump—finally. The minute he heard his cattle were out, he said he remembered he hadn't shut that gate because he was talking on the CB when he left the pasture. It wasn't your fault. Besides, we rounded up all the cattle and got them back in the pasture, safe and sound. They're all fine."

"What a relief. But I admit I was daydreaming a little in the pasture, so I could have forgotten. I need to be more serious."

"But you didn't forget, and there'll be time enough to face the harsh realities of this old world."

Ann smiled feebly. "That sounds like something Matthew Cuthbert said to Anne Shirley."

"He must know what he's talking about. Come on. Let's go down and have some ice cream and forget about it."

"I'm not sure ice cream can 'minister to a mind diseased.'"

"Give it a try," said Grandpa. "It's always been my experience there's not much in this world that can't be made better with ice cream."

"You go on. I'll be there in a second."

Ann listened to Grandpa's heavy steps on the stairs. She was relieved nothing had happened to the cattle and that she had not been to blame for the open gate. But Grandma's stinging words still rang in her ears.

"She doesn't trust me." Ann leaned her elbows on her windowsill and rested her chin in her hands. "Even after all this time, no matter what I do right, even after doing our skit together, she still thinks I can't be trusted."

She saw John Alexander's truck and horse trailer go north across the highway. Cameron was probably with him, had probably helped with the round-up.

"And if she can't trust me enough to believe me when I said I closed the gate, she'd never trust me enough to be more than friends with Cameron."

33

The Truth

Ann had put the last dish away and triple-checked the kitchen. It was a Tuesday evening, and Grandma and Grandpa were at a meeting to begin planning the senior citizens' float for the Labor Day parade. Grandma had left her in charge of cleaning up after supper, and Ann had no intentions of making another mistake. She'd already gotten in trouble for not getting the counter clean enough after helping make supper. One dressing down was always more than enough for one day. Grandma seemed to be especially critical this week; she seemed fed-up with having a teenager around.

Ann was rinsing the dishcloth after one last wipe of the table when the phone rang.

"I hope it's not Herman Bentley. He never believes I'm not Grandma when I answer, although I don't think I sound much like her," said Ann as she hurried to answer. "Hello?"

"Hey, kiddo. It's Dad. What's up?"

Ann was so surprised she was speechless for a moment. "Oh, hello. Not much," she said.

"Are your grandparents there? I need to talk to them." He slurred his words.

Straight to the point, and drunk as well. "No, they're at a meeting. Could I take a message?" she said in her best farm implement store sales voice.

"Yeah, sure. I'm touring right now, so I don't have any idea when I could call again."

"Of course," said Ann, a bitter edge to her voice.

"Look, the band is just about to go big, you know?"

"Mm hmm?" said Ann. *That's what you told me last summer. Come to think of it, that's what I've heard about every single one of your second-rate bands my whole life.*

"So you know, I gotta follow that dream. You know me. I've always been an artist. I just can't see myself tied to a nine-to-five."

"Not even to get your daughter back." It was a statement, not a question.

"You're out of line." Dad's tone hardened.

"And what exactly is the message you'd like me to give to Grandma and Grandpa?" Anger seethed through every syllable.

"Tell them they can keep you. It's not like I ever wanted you anyway. I already had Sabrina. Your mother's the one who wanted kids. You were just an unwelcome surprise a year after we got married. And you killed her."

Anger and hurt surged through Ann in parallel waves. *I will not cry; I will not.* She cleared her throat and forced herself to speak as if she were only dealing with a grouchy customer in Uncle Edward's store. She would not give him the satisfaction of knowing he'd upset her.

"Then why didn't you just let me come to Sunflower Lane years ago?" Ann countered. The different life she might have led pierced her heart.

"And let them think I wasn't good enough for their precious daughter?"

"So you were selfish," Ann said.

"Young lady . . ."

Ann cut him off. "Just stop. Look, I'll be happy to relay your message to Grandma and Grandpa. Is there anything else?"

"No. I've already talked to my lawyer, so they'll hear from him about custody."

And then he hung up.

Ann sat, a mix of rage and hurt and confusion roiling inside her. She pressed her lips together, willing herself not to shed a single tear over her father's cruelty—not just for how he'd treated her now. She would not cry for all the ways he'd neglected and mistreated her across the years, all the ways she'd forced herself to discount or minimize his actions to survive. When child services and the judge had put a name to his behavior, she'd refused to acknowledge it because she knew it was true. They'd been right all along—he *had* failed to provide for her basic needs; he *had* neglected her. All the times he'd left her hungry, cold, sick, in deplorable living conditions, with her abusive older sister, and above all, alone, flickered across her mind's eye in a fast-playing reel of film.

The phone rang again. Ann snatched it up.

"Forget to tell me something?" she said hotly.

"Ann?"

Ann let out a breath. "Corrie. I'm sorry."

"Who did you think I was?"

"My father."

"Oh, no. What did he do now?" asked Corrie.

Ann exhaled harshly. "Where to begin?"

"How about with a drive in my new car? You can tell me all about it."

"You have a car?" said Ann.

"Yeah. It's really a used car, but it's new to me. Dad got it for me for my birthday. Wanna take a ride?"

Ann hesitated for a second. She knew the rules. She knew she wasn't supposed to go anywhere without asking for permission. But Grandma and Grandpa wouldn't be back for a couple of hours, and if she didn't tell someone the horrible things her father had said, she'd implode.

"Yes. Let's go," said Ann.

"I'll be right over."

Ann grabbed her purse, locked up the house, and was waiting for Corrie on the front porch when she pulled into the laneway in a small, blue compact.

"Nice ride," Ann said.

"Thanks. Where to?"

"Wherever. I just want out."

"Let's take the back roads into town and go get ice cream," said Corrie.

"Sounds good."

Corrie slipped a cassette in and hit play. "I can even listen to my own tunes."

"It really is a nice car. You'll be in charge of driving us everywhere now unless you want to ride in Bessie."

"Thanks. I love it. Mom was not happy with Dad for getting me a car, and John was really ticked about it. I think he's just jealous my father can afford to give me nice things. I am so sick of having to deal with him. I swear, sometimes I wish I could go live with Dad in KC, especially if you do end up back in Denver."

"That's not going to happen," said Ann.

"Is that what your dad said when he called?"

"That, and more. He's giving my grandparents custody so he can pursue his dream of being a worthless, second-rate musician fulltime. And then he told me that he'd never wanted me."

"What?"

"Yes. Just what everyone wants to hear from their parent."

"Ouch. Like, seriously. I can't imagine hearing that. Even John wouldn't say something like that, and he's an ogre. Do you think you'll ever speak to him again?"

"I honestly don't know. I sure don't want to talk to him now, and maybe ever. You know, the truth is, I didn't want to go back to Denver. I haven't wanted to for a long time. I've never had it as good as I do at Sunflower Lane. I just wanted my father to care enough to try. I suppose, somewhere deep inside, I've known all along he'd never wanted me. But to hear I was just a mistake a year after they got married . . ." Ann stopped short as the meaning of her words made its full impact.

"What's the matter?"

"A year, Corrie! A *year!*"

"Ann, I'm not following you."

"The Misses Page told me my parents eloped. I didn't know that, and I started wondering if they'd had to get married because Mom was expecting me. I never knew their anniversary, and I couldn't think of a way to ask without upsetting Grandma. Besides, I wasn't even sure I really wanted to know the truth. But it would've made sense, wouldn't it? You know how no one ever seems to want to talk about her. But if I was born a year after, that wasn't the case."

"How come you never told me any of this?" asked Corrie.

"Because it was all so overwhelming."

"No more secrets. Trust your bosom friend, OK?" Corrie turned and smiled.

Ann opened her mouth to respond when she saw the flash of white just beyond Corrie's face.

"Look . . . !"

The one-ton pickup lurched out of the pasture entrance before Corrie could react. Ann heard the crash, the screech of contorting metal, and the shattering of glass as the car bumped off the road and into the ditch. The world spun for a moment. Then, everything was silent.

Ann opened her eyes against the pain she felt throughout her entire body. She looked, stupefied, around her. The roof was caved in from the roll, safety glass littered the floorboard around her feet, and the decorative trim had blown off the vents in front of her. They were sitting upright in a pasture. She looked across to Corrie.

"Corrie?" Ann said.

Corrie didn't respond or move.

"You OK?" A farmer Ann didn't know was at the window. He'd left his truck up on the road and scrambled down the ditch and into the pasture.

"My friend's not answering," Ann said, her throat thick.

"I already called for an ambulance on the CB. They're on their way," he assured her.

Ann tried to open her door, but it wouldn't budge. "I can't get out. Please check on my friend," she said, choking on her tears.

"You stay put. It's better not to move." He gently laid his rough fingers on Corrie's neck. "She has a pulse. Looks like she bumped her head."

"Will she be OK?" Ann said, the tears running down her face. They carried the taste of blood with them.

"I hope to the good Lord above she is. I didn't see you. I wasn't looking." He rubbed a hand over his eyes. "I'd better call your parents."

"My friend is Ellen Alexander's daughter. And I live with my grandparents, but they're at a meeting at the senior center."

"Who are your grandparents?"

"The Holmbergs. They're all I have," Ann said. She choked on the words.

"I'll be right back," he said. He jogged up to his waiting truck.

Ann looked at her bosom friend, immobile and silent. She reached out a hand and held Corrie's. "Please . . ." she said in a ragged prayer. "Please . . ."

34

Revelations

Ann couldn't stop the flow of tears. They streaked her face, and her nose ran. She was a blubbering mess. Every single fiber of her being ached. But nothing hurt as badly as the avalanche of truths that had hit her that afternoon. Dad didn't want her back, never had intended to try to get her back, had never wanted her in the first place. And now, Corrie was lying unconscious somewhere in the cold, antiseptic-reeking hospital.

Ann heard the curtain being slid open, but she didn't open her eyes or raise her head. A hand gently brushed the hair from her forehead above the line of stitches.

"Honey," It was a voice Ann thought she should recognize, but it was so thick with tears she couldn't.

She opened her eyes to find Grandma leaning over her. "Grandma?"

"Oh, Ann, I thought we'd lost you." Grandma dropped to the chair beside her bed and buried her head beside her granddaughter's bruised body. Her shoulders shook.

"Thelma, it's all right. The doctor said she's only going to be sore," Grandpa said quietly. He rested his hands on Grandma's shoulders.

"How can you say that, Bernard?" Grandma looked up, raising her voice far louder than Ann had ever heard her. "She could have died. And it would have been Amelia all over again. It would have been my fault again for not knowing how to protect our girls."

Some glimmer of understanding pierced the fog of Ann's aching head.

"You blame yourself for Mom," she said quietly.

"Of course I do! I never approved of her engagement, but I agreed against my better judgment. Then he convinced her to run off with him before they could have a real wedding. He took her away and made her miserable. He didn't take care of her, but I didn't either. And try as I might, I couldn't take care of you, either."

"Yes, you did. It's my fault for going off with Corrie without asking your permission. You've always done your duty by me."

"Duty?" Grandma wiped a hand across her eyes. "Do you think that's all you've been to us?"

Ann looked down at her hands, watched the IV drip into her veins, wondered if the pain medication could numb a hurting heart. She nodded silently.

Grandpa spoke softly. "Surely by now you know that's not true."

Grandma reached for Ann's hand. "No, she probably doesn't. Not after all my rules and how strict and critical I've been. I was afraid—afraid of not taking care of you, and afraid I'd grow to care too much for you. Your father could come and take you away whenever he got his life together, and then I'd never see you again. Just like Amelia. You do favor her, you know—you look so much like your mother, and you have so many of the same expressions and gestures. But it happened anyway—you made me love you, and I love you just as much as ever I did your mother and Janis."

"You do?"

"Yes, I do."

"We both do," said Grandpa.

"I don't know what I'll do if Jake takes you away," Grandma said.

"I wouldn't worry about my father taking me anywhere. That's not happening."

"We can't know that," said Grandma.

"Oh, yes we can. He called while you were gone. He's not even trying to get a steady job because he doesn't want me. He made that abundantly clear. He said you can keep me."

"He did?" Grandpa asked.

"Yes. He said he 'just can't see himself tied to a nine-to-five' and that you'll hear from his lawyer. That's what he told me. And that he'd never wanted me. That's why I left with Corrie when she called. I was angry with him, and I thought you were tired of having me here. And more than anything, I want to stay at Sunflower Lane. It's the only place that's ever felt like home."

Grandma grasped her hand and smiled at Grandpa. "She's staying!"

Grandpa laughed his deep, resonant laugh and wrapped them both in his gentle embrace. "So I heard."

"Forever, if it's all right with you," Ann said.

"Of course, it is," Grandpa said.

Grandma kissed Ann's forehead gently. "They want to keep you overnight, just to be safe. But we'll take you home in the morning."

"How is Corrie? No one's told me anything."

Grandma gave Grandpa a worried frown.

"Please just tell me the truth," said Ann.

"She hasn't come to yet," said Grandpa.

"She had a nasty bump on her head, despite the seatbelts," said Grandma.

"Do they think she'll be OK?"

"We're praying for her. We saw John and Cameron in the waiting area, and that's all they knew," said Grandpa.

"We have to trust she'll be fine," Grandma said.

Ann nodded. "Whatever happens, just be straight with me, OK? No more secrets."

"What do you mean?" asked Grandpa.

"Like about my parents eloping. I already knew, by the way."

Grandma furrowed her brow. "I can about guess how you found out. The Page sisters?"

"Yeah. And until today, I thought they might have skipped the wedding because I was on the way. But Dad set me straight when he went on his tirade about never wanting me."

"How you must have suffered thinking that," said Grandma. "But that's not what happened."

"What did happen, then?"

Grandma glanced at Grandpa. He nodded.

"Your father told her if she didn't elope with him, it was over. And Amelia was so in love she let him persuade her," Grandma said.

"So he manipulated her. How very typical of him," said Ann.

"We took it real hard," Grandpa said. "Your mom never had done anything so rash before. She was smart and creative, and real responsible. She loved her home, and she respected us. She was swept off her feet, and she didn't think. But we still loved her. We never cut her out of our lives, and we tried to support her in her new life."

Ann digested the information. "I get the rules now," she said, squeezing Grandma's hand.

Grandma touched her face gently. "And then she died. It's still painful, even after all these years, but we should've told you the truth. I'm sorry we didn't, and I promise: no more secrets."

"And I won't have any secrets from you," said Ann. "Which means I'd better tell you about the Teddy Bear and . . ."

Before Ann could finish, the nurse opened the curtain. "Ready to go to your room?"

"Yeah. These pain meds are making me pretty sleepy."

Grandma and Grandpa followed them to Ann's room. Her eyes were growing heavy by the time she arrived. The last thing she remembered before drifting off to a dreamless sleep was the image of both of them holding her hands.

Ann awoke to the first streaks of dawn. Disoriented, she looked around, attempting to determine where she was. Her eyes tried to focus in the half-light. The multiple aches piercing her body brought everything back in a rush.

"Corrie," she said thickly, trying to sit up. She moaned in pain.

"Are you OK?" Cameron's shadow fell across her.

"Yeah, I think so. I just ache everywhere. Where are my grandparents?"

"They went to the cafeteria for a cup of coffee. They were here all night. They saw me in the waiting room, and the first thing your grandma wanted to do was feed me. But there's no way I could eat a thing. My gut's in a knot."

"How come you're not with Corrie?"

"She's still in ICU. She hasn't come to yet." Cameron's voice broke. "They're only letting Mom or Dad in one at a time, and just for a little bit. John and I are stuck in the waiting room."

The tears welled in Ann's eyes.

"Hey, don't cry. I didn't come in here to upset you." He sat in the chair beside her bed and took her hand.

"You'd probably better leave before my grandma gets back. Things are perfect with her now, and I don't want to mess it up."

"Are you kidding me? She's the one who told me to come."

"Really?"

"Yeah. She walked to the main desk and informed the nurses that I was your best friend's brother and would be good medicine for you, so they'd better look the other way on the visiting hours policy."

"*My* grandma? Thelma Holmberg?"

"Yeah. That's her. I think what she really meant is you'd be good medicine for me. If anything happens to Corrie . . ."

Ann squeezed his hand. They sat in silence for several minutes.

"I should've told her 'no,' you know," Ann said at last. "When she called and suggested we go for a drive. But I was just so mad at my father . . ."

"Hey, now. Stop it. The other driver admitted he was at fault. He was messing with the radio and tore out onto the road without looking."

"But we wouldn't even have been on that road if I hadn't agreed to go."

"Let's be honest: you wouldn't even have been there if my dad hadn't decided to keep trying to buy my sister's loyalty by giving her a car," said Cameron.

"None of it matters as long as Corrie's OK."

"She will be. She has to be."

A soft knock came at the door. John Alexander entered the room, a smile across his face.

"Cam, your sister's awake," he said.

"She is?" Cameron stood.

"Yeah. And as soon as your mom and dad step out, they said you could go see her for a few minutes. Head on down so you can put on all that garb to go in."

Cameron squeezed Ann's hand. "I'll be back."

"Tell her 'hi' from her bosom friend," she said.

John laughed as he watched Cameron leave. Then, he turned to Ann and stood looking thoughtfully at her, his cap in his callused hands. "How're you feeling today?"

"Sore."

"Sorry to hear that. I got tossed by a colt once, and then he jumped on me like a trampoline. It'll hurt like the dickens for a while, but give it time."

"Thanks," said Ann. She studied the kindly face of the man who had loved her mother.

"You sure do look like your mother," John said, as if reading her mind.

"You knew her well?"

John flushed, and looked at his hands, twisting the cap. "Sure enough. We grew up together. We were real good friends. Truth is, I was in love with her. Problem was, she didn't feel the same way. She was real smart, and I thought after she finished college, maybe I'd stand a chance. But then she met your dad. I was devastated when she died. But I'd better hold my tongue. You probably don't want to hear all this sentimental mumbo jumbo from your best friend's stepdad. I guess I'm still a little keyed up over the accident. Don't know what I'd do if something happened to Corrie."

Ann smiled and reached out her hand. John took it awkwardly.

"I think I'll always want to hear about my mother from those who knew her and loved her well."

"That sounds just like something Amelia would've said."

"Sit with me?" Ann pointed to the chair. "Just until Grandma and Grandpa come back. Tell me more of what you remember about Mom."

John sat beside her. "What do you want to know?"

"Everything."

35

The River of a Dream

"**D**o you remember the time the mouse got in your hair?" asked Grandma with a laugh. She and Ann were sitting on the front porch enjoying the breeze, sipping lemonade, and eating cookies as Tiger and Sam napped on the cool concrete beside them.

"I'll remember that until the day I die," Ann said with a shudder. "How about the time I put the biscuits back in the oven?"

"How could I forget? It was the first time in decades there'd been a burned biscuit at Sunflower Lane. But you've learned to be a fine baker," Grandma said.

"As you always say, 'practice makes perfect.'"

"Have you picked up all my sayings this past year?" asked Grandma.

"Maybe one or two," Ann said with a grin over her glass.

Grandma returned her smile. "I guess we're kindred spirts after all."

"I think you might have picked up some of my sayings, too."

"Maybe one or two," Grandma said, reaching out and taking Ann's hand.

They had spent the past two days talking and getting to know each other as they never had during all the months before. Grandma and Grandpa both shared anecdotes about their daughter, and Grandma produced a box of letters they had exchanged when Amelia was at college and in the months before Ann's birth. Between the letters, what her grandparents told her, and the stories John shared in the hospital, Ann now had the clearest image she'd ever had of her mother. All the terrifying what-if's she had allowed herself to imagine vanished. What was more, Ann had the clearest image of herself she'd ever had, too. She was shedding the fictions with which her father and stepsister had cloaked her and those she'd written for herself and becoming her own Ann.

"It looks like someone's coming in the lane," said Grandma.

"It's Cameron. He said he'd let me know how Corrie's doing. I can't wait until I can visit her myself."

"What a nice boy. It's so thoughtful of him to bring you updates. And call to see how you're doing."

"What are you insinuating?"

"Oh, nothing," Grandma said while Cameron parked. He waved as he walked to the porch.

"How is she?" asked Ann by way of greeting.

He grinned. "Hello to you, too."

Grandma laughed. "She goes straight to the point, doesn't she? Cameron, please feel free to sit down before you feel obligated to answer Ann's questions."

"Thanks, Mrs. Holmberg. And Corrie's doing fine. She has a bad headache yet, and she's sore like you are, but she'll be OK. She remembers everything about the wreck, which is a good sign."

"I'm so relieved," said Ann.

"They're keeping her in traction for a while, and she'll have to have some physical therapy for the broken leg. You can imagine how well she'll like being on crutches."

"The important thing is she's going to be all right," Grandma said.

"Agreed," Cam and Ann said in unison.

Grandma offered him a glass of lemonade and some of her chocolate chip cookies. They sat and chatted about Cameron's upcoming year at Kansas State.

"Would you like some more?" asked Grandma.

"No, thanks. I couldn't eat another bite," said Cameron.

"Then, could I ask you to do me a favor?" Grandma smiled sweetly.

"Sure. What is it?"

"The doctor told Ann she should be sure to move around and walk so she doesn't get stiff. We've sat here and talked since supper. Would you be a gentleman and accompany her on a short walk?"

Ann and Cameron stared.

"A walk?" said Cameron.

"Together?" said Ann.

"Yes. Maybe just down Lover's Lane to that spot you call Idlewild. That should be far enough. And if you're tired, sit down there and rest a spell before you come back. Ann needs to walk, but don't overdo it. You two can talk there just as well as here," said Grandma.

"OK," said Cameron. He stood, unable to hide the grin on his face.

Slowly, Ann started to rise. "Ow, ow, ow."

Cameron extended a hand to help her up. She took it, then dropped it as soon as she was standing.

"You're sure you don't want to come along?" she asked Grandma.

"In this heat? No, thank you. I'll leave that to you young folks. Besides, I have a willing walker to go with you. I trust you," Grandma said meeting Ann's eyes. "Both of you."

They made their way slowly across the yard and down the lane. Ann's stiff joints loosened as they went.

"Let me know if you need to stop," said Cameron.

"I will. Once I get moving, it isn't so bad."

"Corrie had a message for you.

"What is it?"

"She said to tell you she's sorry she got you in a wreck."

"Be sure to tell her I don't blame her. Or even the guy who hit us. It was an accident."

"That's what I told her, but you know my sister. She also said to say, 'as long as the sun and the moon shall endure.' Whatever that means. She made me repeat it about a dozen times."

"It's from . . ."

"Wait, let me guess. *Anne of Green Gables?*"

"Of course," Ann said.

They turned into Lover's Lane, the grass alongside it whispering as they passed. They followed the rutted path to Idlewild and stood in the dappled light, watching the softly flowing waters of the creek gliding by as "the river of a dream." Ann leaned her head against the rough bark of the nearby tree. She traced the old scars of Clarence's knife, her finger following the heart he'd carved around his and Lily's initials. They would always be a part of Sunflower Lane, and now, so would she.

"You want to sit a little while?" asked Cameron.

"I'd better." Ann began to lower herself onto one of the rocks in the circle. Cameron reached out a steadying hand to help her.

"Quite the last couple of days," he said at last.

"I could do with something a little less thrilling. I think I'll leave the adventure to the novels."

"Me, too."

"Corrie knows this, but you probably don't yet. I'm staying at Sunflower Lane. Permanently. My dad doesn't want me back. In fact, he made sure to tell me he'd never wanted me."

"That's great! I mean, that you're staying. Not the part about your dad saying that."

"I'll be OK. In fact, I'm really happy. Honestly, I'd have been miserable if I had to go back to living the way I did before. I've never had a home until now, and even with Grandma's rules, I've never had so much freedom."

"So maybe I'll see you when I come back from college on breaks." He concentrated on the creek.

"Maybe you will."

They sat in silence as the first threads of darkness fell, wrapped in the summer symphony of frogs and cicadas and crickets. Finally, Cameron stood.

"I suppose we'd better head back before it gets dark." He offered Ann his hand and helped her stand. This time, she didn't let go.

* * *

"I've come bearing raspberry cordial," Ann said. She peeked around the hospital room door.

"Ann!" Corrie cried from her bed. It was the first time the girls had seen each other since the accident.

Ann deposited a stack of books on Corrie's bedside table along with a bouquet of flowers from Grandma's garden. She hugged her friend. "I've missed you."

"I've missed you, too. I'm so glad I can finally have visitors. And where's that cordial?"

"They wouldn't let me bring the real thing, so I've brought the books instead."

Corrie studied the stack. "The whole series?"

"The whole series. A certain bosom friend I know loaned me hers on the first day she met me, and then she gave me my own set for my birthday."

"She sounds pretty special."

"She is."

"Thanks for the books, and the flowers. Did you see that huge arrangement John brought me?"

"So maybe he's not quite an ogre after all," said Ann.

"Maybe. He was totally freaked out by the accident. He said, 'Corrie, I'm an old dog, but I'll do my best to learn the new trick of being a better stepdad.' It was a typical John statement, but kind of sweet, to be honest."

"I'm glad. I think he is a genuinely nice guy."

Corrie shrugged. "Yeah, you might be right. Listen, I remember everything from the afternoon of the accident, including what you told me about your dad's call and your parents eloping. I meant what I said, too. I'll always be here for you."

"I know. Me, too."

"You're OK? I mean, after what your dad said."

"Yeah, I think am. If there's one good thing to come out of this whole experience, it's that Grandma finally opened up. She's spent years blaming herself for my mother's death. I guess somewhere deep inside, I always blamed myself, too. But now, we talk about everything. I never dreamed she and I could be this close. She laughs, and she's understanding and patient. It's like I've found another grandmother entirely hidden under the skin of the old one."

"That's so awesome. Do you think she'll still have all her rules?"

"I don't know. But if she does, I'll at least understand her reasons now. That makes a big difference."

"Because you know, if she eased up on the 'no boys' rule, you and Cam could go out."

"You really aren't going to let that go, are you?"

"Nope. I want my happy ending."

Ann laughed. "Are we seriously going to sit here and talk about your brother? Come on, I haven't seen you in an eternity! Let's discuss everything we're going to do now that we know I'm staying."

"You mean once I'm out of here and can walk on those stupid crutches without falling."

"You won't let a little thing like crutches stop you, and you know it. Come on. Let's start planning."

Corrie grinned. "Well, I think we should do another skit for next year's talent show. Maybe this time we could recruit Cam and do the slate-breaking scene."

"That has potential. As long as I really get to break a slate over his head."

"And we need to have an honest-to-goodness tea party for the other girls. With fancy dresses and all the food and everything."

"I know just the recipes. The Misses Page gave them to me."

"And we need to start saving money, because someday, you and I are going to Prince Edward Island."

"Promise?"

"Promise."

36

The Open Door

Ann sat once again on the swing at the edge of the garden, just as she had on her first day at Sunflower Lane. That afternoon seemed a lifetime ago. She rocked gently back and forth, her feet never leaving the ground as she looked out across the now-familiar panorama of limitless views. Butterflies and dragonflies danced among the fragrant purple blossoms of the nearby butterfly bush, and the wind whispered in the leaves of the oak tree overhead.

"I guess that old swing still works," Grandpa said.

Ann smiled softly up at him. She cherished this kindred spirit who had given her a home, a beloved novel, and somewhere in between, a sense of belonging.

"Still does," Ann said.

"Can't believe how fast this past year has gone. It seems like you just came to live with us here at Sunflower Lane, and this time next year, you'll be leaving for college." He laid his work-worn hand on her shoulder.

"Grandma would tell you not to borrow trouble and that 'tomorrow will take care of itself.'" She took his hand. "That's a whole year away. Besides, you can't get rid of me that easily. I'm going to K-State, just like Mom did, and I'll come home for all the breaks."

"Sunflower Lane will always be your home, even when you go off to college, so you come as often as you want," Grandpa said.

"Thank you, Grandpa—for everything you and Grandma have done for me this past year. I can't imagine what my life would be like if I'd never come to Sunflower Lane."

Grandpa smiled into her clear, blue eyes. "We can't either. And you're welcome."

The sound of gravel crunching under tires drew their gaze back to the laneway where Cameron was pulling in.

"Looks like you've got company." Grandpa grinned.

Cameron had been a regular visitor since the accident, at first to bring news of Corrie to Ann, and then to check on Ann's recovery. He had helped Ann through the rough days after the wreck and her father's revelation, when she was unable to visit Corrie. Later, when Corrie was home, he offered to pick Ann up to visit her and drop her off afterwards. He even helped a convalescing Corrie make a cake for Ann's birthday that week. Despite Ann's first misgivings, Grandma had welcomed Cameron. Just last night, she told Ann the "no boys" rule was no longer necessary, as long as Ann was always open and truthful about whom she was seeing and where she was going.

"Think I'll head in and see what Grandma is up to," said Grandpa.

"You're welcome to stay."

"No, you two clearly have a lot to talk about."

Grandpa turned before Ann could reply, walking to the house with a wave to Cameron as he approached.

"Hello, Ann." Cameron leaned against the towering oak tree while Ann swayed in the swing. A warm, sweet breeze tousled her hair, and the cicadas hummed around them, singing the nostalgic song of the approaching end of summer. "I hope I didn't run your grandpa off."

"No, he said he was just leaving." Ann felt her cheeks warm. She twisted back and forth in the swing to hide her discomfort.

"Well, I'm off to K-State tomorrow."

"Are you nervous?"

"Not really. You ready for your senior year?"

"Yes. I want to do well in school to earn scholarships, but I'm going to keep working for Uncle Edward, too. I want to enjoy my time here. I've spent the better part of my life moving around, and it's good to feel I have roots. I hope I can find the right balance."

"Don't worry; you'll be fine."

"You think so?"

"Of course. Here, let me push you. All your twisting around is making me dizzy." Cameron reached down to grasp the rope below Ann's hands.

"No pranks," she warned.

"I wouldn't dream of it."

He pulled the swing, and Ann swung evenly back and forth, Cameron's steady hands gently pushing against the small of her back. Several moments passed in silence before she glanced back, the bright heads of the sunflowers in Grandma's garden a blur behind him. She leaped lightly from the swing and turned to face the frank eyes of the boy who had become such a part of her life in the last year. She hesitated for a moment before wrapping her arms around him.

"Thanks, Cam," Ann said quietly against his chest. His arms held her close.

"For what?"

She stepped back and looked up at him. "You've always been there, even when I pushed you away. You helped me get through these last few weeks—and the entire year, really. Grandma was right: you're good medicine."

"It's mutual," he said.

Ann's gaze faltered under the seriousness of Cameron's eyes. Why, oh, why was this so much harder than in books?

"Listen, I came over and talked with your grandparents this afternoon while you were with Corrie," he said.

"Trying to get a care package out of Grandma before you leave for K-State?"

"Well, I wouldn't turn it down. But no. I had a question for them."

"Oh?"

"Yeah. I wanted to know if it'd be OK if I call you sometimes from college. And visit when I'm back. And maybe take you to a movie or for dinner."

Ann felt the same fluttery feeling as she had the night they stood on the front porch after prom. "And what did they say?"

"They said it's fine. I mean, if it's OK with you."

"Sure," she said. Her mouth felt suddenly dry.

"Ann?"

"Yes?"

"Let me clarify: I want to call you and visit you and go out with you exclusively. I want to be more to you than your best friend's brother."

Ann felt a rush of happiness pulse through her. She was sure she should give some romantic speech, but in that moment the only thing she could utter was a simple answer.

"I want that, too."

Cameron grinned.

"You do realize this is the part where the hero kisses the heroine," Ann said.

"Oh, is it?" He raised an eyebrow.

"Or maybe not. It is 1990 after all. Maybe it's up to the heroine." Ann reached for his shirt collar, pulled him toward her, and kissed him with all the emotion she'd felt building since the very first day they'd met on the dusty road.

"Wow," Cameron said at last, leaning his forehead against hers.

"Not what you expected?"

"Better."

They laughed. Cameron might not have stepped off the pages of a novel, but Ann knew she would always be able to laugh with him. He respected her, and she was safe. She leaned her head against his chest, and he held her.

"There were times I never thought I'd see this day," Cameron said.

"You mean, like when I gave you a black eye?"

"Oh, I was a goner from the first moment I saw you walking along the road soaking wet and covered in mud. And even I have to admit I had that black eye coming."

"You really can be insufferable at times," Ann said with a grin.

"Yeah, I know," he kissed the top of her head.

"And I know I didn't make it easy. I don't know why you didn't give up on me."

"Because you're extraordinary." He tucked a strand of hair behind her ear and cupped her chin.

Ann smiled back at his sparkling eyes. "You're pretty special yourself."

She snuggled her head against his chest. They stood in the gathering dusk looking off across the fields to some indefinable point in the future, to that still unseen but open door. They remained several minutes so, as the sun slipped toward the horizon, painting the western sky with its brilliance. Cameron looked at his watch and sighed. "I suppose I'd better head home. I still need to pack some things. I'll call you tomorrow night. But first, I should make this official." He removed his class ring and took her hand. "Ann Alwyn, will you be my girlfriend?"

"Yes!"

He slid the ring on her finger, and they laughed again when it spun on her tiny hand.

"Maybe I'd better put it on my necklace," said Ann.

"I don't care how you wear it as long as you do."

Ann placed his ring on the simple chain with her mother's locket. "Does that look OK?"

"Looks awesome."

He kissed her again—long, deeply, slowly—just like Ann had always imagined a kiss should be.

"Goodnight, Ann of Sunflower Lane," he whispered. Then he took her hand, kissed her palm, and closed her fingers around his promise.

Ann waved as Cam pulled out of the drive, her hand gently holding her necklace where his ring and her mother's locket hung in harmony. She sat pensively on the swing and turned her gaze up to watch the first stars, "the forget-me-nots of angels," sparkle out. Love and friends and family and especially, home—all those things she'd imagined and never had before were hers now.

"It really is 'delightful when your imaginations come true,'" Ann whispered to the stars.

Slowly, she began to wind the rope above her, just as she had on that first afternoon at Sunflower Lane a little over a year before. So much had happened in that time. She was not the same girl she was then, but she was finally discovering the many facets that had always been part of her nature.

Ann pulled herself back onto the tips of her toes and looked across the canvas of greens and browns and yellows of the land to the palette of colors staining the sky. She let the swing fly, unwinding at a dizzying pace as all the hues of that great unbounded vastness swirled before her. A smile blossomed on her face as she swung back and forth, gazing out across the land of Sunflower Lane to the shimmery edge of the Kansas horizon, all of it hers, all of it home.

The End

Literary Allusions

Literary allusions not identified within the text. *AGG* refers to *Anne of Green Gables.*

Chapter 1

"Wherever you are, there is another door"—"Smoke," William Stafford

Chapter 2

every bit as fond of maxims: "Marilla was as fond of morals as the Duchess in Wonderland"—*AGG* Chapter VIII

If Anne Shirley were here—*AGG* Chapter II, "'Pretty doesn't seem the right word to use. Nor beautiful, either. They don't go far enough'"

Chapter 4

the luxury of thinking in exclamation points: "She . . . [Mrs. Lynde] . . . thought in exclamation points"—*AGG* Chapter I

The Lake of Shining Waters is Anne Shirley's name for Barry's Pond in *AGG.*

master of his fate and captain of his soul—A paraphrase from "Invictus," William Ernest Henley

Chapter 5

A New Departure in Biscuits—*AGG* Chapter XXI, paraphrase of
chapter title, "A New Departure in Flavourings"

"Poetry is the achievement"—"Poetry," Carl Sandburg

"genius took to burning"—*Little Women,* Louisa May Alcott

Chapter 6

new moves: "some new move will appear. / Wherever you are,
there is another door"— "Smoke," William Stafford

"[A]ngry people are not always wise"—*Pride and Prejudice*, Jane
Austen

Chapter 7

A bosom friend is Anne Shirley's term for a best friend.

"Two roads diverged"—"The Road Not Taken," Robert Frost

Chapter 9

"in the depths of despair"—*AGG* Chapter III

"Even I have to admit it's better to be Ann of Sunflower Lane
than Ann of a Foster Home"—*AGG* Chapter VIII,
paraphrase of "'It's a million times nicer to be Anne of Green
Gables than Anne of nowhere in particular'"

"*Et tu*, Grandpa?"—paraphrase of Shakespeare's *Julius Ceasar*

'lifelong sorrow'—*AGG* Chapter II

break a slate: In *AGG* Chapter XV, Anne Shirley cracks her slate
over Gilbert Blythe's head when he calls her "Carrots."

Chapter 10

"But I'll just have to endure the presence of that caterpillar"—
The Little Prince, Antoine de Saint-Exupéry, paraphrase of
"'I must endure the presence of a few caterpillars if I wish to
become acquainted with the butterflies'"

"hadn't a spark of imagination"—*AGG* Chapter IX

Chapter 11

"There surely I shall speak for mine own self, / And none of you can speak for me so well"—"Lancelot and Elaine," Alfred Lord Tennyson

Chapter 13

Ann's Imagination Goes Wrong—*AGG* Chapter XX, paraphrase of chapter title, "A Good Imagination Gone Wrong"

"stare into the night / While others take their rest"—"Night Journey," Theodore Roethke

that would get a slate cracked—In *AGG* Chapter XV, Anne Shirley cracks her slate over Gilbert Blythe's head when he calls her "Carrots."

Jane Andrews, one of Anne Shirley's friends, proposes to Anne on behalf of her brother, Billy, in *Anne of the Island.*

"not even fear of punishment / can stop the giggle in a girl"—"Young Girls," P. K. Page

Chapter 14

"'I'd rather look ridiculous when everyone else does'"—*AGG* Chapter XI

"like a fashion magazine:"— *Anne of the Island* Chapter V, paraphrase of "like a head-on collision between a fashion plate and a nightmare"

"'ever so much gratefuller'"—*AGG* Chapter XI

"I've found it's easier to be good"—*AGG* Chapter XXIX, paraphrase of "it is ever so much easier to be good if your clothes are fashionable"

Chapter 15

smallpox: Anne Shirley imagines herself nursing Diana through the smallpox in *AGG* Chapter XVI.

"I am excessively diverted"—*Pride and Prejudice*, Jane Austen

Chapter 16

"spirit and fire and dew": "The good stars met in your
horoscope / Made you of spirit, fire and dew"—"Evelyn
Hope," Robert Browning, and the epigraph to *AGG*

Ruby Gillis's sting of beaux—In *AGG* Chapter XVIII, Anne
Shirley says of a friend, "'Ruby Gillis says when she grows up
she's going to have ever so many beaus on the string and
have them all crazy about her.'"

Chapter 17

Green Gables perfection—*Don Quixote*, Miguel de Cervantes,
Translated by Edith Grossman, paraphrase of "'I deduce,
friend Sancho, that the knight errant who most closely
imitates Amadís will be closest to attaining chivalric
perfection.'"

"up on the wings of anticipation"—Anne Shirley admits in *AGG*
Chapter XVII, "When I think something nice is going to
happen I seem to fly right up on the wings of anticipation;
and then the first thing I realize I drop down to earth with a
thud.'"

Chapter 18

the storm Uncle Abe didn't predict—In *Anne of Avonlea*
Chapter XXIV, Uncle Abe is a local man notorious for his
weather predictions that are the opposite of what happens.
Anne Shirley and her friends publish a forecast for a storm
supposedly made by Uncle Abe, and it is the only time his
forecast is accurate.

Chapter 19

Golden Picnic—*Anne of Avonlea* Chapter 13

"roam'd from field to field"—"How Sweet I Roamed," William
Blake

"Mending Wall" is a reference to the poem of the same name by
Robert Frost.

Jimmy book—In *Emily of New Moon*, also by L.M.
Montgomery, aspiring author Emily Starr's Cousin Jimmy
gives her blank books for her writing.

written herself out—*Emily of New Moon,* L.M. Montgomery,
paraphrase of Chapter 1 title, "Writing Herself Out"

like the free bird: "A free bird . . . / . . . dares to claim the
sky"—"Caged Bird," Maya Angelou

Stafford's other door—"Smoke," Williams Stafford, "Wherever
you are, there is another door"

Idlewild—*AGG* Chapter XIII

Chapter 20

I tend to scorn romance—*Little Women,* Louisa May Alcott,
Chapter Thirteen. The narrator observes that Jo "rather
scorned romance, except in books." Jo goes on to say, "'I
want to do something splendid before I go into my castle—
something heroic or wonderful that won't be forgotten after
I'm dead.'"

there "is no use trying to be romantic"—*AGG* Chapter XXVII,
quote and paraphrase of "'I have come to the conclusion that
it is no use trying to be romantic in Avonlea. It was probably
easy enough in towered Camelot hundreds of years ago, but
romance is not appreciated now'"

Chapter 21

"I can assure you, it is uphill work"—*AGG* Chapter XVI

"after a good dinner"—*A Woman of No Importance*, Oscar
Wilde

"souls of good violets"—*AGG* Chapter XIII

Chapter 22

"poem of the air"—"Snowflakes," Henry Wadsworth
Longfellow

"more romantic to end a story with a funeral than a wedding"—
AGG Chapter XXVI

Chapter 23

pudding sauce—A mouse drowns in the pudding sauce Anne
Shirley forgets to cover in *AGG* Chapter XVI.

harrows up my very soul—*AGG* Chapter XV, paraphrase of
Anne Shirley's response to Diana Barry in when she asks
Anne to return to school after Anne gets in trouble for
breaking a slate over Gilbert Blythe's head: "You harrow up
my very soul."

Diana Barry's ridgepole—In *AGG* Chapter XXIII, Josie Pye
dares Anne Shirley to walk the ridgepole of Diana's kitchen
roof. Anne tries and falls, breaking her ankle.

"perish in the attempt"—*AGG* Chapter XXIII

I'm neither killed nor rendered unconscious—*AGG* Chapter
XXIII, paraphrase of Anne Shirley's response to Diana after
she falls from the kitchen roof

Acacia, like Josie Pye before her, had enough imagination—
AGG Chapter XXIII. After Anne Shirley falls from Diana's
kitchen roof, the narrator notes that Josie had enough
imagination to envision being forever known as responsible
for killing Anne.

Chapter 24

"'sink through the floor with mortification'"—*AGG* Chapter
XVI

Chapter 25

"'just as if I was a heroine in a book'"—*AGG* Chapter V

Chapter 27

"'it's easier to be cheerful'"—*AGG* Chapter IV

a "dream the world is having about itself"—"Vocation," William Stafford

Chapter 28

"obscene travesty"—"The Waltz," Dorothy Parker

"tomorrow is a new day"—*AGG* Chapter XXI

Chapter 29

Tea with Tragic Results—*AGG* Chapter XVI, paraphrase of chapter title, "Diana is Invited to Tea with Tragic Results"

We decided to end with the line about new days and no mistakes—*AGG* Chapter XXI, paraphrase of "tomorrow is a new day with no mistakes in it yet"

Chapter 32

"fitting floor for this magnificent temple of the sky"—"The Prairies," William Cullen Bryant.

Selling the neighbor's Jersey Cow—*Anne of Avonlea* Chapter II

That sounds like something Matthew Cuthbert said—*AGG* Chapter XXVIII, reference to "'Don't give up all your romance, Anne.'"

"'minister to a mind diseased'"—*Anne of the Island* Chapter XII

Chapter 35

She was shedding the fictions—*The Awakening*, Kate Chopin, paraphrase of "She was becoming herself, casting aside that fictitious self which we assume like a garment"

"the river of a dream"—"Maidenhood," Henry Wadsworth Longfellow "as long as the sun and the moon shall endure"—*AGG* Chapter XII, from the oath of friendship between Anne Shirley and Diana Barry

Chapter 36

"tomorrow will take care of itself"—Matthew 6:34

"the forget-me-nots of angels"—*Evangeline: A Tale of Acadie*, Henry Wadsworth Longfellow

"It's delightful when your imaginations come true, isn't it?"—*AGG* Chapter II

Acknowledgments

Ann of Sunflower Lane is a reality thanks to the unwavering support of so many kind and kindred spirits. Thank you to readers of early versions of the novel who provided me with invaluable feedback: Nancy Julien-Kopp, Christopher Renna, Lesley Sieger-Walls, Betty Brewer, Tracy Million Simmons, and Dr. Darin Allen. Thanks also to Grant Overstake for talking with me about my original idea and encouraging me to keep on, to Elizabeth Rollins Epperly for a long-distance pep talk when I needed it, to Michel Alexandre, Liz Lane, and my group of Koady's Friends for always enthusiastically believing in me, and to Annette Starr and Pastor Michael Strickland for prayers along the way. I am grateful to Kim Stafford and Zachariah Selley for helping me find bibliographic information for several of William Stafford's poems. A special thank you to Kate Macdonald Butler for her support of my creative work. Thank you to Onalee Nicklin for creating the beautiful cover art that so tenderly depicts Ann and Sunflower Lane. Lesley Sieger-Walls, I cannot thank you enough for the treasure trove of memories (many of them Green Gables inspired) that we share from across the years and for our enduring friendship. Love and thanks to my husband, PJ Vaske, for his patience in tolerating my brainstorming out loud on our walks and for reading drafts and rewrites, and to my dog, Mozzie, for being a willing listener and calming presence while I wrote. Special thanks to Tracy Million Simmons and Meadowlark Press for believing in Ann Alwyn's story and helping bring her to life.

Julie A. Sellers was raised in the Flint Hills near the small town of Florence, Kansas. Those great expanses of tallgrass prairie and reading fueled her imagination, and Julie began writing at an early age. After living in several states and countries, Julie resides in Atchison, Kansas. Julie has published three academic books and a variety of articles. Her creative prose and poetry have appeared in publications such as *Cagibi, Wanderlust, Unlost, The Write Launch, 105 Meadowlark Reader,* and *Kansas Time + Place.* Julie was the 2020 Kansas Authors Club Prose Writer of the Year. In the Kansas Voices Contest (Winfield), she was the Overall Poetry Winner (2022) and Overall Prose Winner (2017, 2019). Julie's first book of poetry, *Kindred Verse: Poems Inspired by* Anne of Green Gables, was published by Blue Cedar Press in 2021. *Ann of Sunflower Lane* is her debut novel.

Discussion Questions

- What made your book club or reading group select *Ann of Sunflower Lane*?

- Which character resonated most with you and why? Which character did you like the least and why?

- How did the allusions to *Anne of Green Gables* and other works of literature impact your reading and interpretation of the novel?

- There are several themes that weave throughout the novel: sense of place, identity, community, family, friendship, love, and home. Discuss these and other themes you noticed that intrigued you as you read.

- There are several secrets and truths that are revealed throughout the story. Did you foresee any of these revelations? Which was most surprising?

- Objects (such as the copy of *Anne of Green Gables*, the trunk, R.J.'s letter, the rose jar, the locket) aid in creating the setting and in the action. Which of these or other objects did you find most important or interesting to the story and why?

- Ann is always on the lookout for what she envisions as an open door. What does this symbolize to you?

- Ann is a reader and a writer. How did these aspects of her personality influence her reading of her world?

- What are your favorite quotes from the novel? How do they represent Ann's way of thinking, being, and interacting with her world?

- What will you take away from *Ann of Sunflower Lane*?

Recipes

Sunflower Lane Biscuits

2 c. sifted all-purpose flour

1T. + 1 tsp. baking powder

½ tsp. cream of tartar

½ tsp. salt

½ cup cold butter, cut into small cubes

$^2/_3$ c. milk

1. Preheat oven to 450° F.

2. Sift together dry ingredients; set aside.

3. Use a pastry blender to cut in the butter until the mixture resembles coarse crumbs.

4. Add milk using a fork and stirringly lightly just until the mixture follows the fork around the mixing bowl.

5. Turn out on lightly floured surface.

6. Knead very gently for only 30 seconds.

7. Pat to ½ inch thickness.

8. Cut biscuits with round cutter.

9. Place on ungreased baking sheet.

10. Bake 10-12 minutes. *Note to Ann:* Always set a timer!

11. Makes approximately one dozen biscuits, depending on size of cutter.

Great-Uncle Pete's Favorite Blonde Brownies

Ingredients

2 c. all-purpose flour

1 tsp. baking powder

1 tsp. salt

¼ tsp. baking soda

½ c. butter (softened)

1 c. brown sugar (packed)

2 large eggs

1 tsp. vanilla

1 c. chocolate chips

Preparation

1. Preheat oven to 325° F.

2. Sift together dry ingredients; set aside.

3. Place butter and brown sugar in a mixing bowl. Use the butter wrapper to grease an 8-inch square glass baking dish; set aside.

4. Using an electric mixer, cream together butter and brown sugar.

5. Add eggs, one at a time. Blend well after adding each egg.

6. Blend in vanilla.

7. Gradually add dry ingredients to the creamed mixture, approximately ½ cup at a time. Mix well after each addition.

8. Stir the chocolate chips in by hand—the batter will be stiff.

9. Spread evenly in the prepared baking dish.

10. Bake for 35 minutes or until no imprint remains when lightly touched. Cool in the baking dish on a baking rack. Cut into 16 pieces.

Amelia's Rose Jar

Materials:

Unique jar with lid

Dried rose petals

¾ tsp. each: cinnamon, cloves, and nutmeg

perfume

Preparation:

1. Separate the rose petals from the flower and place them flat on sheets of newspaper. Dry completely in the sun.

2. In a small bowl, mix the spices together.

3. Alternate layers of rose petals, a sprinkle of spices, and a spritz of perfume in the jar.

4. Seal with the lid and decorate with fabric, ribbon, and lace.

Cameron's Mix Tape Playlist

Available on Spotify at Cameron's Mix Tape—Ann of
Sunflower Lane
https://tinyurl.com/cameronmixtape

"When I'm with You"—Sheriff
"Never Gonna Give You Up"—Rick Astley
"Anything for You"—Gloria Estefan & Miami Sound Machine
"Tell Me True"—Juice Newton
"Mountain Music"—Alabama
"It Ain't Cool to be Crazy About You"—George Strait
"Could I Have This Dance"—Anne Murray
"Right Here Waiting"—Richard Marx
"Eternal Flame"—Bangles
"The Next Time I Fall"—Peter Cetera & Amy Grant
"Take My Breath Away"—Berlin
"One Friend"—Dan Seals
"Give Me Wings"—Michael Johnson
"When you Say Nothing at All"—Keith Whitley
"I'll Still be Lovin' You"—Restless Heart

If you loved this book,
you might also enjoy . . .

OPULENCE
— KANSAS —

Julie Stielstra

Daughter of privilege, Katie Myrdal's world is rocked when her finance-wizard father is found dead in his Porsche. There's more wreckage to clean up than she could have imagined. Katie escapes to the Kansas farmstead of her aunt and uncle, whom she barely knows, near the small town of Opulence. Plummeting from a high-rise, big city condo to a tree-shrouded, yellow house on the prairie, Katie discovers other kinds of richness—the wealth of friendship, her own hidden gifts, tragic family secrets, and how the balm of time will help her turn her life in a new direction.

• • • • •

A recommended title by the
Kansas National Education Association's Reading Circle Commission.
Midwest Book Award Winner • High Plains Book Award Winner

Books are a way to explore, connect, and
discover. Reading gives us the gift of living lives
and gaining experiences beyond our own.
Publishing books is our way of saying—

We love these words,
we want to play a role in preserving them,
and we want to help share them with the world.